MURDER AT THE FOUNDLING HOSPITAL

IRINA SHAPIRO

Storm
PUBLISHING

Ebook ISBN: 978-1-80508-659-8
Paperback ISBN: 978-1-80508-660-4

Cover design: Debbie Clement
Cover images: Arcangel, Shutterstock

Published by Storm Publishing.
For further information, visit:
www.stormpublishing.co

ALSO BY IRINA SHAPIRO

PROLOGUE

DECEMBER 26, 1858

Boxing Day

The sky beyond the window was nearly black, the quiet absolute, as Horace Fletcher left his tiny room and grabbed the bucket he used for coal in one hand and an oil lamp to light his way in the other. The cellar was chilly on the warmest of summer days, but at the end of December it was as frigid as a winter grave, and Horace wore nearly every article of clothing he possessed beneath the shaggy sheepskin he'd inherited from his father nigh on twenty years ago.

Horace walked slowly, his knees creaking and his arthritic joints aching and burning in protest as he set down the lamp, opened the coal chute, and lifted the shovel. His day started early, hours before sunrise, but he didn't mind. He had a job and a roof over his head, and received three meals a day. What more could a relic like him ask for?

Horace filled the buckets, and was about to head upstairs to light the fires before everyone woke when he noticed that the door to the laundry room stood ajar. Setting down the buckets, he held the lamp aloft, approached the door, and slowly pushed it open. At first glance, nothing seemed amiss. Elongated metal tubs resembled tombs in the nearly impenetrable darkness, and the air smelled of damp and lye.

Horace was just about to shut the door and return to the task at hand when the light from his lamp fell on the tub closest to the outer wall. Something rested on the lip of the tub, and the pale links reminded Horace of fat grubs. He inched further into the room and was halfway to the tub when his bleary brain finally understood what he was looking at. The links were thin fingers, the nailbeds bluish against the nearly translucent skin.

His breath catching in his throat, Horace held the lamp over the tub and peered down. A scream tore from his chest when he saw a pale face, blue eyes staring through a layer of ice that had formed during the night. Even without touching the body, Horace knew the child was dead and there was nothing to be done. There had been a few children who'd taken their own lives in a fit of despair, but Horace knew in his aching bones that what he was looking at was an act of murder.

ONE

A hush hung over the corridor that seemed unnatural in a place that housed hundreds of children. Although he saw no one, Sebastian Bell was sure he was being watched as he strode down the corridor after Matron. He had been to the Foundling Hospital only a fortnight ago to visit Gemma Tate to consult her on a case he was investigating, but this time he'd been summoned for a wholly different reason. The caretaker had discovered one of the children dead, the body left in the laundry, the child as yet unidentified. The man, Mr. Fletcher, had raised the alarm, then kept vigil over the remains and refused to allow anyone in until a detective from Scotland Yard arrived.

Because Matron Holcombe had recalled him from his previous visit, Sebastian was the one she had asked for, so here he was, about to come face to face with an innocent life cut short, another defenseless child gone from the world. The matron was white-faced and silent, her shoulders rigid with tension as she pushed open a door and began to descend a flight of stairs that led to the cellar. It was a warren of small rooms, mainly used for storage. The largest was the laundry, a windowless stone box with a door that led to the outside, where a dozen clotheslines had been strung from wooden poles. The room contained six large tubs, a wringing apparatus, several irons, and a wide hearth that allowed a number of kettles to be heated at once. The sharp smell of lye soap permeated the frigid air and mixed with the scent of sweet tobacco and stale sweat that emanated from Mr. Fletcher, who had silently followed Matron and Sebastian inside and positioned himself by the back door.

Sebastian sucked in a sharp breath as he drew closer and leaned in to get a better look. The child lay on her back, one pale hand still gripping the side of the tub. The layer of ice was beginning to thaw to reveal a face that was unnaturally white and slightly distorted by the water above it. The girl's eyes were open, long hair floating around her head like blades of seaweed. Sebastian could see no obvious wounds or ligature marks, but only the girl's wrists, hand, and neck were exposed. He would need to see the rest of her body to determine if there had been a struggle, but frozen puddles next to the tub were indicative of water sloshing around when the child had gone in.

The girl wore a plain brown dressing gown over a round-necked nightdress, and one well-worn slipper over a bare foot. The second slipper lay on its side on the floor, heartbreakingly small in the shadow of the tub. Had the girl gone into the tub herself, she would have either taken off both shoes or kept them on, and, since the tub was only half full, water wouldn't have splashed over the sides unless the girl had been pushed in and possibly thrashed about. She might have grabbed onto the side of the tub to gain purchase but been unable to rise above the water to draw breath.

Matron gripped the sides of the tub and bowed her head, her breathing ragged as she tried to regain control of her feelings. At their last meeting, Matron Holcombe hadn't struck Sebastian as someone who gave in to emotion, but her shock and sorrow appeared genuine, and Sebastian felt an echo of her grief in his own heart. But he had a job to do, and, in order to do his best for this young girl, his faculties and instincts had to remain razor sharp. Sebastian pushed down his feelings and turned to Mr. Fletcher. He needed to hear his account before he questioned the matron.

"What do you need from me, Inspector Bell?" Matron Holcombe asked once Mr. Fletcher had recounted the details. The initial shock had passed, and she was now clearly ready to take control of the situation and the institution she was in charge of.

"We'll need to start with the identity of the victim. I trust you know every child in your care?"

"Of course I do," the matron replied haughtily. "We'll discuss the identity in private."

Sebastian got the feeling she didn't want to name the child in front of Mr. Fletcher for fear that the news would spread before she had decided how to present it to the rest of the students and the staff.

Matron sighed heavily. "Of all the ways a child can die, I never imagined we'd have death by drowning," she said wearily.

"We don't know that she drowned, Matron."

Matron Holcombe stared at him, shock written on her face. "But she's lying in a tub of water. How else could she have died?"

"I won't know for certain until a postmortem has been performed."

Matron sucked in her breath. "Is that really necessary, Inspector Bell?"

"I'm afraid it is. Is there a wagon I can commandeer for a few hours?" he asked.

"I would be happy to drive you wherever you need to go," Mr. Fletcher volunteered, and received a sharp look from Matron for speaking out of turn.

"I will need some sacking to wrap the body, and straw to lay it on," Sebastian said. He considered the benefits of taking the child out of the water, then decided she was better off where she was until he was ready to take her away. And he wanted Gemma to see the body as Mr. Fletcher had found it.

"Where are you taking her, Inspector?" Mr. Fletcher asked sorrowfully. "To the city mortuary?"

"No. I will deliver her to a surgeon of my acquaintance. The child will be treated with consideration and respect," he added when he saw doubt in the old man's eyes. "And she will return to her Maker exactly as He made her."

"God bless you, sir," Mr. Fletcher said. "You seem a kind man, so it's only fitting that you should investigate the death of this poor child."

"I think perhaps it's best if we speak in my office, Inspector," Matron said.

"Mr. Fletcher, kindly lock the room while you fetch the sacking and prepare the cart," Sebastian said. "I don't want anyone to either see or interfere with the body."

"My God, who do you imagine would do such a thing?" Matron demanded, but Sebastian didn't bother to respond. She was an intelligent woman and could deduce for herself the dangers of leaving the body unattended.

Matron's back was ramrod straight, her head held high as she walked through the door, and Sebastian couldn't help but wonder if she had experienced a moment of doubt before she sent one of the porters to fetch the police. The girl's death could have been explained as a terrible accident, making it easier for the children to comprehend and the administrators to sweep under the carpet.

Sebastian didn't inform Matron that he'd sent for Gemma, but the reason for dispatching Constable Bryant to fetch her was twofold. For one, he needed the benefit of her expertise, and for another he didn't want her to walk into a tragedy unprepared. Strong and self-possessed as Gemma was in the face of violent death, she was still a tender-hearted, compassionate woman, who not only administered to the children's physical well-being but also genuinely cared for the orphans and would be devastated to learn that an innocent child was dead. Gemma also knew the members of staff, understood the ways in which the institution was administered, and was familiar with the layout of the building, which was massive and one of several that formed the hospital compound.

Sebastian knew some basic facts from Gemma, and recalled what she'd told him as he followed Matron back to her office. The Foundling Hospital was not a hospital in the modern sense. It was a place of hospitality for unwanted children, founded more than one hundred years ago and reserved for the illegitimate offspring of mothers deemed deserving. It was more than an orphanage. The hospital was an institution that not only looked after the children but also educated them, taught them valuable life skills, and prepared them for life beyond its walls.

Each infant was assigned a unique number upon being accepted and was identified by that number for as long as they remained at the hospital. The child was fostered with a respectable family in the country until he or she turned five, at which time they returned to London, were placed in a dormitory, and were expected to work within the hospital walls and attend school until they were ready to go out into the world.

Sebastian wasn't sure who named the babies that were left with the hospital, but he did know that a mother was permitted to leave a token that could be used to identify her child if her circumstances ever changed and she was able to reclaim her baby. The tokens were kept in a register, along with the mother's name, the child's date of birth, and the date of death if the child were to die during their time at the Foundling Hospital.

If there was one thing Sebastian was sure of, it was that this child's death had not been self-inflicted.

TWO

Gemma yanked open the door of the boarding house and hurried down the steps, the flustered constable on her heels.

"Miss Tate, please wait," Constable Bryant implored, but Gemma barely heard him. She took off at a run, the soles of her boots slipping on frosty ground and the folds of her black cape filling with wind and flapping like bat wings. Gemma's breath came in sharp puffs, and her heart pounded in her chest, the awful voice of premonition crying, "Lucy, Lucy, Lucy."

She couldn't say why she feared for Lucy. Who'd have reason to harm a five-year-old child? But the fact that Sebastian had sent a constable to fetch her didn't bode well, and now Gemma understood that a woman didn't have to be a mother to be endowed with maternal instinct. Had she been calmer and felt more rational, she would have scolded herself for allowing her emotions to get the best of her and would have acknowledged that she had grown inappropriately attached to the child, but all she could do was think of her young charge and pray for her well-being.

Gemma dashed out in front of a dray wagon, ignored the cursing of the angry driver, and continued to run, holding up her skirts to keep them from getting splattered with mud. When she finally reached the main entrance to the Foundling Hospital, she fell through the door and nearly collided with Mrs. Dixon, one of the girls' mistresses, who had been walking down the corridor.

"Good grief, Miss Tate," Mrs. Dixon exclaimed. "What's amiss?"

"Is it Lucy?" Gemma cried, unable to contain her fear any longer.

"Lucy?" Mrs. Dixon stared at her as if she'd gone quite mad.

"Was Lucy the child that was found dead?"

"How on earth do you know about that?" Mrs. Dixon asked, her eyes narrowing in suspicion. Her question was answered by Constable Bryant, who exploded through the door, still huffing and puffing, his cheeks ruddy with cold and his chest heaving with the effort of keeping up with Gemma.

"I had no idea you could run so fast, Miss Tate," he said as he tried to catch his breath.

Mrs. Dixon had still not answered her, and Gemma found that she couldn't stop trembling as she looked up and down the deserted corridor, but Mrs. Dixon's disapproving expression brought her to her senses. A display of emotion would be held against her, possibly even to the point where she lost her position, a job she needed if she hoped to survive on her own in a world that wasn't kind to unmarried women who had no family to rely on.

As a member of staff, she had no right to show preference for any one child or to allow personal feelings to get in the way of doing her job, and Matron Holcombe was already aware of Lucy's attachment to Gemma and the bond that had blossomed between them as a result of Lucy's frequent visits to the infirmary. If such a thing were possible, Gemma would gladly adopt Lucy, and then it would be the two of them against the world; but no one would permit an unmarried woman to take in a child and, in any case, Gemma couldn't afford to take on a dependent. She loved Lucy as if the little girl were her own, but, although not nearly as loved there as she would be with Gemma, Lucy's prospects were more secure at the Foundling Hospital.

Gemma drew back her shoulders, nodded curtly to Mrs. Dixon, and walked sedately down the corridor toward Matron's office, followed closely by Constable Bryant, who'd managed to catch his breath and now looked like a stolid representative of the law rather than a flustered, red-faced youth. When she turned the corner Gemma came face to face with Matron Holcombe and Sebastian, and her breath caught in her throat as she sought Sebastian's gaze.

"Miss Tate," he said, bowing from the neck.

Detecting the warning in his tone, Gemma had no choice but to resort to cool formality. "Matron Holcombe. Inspector Bell," she said. "Is there anything I can do to help?"

"I think it's best that you go about your duties, Miss Tate," Matron said. "I will send for you should your assistance become necessary."

Matron Holcombe unlocked the office door and stepped inside, but Sebastian hung back, his gaze warm and sympathetic now that Matron couldn't see his face. He understood Gemma's fear and didn't judge her for her weakness or her inability to retain a sense of detachment that befitted a woman in her position. Instead, he sought to calm and reassure her in a situation that could draw unwelcome attention to their personal relationship and compromise his authority with Matron Holcombe.

"It's not Lucy," he said quietly.

Gemma's knees nearly buckled with relief, but if the victim wasn't Lucy, it was some other unfortunate child, and she couldn't help but hope that the death had been the result of an accident rather than something more sinister.

"Who is it, Inspector?" she asked, keeping her demeanor as

calm as she was able to manage. "Who's dead?" As a nurse, she had a right to know what had happened. Matron couldn't censure her for that.

"The child is yet to be identified. I need to gather some basic facts, but then I would like you to examine the body. Any observations would be most helpful, Miss Tate." Sebastian pulled out his pocket watch and consulted the time. "Please meet me by the laundry in, say, half an hour?"

"I thought you intended to carry out a postmortem, Inspector Bell," Matron Holcombe said from inside her office. "If you require an opinion, I can send for our own doctor." Matron was clearly annoyed that Sebastian had stopped to speak to Gemma and was letting her feelings be known, belittling Gemma's expertise in the process.

"I do, but since the surgeon is unable to examine the body at the scene I would welcome the benefit of Miss Tate's experience. She has more practical knowledge of violent death."

Matron snorted like an angry horse but didn't bother to argue any further.

"Constable, I would like you to stand guard by the laundry until I return," Sebastian said.

"Yes, sir," Constable Bryant said, snapping to attention. He was clearly relieved to have been given something to do.

With a brief squeeze of Gemma's fingers, Sebastian walked into Matron's office and shut the door firmly behind him, leaving Gemma with no alternative but to report to the infirmary and go about her duties. In an institution that housed hundreds of children, there were always patients in the infirmary. Today, there were three boys, all suffering from what Gemma believed to be spasmodic croup. The children lay still, their breathing labored and their faces flushed with fever. From time to time, one of them would be overtaken by a bout of barking coughs that would leave them doubled over and gasping for air.

Miss Landry, who was the night nurse, was sitting by the window. She was a colorless woman of middle years who'd been at the hospital for nearly a decade, having been in need of employment after her father died and left her nearly destitute. Miss Landry's dark gaze seemed to be fixed on the street beyond, and her forehead was creased with worry.

"I suppose you've heard," she said, turning to face Gemma. "Terrible business."

"Yes."

"A detective from Scotland Yard has been summoned," Miss Landry said. "That could only mean one thing. It was no accident."

"Do you know what happened?" Gemma asked.

Miss Landry shook her head. "Matron's not divulging any details."

"I expect we'll find out in due course," Gemma said noncommittally, even though her innards were twisting with anxiety and grief as she thought of the nameless child who even now lay dead, the strong, young body that was wonderfully alive only yesterday now nothing but a shell that would be probed and dissected before it was put in the ground. But she didn't want to discuss the case with Miss Landry, who was something of a gossip and would lay the blame for speculating at Gemma's door if rebuked by Matron.

"I expect so," Miss Landry agreed. "I'll be off, then."

Gemma had just checked on the children when Mr. Campbell, the boys' mathematics tutor, walked in, a gangly, fair-haired boy trailing behind him. The boy was about fourteen, one of the older children who would soon be leaving the hospital. Mr. Campbell gave him a reassuring smile and patted him on the shoulder, then turned to Gemma.

"Miss Tate, I'm afraid Michael is rather unwell. I thought perhaps you could have a look."

"Of course. Please, come in, Michael."

Gemma motioned toward the cot furthest from the sick children, and Michael sat down heavily, as if his legs were too weak to hold him.

"What's troubling you?" she asked gently.

"Michael vomited several times, and he says his head hurts," Mr. Campbell hurried to explain. Gemma was gratified to see that the teacher seemed genuinely concerned and had remained to support the boy.

Gemma had met Mr. Campbell before and found him to be pleasant and respectful of both the children in his care and members of staff. He was in his mid-twenties, with dark curling hair, thickly lashed dark eyes, and fine bone structure. She had heard from Miss Landry that he had once been a soldier, but he had been teaching at the hospital for several years now and was a favorite with the boys.

Gemma touched her fingers to Michael's forehead. He didn't appear to have a fever, which was always a good sign.

"Does your stomach hurt?" she asked.

The boy nodded. "I feel bilious," he said.

"Why don't you rest here for a little while, and we'll see how you feel in an hour," Gemma suggested. There wasn't much she could do for nausea and, since Michael had already vomited, she hoped that whatever had not agreed with him had been expelled and he would begin to feel better on his own. "Leave it with me, Mr. Campbell," Gemma said when the man made no move to go. "I will send Michael back once he feels better."

"Thank you, Miss Tate. I trust it's nothing serious."

"I don't believe so," Gemma reassured him.

Once Mr. Campbell was gone, Gemma turned back to Michael. "Is there anything else you wish to tell me? Did anything happen? Did you eat or drink something other than what was served in the dining hall last night?"

If something served at supper had upset Michael's stomach,

there were likely to be other children suffering from the same thing, but so far he seemed to be the only one.

"No, ma'am."

"Does this happen often?"

"No, ma'am."

Michael was deathly pale and looked like he was about to vomit again, so Gemma set a basin by the cot, instructed him to take off his shoes and lie down, and covered him with a blanket. If he didn't begin to feel better, she might give him a teaspoon of castor oil to purge his bowels of whatever had caused the upset. Michael buried his face in the pillow and shut his eyes. As Gemma turned away, she thought she could hear him crying. Perhaps he felt more ill than he had let on, or maybe his symptoms were caused more by hurt feelings and fear than any physical ailment. Children could be cruel and, although bullying was severely punished, there were always those who picked on the more sensitive boys. Gemma drew the curtains, shutting out the bright light. She hoped Michael would sleep.

It was only once she set off for the other side of the ward that Gemma heard another sound. It was like the scratching of a mouse, but it was accompanied by stealthy breathing. Gemma followed the sound, which led her to the storage cupboard in the corner. Inside were sheets, pillowcases, and blankets, as well as several clean nightshirts of varying sizes, and even linen nappies for the incoming babies, should they require a stint in the infirmary before they were sent to the country. A brown woolen blanket lay in a heap in the corner of the cupboard, the fabric shivering like a quagmire. Gemma carefully felt beneath the blanket until she located a small foot.

"It's safe to come out," she whispered. "No one will scold you."

A tousled blond head appeared from beneath, followed by a narrow, chalk-white face. "I don't want to go back," Lucy whispered urgently. "I'm frightened."

"I know, sweetheart," Gemma said, and wished she could pull Lucy into her arms and hold her close until she was no longer terrified, but if someone happened to walk in Gemma was in no doubt that Matron would hear all about her transgression and see that Lucy was punished as well.

"I will look after you," Gemma promised, but Lucy stubbornly shook her head.

"You can look after me in here, but you're not there when I need you," she whimpered.

Gemma was beginning to suspect that Lucy's distress wasn't directly related to the morning's events but was due to something else entirely, and hoped the little girl knew nothing of the tragedy. She would find out soon enough, as would the rest of the children, but hopefully by that time Matron would be able to provide some answers and calm their fears. *Or stoke them*, Gemma thought worriedly, as she recalled the grim look on Sebastian's face. Death stalked the halls of any orphanage but, whereas the children could make sense of a passing caused by illness, death by violence was not something that could be as easily explained away.

"Why don't you come out and tell me what frightened you," Gemma suggested, but Lucy shook her head again. She clearly felt safer in the cupboard.

"I bet you're hungry. Would you like a biscuit?"

Gemma kept a tin of ginger biscuits on hand for those times when she needed to coax a frightened child into taking medicine or to allow her to clean an open wound. The biscuits also helped to quell nausea and settle an upset stomach in cases that were mild and didn't require more drastic measures. Gemma knew she shouldn't be bribing Lucy with treats, especially not when the child was blatantly breaking the rules, but in this case a biscuit might be as effective as a dose of medication, and, even though Lucy wasn't physically ill, something was clearly ailing her. Unable to resist the lure of the biscuit, or maybe just desperate to be comforted, Lucy finally allowed herself to be coaxed out of the cupboard and sat next to Gemma on an out-of-the-way cot. She looked like a little rabbit as she gnawed on the biscuit with her front teeth to make it last longer. Gemma waited patiently until she was done. Finally, Lucy looked up, her eyes huge with anxiety, but it seemed she needed a bit more cajoling before she was ready to confide her fears.

"What frightened you, sweetheart?" Gemma asked gently. "If you tell me, then maybe I can help."

Lucy sighed heavily. "Sometimes I wake in the night and can't get back to sleep because I'm frightened."

"Are you afraid of the dark?" Gemma asked. She had been terrified of the dark at Lucy's age, and she imagined that being the only child awake in the cavernous dormitory could be very scary indeed.

"No," Lucy replied. "I'm afraid of being alone."

"But you're not alone. All your friends are sleeping right next to you."

"They're not my friends," Lucy said defiantly. "You're my friend, but you're not allowed to come. I heard Matron scold you for being kind to me."

Gemma's heart ached for this sad little girl, and she wished she could hold her and rock her and sing to her until she had dispelled her fears; but, even if she got away with breaking the rules, mollycoddling Lucy wouldn't solve the problem in the long term. Having been torn from the only family she had ever known, she was understandably lonely and afraid, and, although she was surrounded by people all day long, those people didn't belong to her any more than she belonged to them. She had yet to make friends with the other girls or grow thicker skin that would help her to survive in an environment where she was hardly more than a number.

"I can't come to your dormitory at night, but I can teach you a trick you can try when you feel afraid," Gemma offered. "My father taught it to me when I was small, and I still use it whenever I'm sad or frightened."

"Really?" Lucy asked, looking more hopeful. "What is it?"

"You lie still, close your eyes, and picture something that made you very merry. You don't just think about it. You recall every detail until you're there once again and you feel happy and safe. And then you remind yourself that there will be many more wonderful days in the future. You will be able to fall right back asleep. I promise."

Lucy looked dubious, since this clearly wasn't the magical solution she had anticipated, then asked, "What do *you* think about, miss?"

"Me? Well, when I was seven, my parents took me and my brother on holiday to the seaside. It was the first time either of us had seen the sea. That first day, Victor and I played on the beach for hours. We took off our shoes and stockings, Victor rolled up his trousers, and I pulled up my skirt so it wouldn't get wet, and we jumped in the surf and ran up and down the beach like little savages. I can still remember how cold the water was and how rough and slippery the pebbles felt beneath my feet as I chased Victor. And then, once we got hungry, we sat down on a blanket and my mother gave us ham sandwiches and lemonade that she brought from the hotel in a wicker basket, and there were ripe, juicy plums for after. It was one of the happiest days of my life," Gemma said wistfully.

"I've never seen the sea," Lucy whispered.

"But you will. You have your whole life ahead of you, and you will do many new and exciting things. Now, tell me your happy memory," Gemma invited her. "If you can't find one, then the trick won't work."

Lucy didn't need to think for very long. "Just before I left my foster family, there was a wedding, and everyone in the village came. The bride was so lovely. She wore a veil and carried a posy of wildflowers. And the groom couldn't stop smiling when he saw her," she said dreamily. "There were long tables set up on the village green, and once the sun went down and everyone had eaten there was music and dancing."

"Did you dance too?" Gemma asked. Her voice was thicker than usual, and she needed to look away for a moment to blink away the tears that pricked at her eyes. Lucy had been part of a family and a community, and she had believed that she would remain among the people who had cared for her until she was old enough to fend for herself. Little did she know that only a short time later all those people would be nothing more than a memory and she would be thrust into an institution where every bit of vulnerability and individuality would be stripped from her over time.

"No," Lucy said. "I didn't want to dance, but I sat on the grass with some other children and listened to the music, and it made me happy because everyone looked so gay. I fell asleep and woke up in my own bed. And there was left-over kidney pie for breakfast. I like pie. It's so much nicer than porridge."

Lucy looked up at Gemma and brushed away a tear that slid down Gemma's cheek with her little hand.

"Are you sad because you never had a wedding, Miss Tate?" she asked, mercifully misinterpreting Gemma's sorrow and mistaking it for self-pity.

"Yes," Gemma said, and knew it to be true. She was sad never to have known such joy, and sadder still to be reminded that, even if she married someday, none of the people she had loved would be there to witness her happiness. They were all gone, their features forever unchanging and their voices fading to barely discernible whispers in her mind.

"There will be more happy days for you too. You're not so old yet." Lucy slid off the cot and reached for Gemma's hand. "I don't like Mrs. Baker. She will hit me with a ruler for running away, but I don't want you to get in trouble."

"Thank you," Gemma muttered, still choked up.

"I will think of my memory when she hits me," Lucy promised. "I don't think I will be happy, but maybe I won't be so miserable."

More than anything, Gemma wished she could allow Lucy to remain in the infirmary, but Lucy wasn't ill and the longer she stayed away the more severe her punishment would be. She was understandably afraid to go back, but by the time she got back the other children would have no doubt heard the terrible news and would be frightened too, so Mrs. Baker would have her hands full.

"Where's your cap?" Gemma asked.

"In the cupboard."

Lucy found her cap and pulled it on, tucking loose strands of hair inside until she looked presentable. Then Gemma took her hand and together they walked out into the corridor and toward the stairs that led to the upper floor where Lucy's dormitory was located.

"I'll have a word with Mrs. Baker," Gemma promised when Lucy's fingernails bit painfully into her hand as they neared the door.

But her entreaty would probably do little good. Mrs. Baker wasn't a cruel woman but, like Gemma, she had to follow the rules if she hoped to retain her position as well as the respect of the girls in her charge. Children weren't allowed to roam the corridors or take themselves to the infirmary. They had to be escorted by their master or mistress if they thought the child was truly ill, and the other children needed to see that Lucy couldn't get away with thwarting the rules without suffering the consequences. Lucy reluctantly entered the room, where all the girls in her age group sat huddled on their cots, silent and staring like tiny widows. Mrs. Baker stood by the window, looking out over the street, which was coming to life now that the shops were open. Perhaps in times of sorrow, people needed to look outward rather than inward, too frightened of what they'd find should they examine the situation too closely.

Gemma didn't bother to tell Mrs. Baker where she had found Lucy but simply explained that Lucy was frightened and would benefit from the mistress's leniency. Normally, Mrs. Baker would have punished the child regardless, but this morning she gave a cursory nod and told Lucy to sit on her cot and keep quiet. It seemed that the morning activities had been suspended and the children were to be confined to their dormitories until breakfast, which was served at eight o'clock.

Gemma gave Lucy a gentle pat on the shoulder and left her with the other girls, then stepped out into the corridor and headed toward the stairs. It was nearly time to meet Sebastian.

THREE

Now that Matron Holcombe was over the initial shock, her thoughts had clearly turned to safeguarding the reputation of the institution and protecting her own position. She answered Sebastian's questions succinctly but was less than forthcoming, and was clearly trying to work out what could have happened and how it could be explained away. She did identify the victim, though.

"Amanda Carter, aged fourteen," Matron said.

Amanda was in Mrs. Dixon's dormitory and was not known for disobeying the rules or talking back to her betters. The mystery of what she had been doing in the laundry on Christmas night hung in the air like a giant question mark that Matron had no answer to.

"What would Amanda's day be like?" Sebastian asked.

Matron sighed. "The children are up at six and perform their chores until eight, when they go to breakfast. After breakfast, they attend classes until lunch, then have some free time to rest, followed by housework and dinner at six. They are in their dormitories by eight and go to bed at nine."

"But yesterday was Christmas," Sebastian reminded her.

"There were no classes scheduled for yesterday. There was a morning prayer service, and in the afternoon there was a service held in the chapel followed by a Christmas concert. After the concert, the children returned to their dormitories and were given free time until lights out."

"How many people do you employ?" Sebastian asked. Amanda could have had an altercation with another child, but she could have also been the victim of an adult.

"There are dozens of employees, Inspector. There are the masters and mistresses, the teachers, the porters, servants who work in the kitchens and the laundry, nurses in the infirmary, and those who see to provisions and repairs. There is also the chaplain and Dr. Platt, who's not here full time but comes when summoned. Some employees reside at the hospital, while others are day workers."

"Do the girls and boys interact during the day?"

"They do not. The boys and girls are kept in separate wings and follow their own schedule of classes and chores."

"Do they ever see each other?" Sebastian pressed.

"I really don't see how this is relevant, but they do see each other in chapel and also at meals, although they sit on opposite sides of the dining hall and do not speak to each other."

"And the teachers?"

"The boys and girls have their own teachers, who keep to their sides of the building. There are several teachers who teach classes for both, but separately."

"And who are those teachers?" Sebastian asked. He was noting everything Matron said in his notebook.

"There's Miss Parish, who teaches music and oversees the choir. There's no call for two music teachers, since not that many pupils are musically gifted, so Miss Parish has plenty of time for both groups," Matron explained. "And there's also

Mr. Simms, who teaches geography. We don't spend too much time on the subject since most children will never travel further than a few miles from where they are now. Except for the boys who are slated to go into the army," she added. "But they will not be in foreign parts to sightsee, only to serve."

And die, Sebastian thought, but kept his opinions on sending children into the army to himself.

"Is there anyone I need to notify about Amanda's death?" he asked.

"Such as?"

"Such as her mother. Surely you have a record of the woman's name."

Matron Holcombe sighed wearily. "Inspector, most women who leave their children with the hospital cry bitter tears of maternal anguish and swear they will come back to reclaim them, but few ever do. In fact, I can think of only two in the time I've been working here who returned."

"But you do have the information," Sebastian pressed.

"I'm afraid I'm not at liberty to reveal it."

"Why not?"

"For one, the information is not pertinent to your investigation. For another, the register is kept under lock and key and not shown to anyone without permission from the committee."

"Surely this is a special case."

"I can tell you that Amanda's mother has not been heard from in fourteen years, so her whereabouts are not relevant."

"Who names the children?" Sebastian asked. His inquiry clearly surprised Matron and she paused briefly before replying.

"Some women name their babies, and we keep their names. Other children are named by the families they foster with. Most often they take the surname of the family, since they don't have one of their own."

"So Amanda was fostered with a family named Carter?"

"She was."

"Has she seen or heard from them since she was returned to the hospital?"

"She has not."

"You seem very sure. Should you not check?" Sebastian asked.

"I'm sure because none of the children remain in contact with the families. It's forbidden."

"I will need to see Amanda's information," Sebastian said. "I need to know everything there is to learn about Amanda Carter and her mother, even if you don't believe the information to be relevant."

"I will bring your request to the committee."

"Matron, do you have a theory on what happened to Amanda?" Sebastian asked. Perhaps asking for her opinion would yield better results than simply asking for facts.

Matron's expression softened for just a moment, but the rigid set of her shoulders forewarned Sebastian that she wouldn't reveal too much.

"Whatever happened had to be her own fault," she said at last.

"How did you come to that conclusion?" Sebastian asked, seething inside that a fourteen-year-old girl was being blamed for her own death.

"If Amanda had followed the rules, she'd be in the dining hall right now, enjoying her breakfast."

Sebastian swallowed down his exasperation. "Was there anything at all unusual about Amanda Carter's recent behavior?"

Matron looked conflicted but then seemed to relent, clearly judging that the information she was about to reveal was not damaging to the institution. "Amanda came to see me last week."

"What about?"

"She asked for domestic placement. Normally, we don't place girls in service until they're sixteen, but there are positions for girls as young as fourteen. Amanda was willing to go in as a scullion."

"What was the rush?"

"She said she wanted to leave."

"Why? Was there someone here she wished to get away from?"

"No!" Matron exclaimed. "Amanda was well liked and got on with everyone. I've never had a word of complaint from her mistress or her teachers. She did not appear frightened when she came to see me."

"How *did* she appear?"

Matron Holcombe considered the question. "Excited," she said at last. "Happy, even."

"Why would a fourteen-year-old orphan be happy to leave the only home she's ever known?" Sebastian asked.

Matron compressed her lips, her brow furrowing as she obviously came to the same conclusion as Sebastian. "She had something waiting for her on the outside."

"Such as? Is it possible that she had been contacted by her mother or some other member of her family?"

"I don't see how they could contact her without going through me."

"Do the children ever receive post?" Sebastian inquired.

"They do not."

"Do they ever leave the premises?"

"We do take them out occasionally, as a special treat, but they never go out on their own."

"When was the last time Amanda left the building?" Sebastian asked.

"We took the older children to the British Museum last week. The teachers thought it educational."

"Were the children left unattended at any time?"

"Of course not. We take our responsibility to the orphans very seriously, Inspector."

"I seem to recall that one of your girls was viciously abused at the hands of the mistress you placed her with and subsequently died."

"That was decades ago, and the woman was convicted and hanged for murder," Matron Holcombe protested. "We review potential employers very carefully."

Sebastian nodded. There wasn't much more he could ask Matron at this juncture except for one thing. "How difficult would it be for Amanda to sneak out and get into the laundry after hours?"

"Difficult, but not impossible. The mistresses do sleep, Inspector."

"I need to see Amanda's dormitory and her bed."

"Right now?" Matron asked.

"If you would be so kind."

"Of course. Come with me."

Matron took Sebastian to the upper floor, where there were several doors, all closed. She pushed open the second door on the right and went in. The room was clean and bright, with high ceilings and two tall windows facing the back of the building. Twenty-four beds stood in two rows, twelve on each side of the room. Twenty-three of the beds, or more accurately cots, were neatly made, with the pillows fluffed and the blankets tucked in. Only one bed remained unmade, the blanket pushed back, the indentation of a head still discernible in the pillow.

"Is this Amanda's bed?" Sebastian asked.

"It is."

Sebastian stood over the bed, then checked beneath, cast a glance over Amanda's clothes, which were carefully folded on a narrow wooden locker by the bed, then turned to Matron.

"Thank you. I will expect the details on Amanda's mother by tomorrow."

"I'll see what I can do," Matron replied evasively.

The two of them returned in silence to the ground floor, where they parted ways.

FOUR

Gemma tried to control the trembling that set in as soon as she approached the door to the laundry. She had seen plenty of death while nursing in Crimea and had unwittingly become involved in two of Sebastian's murder investigations, but this time the victim was a young girl, and it broke her heart. Sebastian hadn't shared any conclusions but, whether the child had died by her own hand, as a result of a terrible accident, or by intended violence, Gemma knew that she would never be able to unsee what lay beyond the door.

She wished she could reach for Sebastian's hand and confess her feelings of horror and dread, but Sebastian was there in his professional capacity, as was she, and to expect him to comfort her in this moment would be both inappropriate and unfair. The magic of last night's moonlit carriage ride seemed very far off and the kiss that had left her breathless had to be set aside to be savored and examined at a later date, when the fragile feelings that had blossomed between them weren't overshadowed by murder.

Sebastian was grim-faced and silent as he waited for Mr. Fletcher to unlock the door, but he seemed to sense

Gemma's apprehension and moved a little closer, touching her bare hand with his own. His warm thumb brushed against Gemma's wrist, the intimate gesture meant to shore her up and remind her of his support. Then the moment passed, and Sebastian turned to Constable Bryant.

"Constable, I need you to speak to all the girls in Amanda Carter's dormitory. Did anyone see, hear, or know anything about Amanda's plans to sneak out?"

Gemma felt a jolt of recognition when she heard the name. She didn't know Amanda well. She had treated her only once, when the girl had cut herself on a shard of broken crockery and the wound needed to be cleaned and bandaged, but she remembered Amanda as being brave and immensely likable. And she recalled hearing her sing. She had passed by Miss Parish's classroom only last week and had seen Amanda through the open door, her hands clasped before her and her eyes cast heavenward as she rehearsed the carol she would perform at the Christmas concert. And now she was gone, her sweet voice silenced forever.

"Are you sure she sneaked out, guv?" Constable Bryant asked.

"I doubt she was taken by force from a room full of sleeping girls. Amanda threw off her covers, got out of bed, put on her dressing gown and shoes, and slipped out. There were no scuff marks in the corridor or on the stairs, and Amanda was still wearing her shoes when she went in the tub, losing one shoe as she fell. The most likely scenario is that she had agreed to meet someone and then something went terribly wrong."

Constable Bryant nodded. "Understood, guv."

"You can return to Scotland Yard once you're finished," Sebastian said. "I will meet you there once I deliver the body to Mr. Ramsey."

"Yes, sir."

Once Constable Bryant had disappeared up the stairs,

Sebastian turned to Gemma and looked down at her upturned face.

"I will understand if you don't want to do this," he said. "It's not a pleasant sight."

"You know full well that I've seen much worse."

"But this is a child."

"Which is all the more reason to understand what happened here last night. I'm ready," Gemma assured him, even though her stomach clenched with apprehension and she suddenly found it difficult to breathe.

Sebastian nodded. "All right, then."

He pushed open the door and walked inside, Gemma behind him. She walked slowly, bracing herself for the horror that awaited her, but, even though she had thought she was prepared, she still cried out when she saw Amanda's body. The water had done its work and the flesh was pale and wrinkled, but Amanda was still recognizable, her wide blue eyes looking up at Gemma as if she would suddenly sit up and brag that she could hold her breath underwater.

"May I examine the body?" Gemma asked once she had recovered herself. There was little she could tell from a distance, and she needed to do her best for Amanda and for Sebastian.

Sebastian picked up the sacking Mr. Fletcher had left for him and spread it on the floor, then removed his coat and tossed it over an empty tub, and rolled up his sleeves. He reached into the tub and lifted out the body. Amanda was a slight girl, but a dead weight was just that, and the strain of lifting could set back Sebastian's recovery by weeks. He'd only just returned to work, and had been advised by Colin Ramsey to tread carefully unless he wanted to refracture his shattered collarbone.

Rivulets of water poured from Amanda's hair and dressing gown and formed puddles on the stone floor as he gently set her down. The sleeves of Sebastian's shirt, his waistcoat, and the bottoms of his trousers were soaked, and his shoes squeaked as he stepped aside to allow Gemma better access. Not bothering to lift her skirts to keep the hem dry, she knelt next to the body and gingerly reached out until her fingers came in contact with cold, wet flesh. Gemma touched Amanda's cheek, then passed her hand over the girl's staring eyes, closing the lids. She worked in silence as she carried out a cursory examination, determined not to allow her grief to get the better of her. Colin Ramsey would autopsy the body and learn its secrets, but there were things Gemma could learn that Colin couldn't, not being present at the scene.

Finished, Gemma stood and smoothed down her damp skirts. Sebastian hadn't uttered a word while she'd examined Amanda, but now he looked down at Gemma, his expression pained, his voice hoarse.

"Well?" he asked.

"The collar of the nightdress is torn, and there are bruises on her neck, which were covered by the fabric and not immediately visible. I don't think Amanda was interfered with, but there's a lump on the back of her head."

"The heels of her slippers look freshly scuffed, as if her feet went from under her when she was pushed backward, and the pockets of the dressing gown are turned out," Sebastian said.

"Well spotted," Gemma said, impressed. She hadn't realized that Sebastian had been coming to his own conclusions while she had been checking over the body.

"Perhaps she was forced to turn out her pockets, or someone did it after she was already dead."

"What would a foundling child have that's worth taking?" Gemma asked. "They have nothing of their own."

"It could be that whatever she had was worth killing for," Sebastian replied.

Gemma thought he would take the body away then, but Sebastian walked around the laundry, looking closely at the floor, and examining the walls and every piece of equipment. He peered at the clothes mangle, then fixed his gaze on the wall next to it. He licked his finger, then touched the wall. His finger came away red, his saliva having liquefied dried blood.

"I think she was hit against the wall just here," Sebastian said, "and then either staggered toward the tub or was dragged."

"That sounds plausible," Gemma replied as she worked to keep the image of a frightened, injured Amanda from unbalancing her completely.

"What isn't plausible is the water in the tub," Sebastian observed. "Why would there be water in the tub in the middle of the night? Would they not get emptied after the laundry was done?"

"I've never been down here before, but that would make sense. And yesterday was Christmas, so no laundry would have been done," Gemma replied, eager to focus on the practicalities.

"Either someone forgot to empty the tub or whoever met Amanda had filled it in advance."

The laundry was equipped with several sinks and an iron water pump, and there were several buckets that could have been used to fill the tub with water.

"They would only need a few bucketfuls," Sebastian observed. "There wasn't that much water, just enough to close over Amanda if she was forced onto her back."

"Which was enough for her to drown," Gemma replied. "So, you think this was premeditated?"

"Could have been. Until I learn more of Amanda's life and a possible motive, it's impossible to say."

"How can I help?" Gemma asked.

"You can help by returning to the infirmary and keeping clear of the investigation," Sebastian said.

"I'm already involved," Gemma protested.

"There's nothing unusual about a nurse examining the

victim, but if you start asking uncomfortable questions you might make yourself a target."

"Sebastian—" Gemma began, but he cut across her.

"The hospital is locked up securely for the night, so chances are that whoever killed Amanda is still on the premises and will remain here for the foreseeable future. It could be another orphan, or it could have been an adult, one of the many who work here. Until I know more, I need you to keep away from my inquiry. I can't focus on solving this murder if I have to worry about your safety."

"I'll be fine," Gemma protested, "but if it's someone on the inside, other children might be in danger, and I cannot bear it if another child were to get hurt."

Sebastian looked utterly exasperated. "The killer is more likely to strike again if they feel threatened, and few things make a guilty person feel more cornered than knowing that they are in the company of someone who's helping the police."

"You said yourself that it's perfectly acceptable for a nurse to examine the body. Just as it's perfectly natural to speculate about the circumstances that brought about the victim's death." Gemma paused, her gaze going to the door that led to the yard. "Amanda could have let someone in."

"She could have, or someone might have gained access some other way. Perhaps they had a key." Sebastian sighed. "I had better get her over to Colin."

He put on his coat, then leaned down and wrapped the body in the sacking, making certain Amanda's face was completely covered. Looking at the pitiful parcel at her feet, Gemma suddenly felt blinding fury and realized she had balled her hands into fists.

"Find out who did this, Sebastian," she exclaimed. "Amanda deserves justice, and the rest of the children need to know they are safe."

Sebastian nodded, then kicked the door open and walked

out into the yard with the body, where Mr. Fletcher was waiting with the wagon. The man resembled an ancient sheepdog as he sat huddled on the wagon bench, his hat pulled down so low it all but obscured his eyes. Sebastian gently laid the body in the wagon bed, then climbed onto the bench next to Mr. Fletcher, his hand going to his injured shoulder as he did. Mr. Fletcher snapped the reins, and the wagon lurched forward, the wheels creaking and puffs of vapor erupting from the horse's muzzle as its breath met with frigid air.

Gemma watched until the wagon disappeared around the side of the building, then reentered the laundry and headed toward the stairs. She wasn't going to challenge Sebastian's authority, but that didn't mean she couldn't find ways to help move the investigation along and do her bit to safeguard the children in her care.

FIVE

When Sebastian arrived in Blackfriars and knocked on Colin's door, Mabel answered almost immediately. She looked surprised, but her look of consternation was immediately replaced with a smile of welcome.

"Do come in, Inspector. I'll just let Mr. Ramsey know you're here."

"Thank you, Mabel," Sebastian said as he stepped into the narrow foyer.

The house was pleasantly warm and smelled of pine, freshly ground coffee, and baking, and Sebastian's mind instantly went to last night's Christmas celebration and the kiss he had shared with Gemma before he saw her safely to her lodgings. He'd been happy last night and had lain awake for a long while, dreaming about the future. It had been years since he had allowed himself to hope, and the images that had filled his mind had left him feeling not only excited but a little frightened too. Hope and love made one vulnerable to pain and susceptible to loss, and he and Gemma had both been dealt so much grief these past few years.

Sebastian wanted to comfort Gemma and protect her as he

hadn't been able to protect Louisa, but, for all her intelligence and generosity of spirit, Gemma was also obstinate, entirely too independent, and alarmingly fearless for a woman who'd seen what men were truly capable of. Sebastian had seen the determination in her eyes and the stubborn set of her chin as she looked after the departing wagon and knew that no amount of warning Gemma off would make the slightest dent in her resolve to unmask Amanda's killer, and that knowledge made him extremely uneasy. He longed to share his thoughts regarding Amanda's death, and he valued Gemma's opinion, but perhaps involving her in the investigation had been a terrible mistake. She had proved instrumental in solving his two previous cases, but had remained on the periphery of the investigations, speaking to people of her acquaintance and searching for obscure associations. This time Gemma was in the thick of it, locked in a building with a possible murderer, her connection to the police obvious to anyone who cared to look.

Sebastian could hardly demand that Gemma leave her post and bide at the boarding house until the investigation was concluded—not that she would listen to him if he did—but he had to make certain she was as far removed from the inquiry as possible and didn't convince herself that it was her responsibility to protect the rest of the children—or, worse, that Lucy was in any immediate danger. He could understand Gemma's attachment to the little girl and feel her desperate need to comfort and reassure a child who was so vulnerable and emotionally isolated from her peers, but her desire to protect Lucy could draw attention to the child and endanger her instead.

Sebastian sighed heavily. Gemma Tate had brought him back to life and had offered him a glimpse of a future in which he could be genuinely happy, but she had also unbalanced him to the point where he was forever torn between wanting her as a partner in all aspects of his life and constantly worrying about her safety and well-being.

"Mr. Melville, is that you?" Mrs. Ramsey's reedy voice called from the parlor. Sebastian had no choice but to acknowledge the greeting, even though all he really wanted was a few moments to himself to deal with his thoughts.

"I thought I recognized your voice," Mrs. Ramsey said when Sebastian stepped into the parlor. She was sitting in her favorite chair by the window, watching the world she no longer took part in go by. "So kind of you to call. It's been so long since we've seen you and Mrs. Melville. How is dear Amelia?"

Sebastian opened his mouth to remind Mrs. Ramsey that he was not Mr. Melville, she'd seen him just yesterday, and his late wife's name had been Louisa. Then he remembered himself and shut his mouth before he upset the poor woman. She was confused enough as it was, her faculties slipping away bit by bit every day, leaving her no more cognizant of her surroundings than a small child whose life was ruled by the most basic physical and emotional needs.

"Amelia sends her regards," he said when Mrs. Ramsey gave him a quizzical look.

"And how's your little boy? Such a rascal, as I recall," Mrs. Ramsey said with an indulgent smile. "My Colin was such a quiet child. One hardly knew he was in the room. He's away just now, studying medicine in Edinburgh."

"I'm right here, Mother," Colin assured her as he walked through the door, his waistcoat stained with something slimy and brown that Sebastian chose not to focus on.

"Colin, dear, are you back for Christmas?" Mrs. Ramsey exclaimed, her eyes alight with joy. "Mabel got us a goose."

"We had a wonderful celebration, Mother," Colin reminded her. "The goose was delicious."

"Ah, yes," Mrs. Ramsey said quietly, suddenly turning inward.

Colin took advantage of the momentary reprieve to fix his gaze on Sebastian, and a wordless conversation took place. Neither man was careless enough to mention in front of Colin's mother what he did in the cellar.

"I'll need you to open the cellar door," Sebastian said.

"Do you need a hand?"

Sebastian was about to refuse the offer of help, but the pain in his shoulder reminded him that he had better set aside his pride and accept Colin's assistance.

"Please," he said. "Good day to you, Mrs. Ramsey," he called out, but the older woman's gaze had that faraway quality, and she was no doubt recalling Christmases past when Colin had been a boy, her husband had been alive, and she had still been happy, vibrant, and full of hope for the future.

Once Colin had hauled the body in its now-frozen sacking from the back of the wagon, Sebastian took out a shilling and held it out to Mr. Fletcher, but the man shook his head. "Keep your money, Inspector. It was the least I could do."

"Thank you, Mr. Fletcher."

The older man tipped his hat and snapped the reins, and the wagon creaked into life as it pulled out of the alley. By the time Sebastian walked into the cellar, Colin had already deposited the body on the table he used for postmortems.

The size of the bundle was not lost on him. "Is it a child?"

"Yes. I have reason to believe she was murdered," Sebastian added.

"Where?"

"At the Foundling Hospital."

"Where Miss Tate works? Is she all right?" Colin hurried to inquire.

"She's understandably upset, but she was nowhere near when the poor girl died."

"Why is the sacking frozen?" Colin asked as he tried to unwrap the body.

"The victim was submerged in a tub."

"I see. Well, I can't begin until the ice melts and I'm able to access the body without causing damage. Have you breakfasted?"

Sebastian shook his head. Constable Bryant had come to fetch him just as the sun had been cresting the horizon. The eager youth had banged on the door of Mrs. Poole's boarding house in a way that had nearly given the poor woman the vapors.

"Come. A strong cup of coffee will set you to rights, and I believe there are a few mince pies left over from yesterday. You can tell me everything you've learned, and by that time the body should be ready. I hope it wasn't exposed to the cold long enough to freeze internally."

"Thank you. I won't say no to a hot drink. Or a mince pie."

Colin clapped Sebastian on the back, and the two men returned upstairs. Sebastian was relieved to see that Mrs. Ramsey was no longer in her chair. Perhaps Mabel had taken her out for a walk or helped her to her room, where she could rest. The coffee Mabel had set to brew was ready, and a covered dish containing six mince pies sat on the pine table next to the sugar bowl. Colin disappeared into the larder and returned with a jug of cream, which he placed on the table before taking down two cups and saucers from the painted dresser.

"Do you mind if we talk in here?" he asked as he set the cups down.

"Not at all."

"Sometimes I like to hide in the kitchen. I know it's cowardly, but it's the only place I can get a bit of peace, aside from my bedroom."

"I understand," Sebastian replied. He could only imagine what a strain Mrs. Ramsey's condition put on both Colin and

Mabel, particularly since Mrs. Ramsey had little to occupy her and longed for company.

"Now, tell me what happened," Colin invited as he poured coffee into their cups and reached for the sugar tongs.

Sebastian relayed the facts but kept the speculation to a minimum. They'd talk more once the postmortem was complete and Colin could present Sebastian with his own set of facts.

"Are you thinking strangulation?" Colin asked.

"Possibly."

"Any evidence of sexual assault?"

"None that Gemma or I noticed, but that doesn't rule out a sexually motivated attack. Amanda had expressed a desire to leave the Foundling Hospital but didn't give Matron a reason. My initial theory was that she had someone waiting for her on the outside, but it's just as likely that she needed to get away from someone on the inside."

"Are you thinking she might have been trying to get away from a man?"

"Maybe."

"Or perhaps she had a falling-out with one of the other girls or had a conflict with a female teacher or mistress," Colin suggested.

"Matron Holcombe said Amanda seemed happy at the prospect of leaving. Could be relief at the promise of getting away, or she might have had plans that had nothing to do with what happened to her."

"The postmortem will tell us more," Colin promised.

"I need to know if she was with child."

Colin looked momentarily sad, then nodded. "Children having children is not unheard of, even in strictly run institutions like the Foundling Hospital. If Amanda managed to get away unobserved this time, she might have done it before."

"But was she unobserved?" Sebastian mused. "Someone

must have seen her leave. There are two dozen girls in the dormitory. Surely not everyone is a sound sleeper."

"Children of a nervous disposition don't tend to sleep as well as those who accept the world for what it is."

"Spoken from experience?"

Colin chuckled. "I was always a light sleeper, even when I was a boy. I still am."

"I used to sleep like the dead when I was young," Sebastian said. "It wasn't until Louisa..." He had no wish to speak the words, but he knew Colin took his meaning. Once violent death had torn a family apart, there was no peaceful slumber or pleasant dreams.

Colin finished his coffee, then rinsed their cups in the sink and set them on the draining board. "I think Amanda should be ready by now. Will you stay for the postmortem?"

"I'll be back in a few hours," Sebastian replied.

He didn't know if Superintendent Lovell had planned to come to the office on Boxing Day, but if he was there he'd need to be apprised of the situation in case the commissioner summoned him. In his years in the police service, Sebastian had learned that members of the highest echelons of bureaucracy tended to belong to a secret club that had informants everywhere and were kept abreast of anything that could undermine their positions or cast doubt on their achievements. The members of the Foundling Hospital committee had most likely already been informed of Amanda Carter's death, which meant the commissioner would feel personally invested in a speedy and satisfactory result since he would feel direct pressure from those who had the power to make his life uncomfortable.

Sebastian would have preferred to walk, but he couldn't afford to dawdle, not when he had to go over what Constable Bryant had learned and apprise Lovell of the latest developments. He walked briskly until he spotted an empty cab and hailed the driver, who pulled over even though the designated cab stop was several streets away. Sebastian climbed in and settled in for the ride.

SIX

Once Sebastian had left, Gemma had no choice but to return to the infirmary. She found Michael sitting on his cot, watching the door, his gaze anxious.

"Can I go now, miss?" he asked.

"Do you feel better?"

Michael nodded. "I'm all right."

He still looked pale, and his expression was pained, but Gemma had no reason to detain him if he felt well enough to return.

"Go straight back to the boys' wing," she said.

"Yes, miss. Thank you, miss."

He practically ran for the door, and Gemma turned her attention to the children in her care. She thought this would be a good time to apply a mustard plaster since the children were now awake. Once the moistened plaster adhered to the skin, it grew warm, stimulating circulation and drawing infection from the body. It wasn't a pleasant experience, especially for small children, who couldn't tolerate the burning sensation as well as adults and complained about the abrasive texture of the mustard seed, but it was highly effective. If the plaster didn't work, she would then try cupping. The children were usually intimidated by the flame that was used to facilitate suction when applying the little jars to the patient's back, but cupping was also very effective when dealing with respiratory illnesses.

Gemma prepared the strips and instructed the children to lift their nightshirts so she could apply the plasters to their pallid little chests. She tried to focus on her task, but all she could see in her mind's eye was Amanda's wide blue eyes and the look of astonishment frozen on her face, the realization that her life was about to end stamped into her features. It broke Gemma's heart, but it also made her incandescently angry.

Unlike so many unwanted children, who died in infancy or before reaching the age of five, Amanda had beat the odds and thrived. She had been accepted into the Foundling Hospital, sent to the country to be raised in a wholesome environment, and returned to the hospital to begin her education. Amanda had been on the verge of adulthood, and, even though she would never have lived a life of luxury or privilege, she would have had a chance, not only at survival but at happiness. She might have found love, married, and had a family, or she might have remained in service for the rest of her life and become part of the below-stairs family that was the closest someone in service could come to that feeling of belonging that eluded so many. She wouldn't have to live in some squalid boarding house or worry every day about whether she would earn enough to put food on the table or purchase a new pair of boots once the ones she'd owned for years had worn through. Now her future had been snatched away from her, her light snuffed out before it truly had a chance to shine.

Gemma sank into a chair and her gaze drifted toward the window. Sebastian was a seasoned detective and could rely on years of experience, but Gemma had inside knowledge of the Foundling Hospital and the sort of access Matron would never allow a policeman. Once again, her thoughts turned to the why.

Why had Amanda left her dormitory in the middle of the night? Whom was she meeting? How had the other person gained access to the laundry, and had this been the first time they had planned to meet? Had Amanda not noticed that her pockets were turned out, or had whoever she'd met been searching for something? And if so, what could it possibly be? The children had nothing of value and were not given the tokens their mothers had left for them. Until she left the hospital, Amanda would have been a blank slate who had no past and as of yet no future. What would someone want with her—other than the only thing any young girl had to give?

Having come to that conclusion, Gemma considered every male who might have had access to Amanda over the past few months and would have the means to sneak into the laundry. Once she had narrowed down the list to a few possible candidates, she returned to the children, who were now squirming and asking her to peel off the burning strips of plaster. She had her suspicions, but now she would have to test them out.

SEVEN

The duty room was empty except for Sergeant Woodward, who was reading a newspaper and sipping from a mug of milky tea. It was Boxing Day, when the masses were still feeling merry and pious after Christmas, and too early in the day for drinking, brawling, and whoring, so no arrests had been made and the building was ominously quiet.

"You all alone?" Sebastian asked as he approached the counter.

"Meadows and Forrest are in the back," Sergeant Woodward said. "Meadows is showing Forrest the evidence room."

"Why?"

"Because the gormless idiot was underfoot, and I needed a few moments of peace to gather my thoughts."

Constable Forrest was a new addition to the Yard. He'd started just before Christmas and had yet to do anything other than make tea and ask pointless questions that poured out of him as if his head were a leaky bucket. The lad was hardly older than seventeen and looked like a strong wind might blow him over. To add to his air of vulnerability, he also refused to shave the fuzz on his upper lip; evidently he was convinced that if he left it alone long enough it would eventually begin to resemble a moustache.

"Is Lovell here?" Sebastian asked.

"Not expected in today."

Lovell's absence offered Sebastian a brief reprieve, and he'd take it gladly. The more he learned in the meantime, the better, since Lovell tended to work himself up into a lather whenever persons of quality were concerned, and, where there were charitable works and orphans, there were always wealthy benefactors who prided themselves on their selfless sacrifice.

Constable Bryant came huffing into the duty room, the bottoms of his trousers covered in bits of straw. He was a resourceful young man who wasn't about to spend his hard-earned wages on cabs. He'd no doubt caught a ride with some farmer and was ready to make his report.

"Did you learn anything?" Sebastian asked once they'd settled at his desk.

Constable Bryant shook his head. "Not a lot, guv. The girls were too frightened to speak in front of Mrs. Dixon. They all said Amanda went to bed at the usual time and no one saw her leave. They didn't know what had happened yet. Just assumed Amanda was in some sort of trouble."

"Someone must know something."

"That Mrs. Dixon was watching the girls like a hawk. If any girl knew something and kept it quiet, she'd get punished for sure. A few girls did mention that Amanda was a particular friend of Doris Dockett, but when questioned Doris appeared to know nothing."

"And what of Mrs. Dixon herself?" Sebastian asked.

"Went to the room she shares with Miss Woodwiss as soon as all the girls were in bed. Says she knew nothing was amiss until she went to wake the girls this morning and found Amanda's cot empty." Constable Bryant sighed. "Then Mrs. Dixon said it was time for me to go and shepherded the girls to breakfast."

"Thank you, Constable."

"Anything else I can do to help?" Constable Bryant asked.

"Not just now."

Sebastian was at a bit of a loss, if he were honest. Any cooperation he received at the Foundling Hospital would depend on Matron and whatever directive she received from the committee. Sebastian was sure that plenty of children had died at the hospital over the years, but deaths caused by illness were to be expected. A murder was something else entirely and would haunt the hospital's reputation for years to come. If he knew anything of privately funded institutions, it was that within a day or two Matron and the hospital governors would close ranks and he would have no way in, which meant he had to act quickly and efficiently if he were to solve this case.

Sebastian left the Yard and began the trek back to Blackfriars. He wished he hadn't wasted time going back and forth, but such was the lot of a policeman. When in the midst of an investigation, he was always in motion and frequently burning through resources of his own, since the police service did not compensate the detectives for expenses incurred.

He consulted his pocket watch. Colin would need another hour at the very least to complete the postmortem, so Sebastian would take his time and walk. Walking helped to focus his mind, and he needed to come up with a plan.

EIGHT

Back in Blackfriars, Mabel directed Sebastian straight to the cellar, wrinkling her nose. Even though they couldn't smell anything upstairs, it was hard not to envision what Colin was engaged in, and the mind unwittingly supplied the rest. Sebastian took a deep breath and headed downstairs, knocking to announce his presence, his stomach churning with apprehension.

Colin had finished the postmortem but was still in the process of closing up the body, a curved needle threaded with silk suspended between his elegant fingers. Amanda lay on her back, her dark hair spread about her head and her eyes mercifully shut. At first glance, she was just a delicate child, all coltish limbs and gently rounded cheeks, but she was a child on the verge of womanhood who would have invited a very different kind of attention from grown men had she not died so suddenly.

Sebastian averted his gaze from Amanda's delicate body, suddenly feeling sick to his stomach at the terrible waste of life and the unspent potential that had reduced a young girl to this hollow shell. Amanda looked like she was sleeping, but another few days and death would set about its ugly work, destroying the loveliness that would never again be appreciated by anyone. Colin tied off the thread, then pulled a sheet over the body, leaving only the shoulders and the head exposed, and Sebastian was glad for that bit of privacy for a girl who no longer cared who saw her nakedness.

Colin cupped Amanda's cheek, as if she could still feel the tender gesture, then allowed his hand to drop away and sighed heavily.

"Tell me," Sebastian said.

"Amanda was in fine health and reasonably well nourished for a child who came from an orphanage. Her teeth were in good condition, and her person was clean and well cared for."

Sebastian waited patiently, since Colin normally followed a particular pattern when delivering his conclusions.

"There's a contusion on the occiput, just here." Colin gently lifted Amanda's head and showed Sebastian the wound Gemma had noticed earlier. "The injury is superficial. The blow wasn't severe enough to cause intercranial hemorrhage, but it most likely stunned the victim long enough for her assailant to maneuver her toward the tub. If the wound bled or if any grit adhered to the skin, all traces were washed away by the water." Colin pulled the sheet a little lower and continued, "There's bruising to the upper arms, and also livid marks on the neck."

"So, what's your conclusion regarding the cause of death?" Sebastian asked.

"Based on the injuries, I would venture to guess that her assailant grabbed Amanda by the arms and smashed her head against something hard, like a wall or the floor, then pushed her into the tub and held her down, their hands around Amanda's throat. There was water in the lungs, so the cause of death was drowning."

"How long would it have taken for her to die?"

"A few minutes."

"Was she conscious, do you think?" Sebastian asked, praying that death had come quickly and Amanda hadn't suffered.

"I believe so. If she weren't, her grip on the tub would have loosened and her eyes would have been closed."

"Time of death?"

"Difficult to say since the body lay in frigid water for what had to be hours. My estimate would be sometime before midnight to a few hours of being discovered by the caretaker, so a six- to eight-hour window."

"Was she interfered with?" Sebastian asked, his gaze sliding to the childish face and snub nose, wondering how anyone could be so cruel as to hold this poor child underwater and watch her die.

"I don't see any bruising or tearing, but any physical evidence such as blood or semen would have been washed away. If sexual congress took place shortly before death, it's impossible to say with any certainty now."

"Was she still a virgin?"

Colin looked apologetic. "Again, difficult to say in the absence of a maidenhead. It's a delicate membrane and sometimes can rupture on its own."

"Is there any possibility Amanda was with child?" Sebastian inquired.

"If she was, the pregnancy was at such an early stage that it's impossible to see with the naked eye."

"Is there anything else you can tell me?" Sebastian implored him. "Are there any historic fractures or scars?"

"Not a blemish on her aside from evidence of the recent struggle."

"What about her clothes?" Sebastian asked, his gaze going to the wet garments Colin had tossed into an enamel basin.

"Nightdress, dressing gown, and cotton drawers. I expect

every girl at the Foundling Hospital is issued with exactly the same items."

"Was there anything of a personal nature at all?"

"Yes, but I don't know what it means."

Colin turned and lifted a small medallion strung on a leather thong out of the biscuit tin he used for personal effects. It displayed the number 8412.

"It's Amanda's registration number," Sebastian said. "It was given to her when she was accepted into the hospital."

Colin shook his head in dismay. "A tag, as if she were a dog."

"It is rather impersonal. And the tokens that their mothers leave are kept locked up, the only connection to the children's past kept hidden."

"Speaking of keeping things hidden," Colin said, and turned around to lift another object out of the tin, "this was clutched in Amanda's left hand."

Sebastian held out his hand, and Colin dropped a tiny wooden pin into his palm. Sebastian held it up for closer inspection. It was as tall as a thimble and as wide at the bottom, but the top was narrower and smoothly rounded. Most of the pin was a glossy red, but a tiny face was painted on one side, yellow hair above round blue eyes and a tiny pink mouth.

"What is that?" Colin asked.

"A toy of some sort."

"But why would Amanda have that in her hand?" Colin inquired.

"Perhaps that's what her assailant was after," Sebastian said, but the answer didn't make any sense. Who would murder a child over a tiny wooden peg? It was pretty but completely worthless, the sort of thing one might find at a craft fair or a country market.

"Perhaps it had sentimental value," Colin suggested.

"It must have, but if that's what the killer was after I can only assume they would have taken it off her."

"Perhaps they didn't realize it was in her hand."

Rage welled up in Sebastian's chest, and he had to take a deep breath to assert control over his emotions. "I will not rest until I find out who did this," he ground out. "This poor girl had her entire life before her, until someone smashed her head into the wall and held her down as she gasped for air. This wasn't an accident. This was an execution."

"Why would anyone want to execute this poor, defenseless girl? Surely she couldn't be a threat to anyone."

"Maybe not a physical threat, but perhaps something much more dangerous," Sebastian replied.

"What could a fourteen-year-old have on someone that would get her murdered in the night?"

"That's what I intend to find out," Sebastian said, and pushed the tiny pin into the pocket of his waistcoat.

As he cast one final look at Amanda, the question he asked all too often popped into his mind. Why did God allow innocents to die? So many children died of hunger, disease, cold, and neglect. What was the point of granting life if it would be snuffed out before the child even reached adulthood? It was heartbreaking and unfair.

Sebastian could still recall the translucent skin of his tiny son's eyelids, the shell-like ears, and the insubstantial weight in his arms as he laid the child in the coffin next to Louisa. At least they would sleep together for eternity, he reminded himself. Not left alone, like him, to cope with crushing guilt and grief.

"Do you mean to involve Miss Tate?" Colin asked, and Sebastian could sense his judgment.

"I will do nothing more than ask for her opinion," Sebastian promised.

"Sebastian, whoever killed that girl is most likely still there, on the premises. Don't put Gemma in harm's way." Colin immediately backtracked when he noticed how affronted Sebastian seemed by the rebuke. "I'm sorry. I didn't mean to imply..."

"It's fine. I know what you meant."

But the implication was clear. Sebastian had been responsible for the death of one woman, and now he meant to endanger another innocent who'd put her trust in him.

"I have to go."

"What about the body?" Colin asked.

He used unclaimed cadavers to teach his students the secrets a body had to tell, but Amanda Carter would not be a subject for study.

"Her body must be returned to the hospital. They will see to the burial."

"I understand," Colin said, still looking contrite. "Sebastian, I didn't mean to imply—" he tried again, but Sebastian held up his hand, then turned on his heel and hurried up the steps before Colin could apologize again.

NINE

Just before noon, Gemma's stomach reminded her that it was time for luncheon. Having left the boarding house in a panic before breakfast was served, she hadn't had anything to eat since Christmas dinner last night. If no one was seriously ill, she normally went down to the dining hall to eat, but when there were patients to look after she had to rely on someone to bring her a tray. Gemma sullenly wished they'd send up someone likely to tattle. Cut off as she was, she had no way of knowing what was happening, and, although she did not as a whole approve of gossip, idle speculation could sometimes be based on valuable kernels of truth. She would also have liked to consult with Sebastian.

Constable Bryant must have returned to Scotland Yard by now, but Gemma didn't think he would have learned anything valuable. She hadn't worked at the Foundling Hospital long, but long enough to get a sense of the children. They couldn't trust the mistresses or their teachers, knowing as they did that they would be reprimanded and punished for any transgression, so they learned early on to rely on each other. In the absence of a traditional family, the other children were their kin, and strong bonds were formed. Amanda would have known the girls in her dormitory since she had returned to the hospital at the age of five, and at least some of them would be trusted friends. Was she the sort of girl to divulge her secrets, or was she someone who guarded her thoughts and feelings? Since Amanda had never spent more than an hour at the infirmary, Gemma had no personal sense of the girl, but, having seen her remains, she was certain that Amanda had been brutally murdered.

Gemma's thoughts were interrupted by the arrival of Ella Boone, who brought her a bowl of pea soup, a slice of buttered bread, and a mug of tea, and cups of beef tea and bread for the sick children. Gemma helped the children sit up so they could eat, then returned to the little table where Ella had set down the tray. Both the soup and the tea were lukewarm, since it was a long walk from the kitchens, but Gemma didn't mind. She was too hungry to care, and hoped Ella would stay for a chat so she could take the tray back with her when everyone had finished.

Ella was about sixteen. She was short, slender, and ginger-haired, her large blue eyes her most striking feature. She was one of the girls who had grown up here and stayed once they came of age. Now she worked in the kitchens and lived on-site, much as she had done when she was one of the foundlings. Gemma supposed in some ways it was preferable to being cast into an unfamiliar world as a servant, where Ella would have had no one to turn to save a housekeeper, who wielded as much power as a monarch in any domestic establishment. At the Foundling Hospital, Ella was still among friends but now had slightly more personal freedom, and shared a room with three other servants rather than two dozen orphans, who weren't permitted a single moment of privacy throughout the day.

Ella smiled apologetically as she set the tray down. "I'm sorry it took so long, Miss Tate. Everything is helter-skelter today, on account of poor Amanda's passing."

"So everyone knows?" Gemma asked. She had wondered how Matron would address what had happened.

Ella nodded. "Matron made an announcement just before lunch."

"What did she say?"

Matron could hardly say that Amanda's death was the result of an accident or a sudden illness. The children might have mistaken Sebastian for one of the hospital's benefactors or a tradesman in his caped coat and top hat, but no one could mistake Constable Bryant for anything other than what he was. In his smart blue uniform and with a wooden truncheon at his belt, he was clearly a policeman, and he had interviewed some of the girls. If Gemma knew anything about young girls, it was that their ability to pass on scandalous news was unrivaled.

"She said that Amanda's death was the result of an altercation with an unknown assailant. She also said that Amanda had broken the rules and had brought about her own downfall, and that should be a lesson to us all."

Gemma nearly choked on her outrage but bit back the criticism. It was only natural that Matron Holcombe would take this opportunity to warn the children about breaking the rules. There was nothing more she could do for Amanda, but it was her responsibility to protect those in her care, and, harsh as her warning might be, she made a valid point. Had Amanda remained in her bed last night, chances were she'd be alive and enjoying her pea soup right now.

"What do you think happened, Ella?" Gemma asked as she lifted the soup spoon to her mouth.

"I'm sure I don't know, miss," Ella said, but Gemma sensed that the girl wasn't being entirely truthful.

"You grew up at the hospital. Did you ever sneak out?" she asked.

"Not me, miss."

Gemma thought that perhaps Ella was too timid to break the rules, but she might know of someone who had.

"Did anyone else?" she asked. "Surely someone broke the rules from time to time."

Ella glanced toward the door, but they were quite alone other than the sick children, who were focused on not spilling their broth.

"There are always those who are prone to mischief, and more often than not they reap a bitter reward," Ella said, sounding like some old-time prophet.

"Where did they go when they sneaked out during the night?" Gemma inquired.

"The kitchens mostly. They'd steal sugar cubes, apples, or pears when in season, or cake, if there was any." Ella sighed wistfully. "Matron Holcombe is very fond of Battenberg cake. Cook bakes it for her once a week, just to keep her sweet."

Gemma had never seen Battenberg cake served at table, so the treat must be reserved for Matron and served to her in her office.

"They'd cut tiny slivers so that Cook wouldn't notice, and then come back with their hands all sticky," Ella said, smiling cheekily. "They always seemed so lighthearted then."

"Is that all it takes, a sliver of cake to lighten a heart?" Gemma asked.

Ella's gaze was filled with longing for a time gone by. "It wasn't the cake, miss. It was the defiance that made them happy. For a few brief moments, they had a say in their lives and did something they wanted."

Gemma understood just what Ella meant. Except for a few hours of rest in the afternoon, the children were kept busy from morning till night. They scrubbed, washed, dusted, mended, and polished in between lessons, meals, and prayers. No child was ever asked what they wanted or how they felt. It was irrelevant, and punishments were frequent and often harsh. Getting caught stealing cake from the larder would probably earn one a caning, but the freedom of those moments had to be intoxicating and the defiance indescribably empowering.

"They're all gone now," Ella said. "Slaving for someone else."

"Why did you decide to remain?" Gemma asked.

"Better the devil you know, miss," Ella replied wisely.

"Did Amanda ever get up to anything that would get her into trouble with Mrs. Dixon?"

"I wouldn't know. Amanda was two years behind me, so I hardly knew her."

The children called out that they were finished, so Ella collected the dirty crockery and stacked her tray. "I'd best be going now, miss."

"Of course. Thank you, Ella."

"You're most welcome."

Once Ella had gone, Gemma's gaze strayed to the patch of blue sky beyond the window. She could imagine how the children felt, spending their days imprisoned by endless rules, grueling chores, and twice-daily prayers that probably felt eternal, especially on fine days when anyone would long to be outside. To break free for even a few moments had to be absolute bliss; but Amanda hadn't sneaked into the larder to steal cake. She had willingly gone down or had been lured to the cellar in the middle of the night, which meant she must have had a compelling motive. Gemma could think of only two reasons a person would agree to such a scheme—the promise of something wonderful or a very real threat. Given that Amanda was dead, Gemma was inclined to think the latter.

She needed to learn more about Amanda Carter, but to appear too interested would arouse suspicion and invite Matron's scrutiny. Gemma had already got on the wrong side of the woman with her unprofessional attachment to Lucy and her connection to the police. But she was a nurse in an institution for motherless children, and their emotional as well as physical welfare fell within her remit. It was only natural that she should inquire about the well-being of Amanda's friends and have a word with Mrs. Dixon, who would have known Amanda as well as anyone. It could be a waste of time, but Gemma thought that the children were more likely to open up to a trusted female than a policeman who had no idea how to talk to adolescent girls.

Gemma checked on her charges, administered doses of balsam of honey, which soothed irritated throats and eased bouts of coughing, tucked the boys in, and left them to nap. The girls were allowed a period of rest after the midday meal, which would be the perfect time to visit the dormitory and have a quiet word.

TEN

Sebastian bought a sausage roll and a mug of chestnut soup from a street vendor, a rare delicacy he didn't come across often and couldn't pass up. He consumed both in record time and was back at the Foundling Hospital just before two o'clock.

Matron Holcombe looked tired and irritable when one of the porters escorted Sebastian to her office. She had been standing by the window and looking out over the empty yard, but now lowered herself into a chair with the air of a woman settling to a highly distasteful task. Death was grim, especially the death of a child, but Sebastian had hoped she would be more invested in finding out the truth.

"I didn't expect to see you again so soon, Inspector," Matron said as Sebastian unbuttoned his coat and sat across from her, placing his hat on his thigh.

"I'm sorry to say that this is now a murder investigation."

Matron Holcombe paled, but her expression remained closed and her posture defensive. "And what makes you believe Amanda was murdered? Her death could have been a dreadful accident."

"The postmortem revealed evidence of a struggle, a wound

to the back of the head, and water in the lungs. Someone attacked Amanda, slammed her head against the wall—" Sebastian held up his hand when Matron looked set to interrupt. "I saw the blood, madam," he said, and continued before she could come up with a plausible excuse for blood smeared on the wall of the hospital laundry. "Her assailant then pushed her into the tub and held her down until she drowned. Once the child was dead, they turned out her pockets, clearly in search of something, then fled."

"What would you have me do?" Matron asked warily.

"I have some questions to put to you."

"I will not answer any questions until I have your word that this investigation will be managed with the utmost discretion," Matron Holcombe replied.

"Do you not care that a child was murdered right under your nose?" Sebastian snapped.

"I do. Very much. But I also bear a responsibility to the other children in my care, which is made possible by the generous donations that enable this institution to continue to operate year after year."

"You mean you care about keeping the donors feeling virtuous and charitable," Sebastian clarified.

"Whatever gets us the funds we need, Inspector Bell. You might know something of that yourself, employed as you are by an organization whose very existence depends on the merit of its reputation."

Sebastian nodded. He did understand, and he had to be mindful of compromising the children who were in the care of the hospital or making things difficult for the matron. Much like himself, she was caught between protecting the vulnerable and keeping her superiors happy, a balancing act that required not only skill but tact.

"Can I see the register?" he asked.

"I'm afraid I cannot give you the name of Amanda's mother.

I have consulted Mr. Crawley, who is the head of the hospital committee, and he feels it wouldn't be appropriate to open our records to the police."

Sebastian could barely contain his annoyance but, unless he had a warrant signed by a judge, Matron and this Mr. Crawley had the final say and did not have to comply with his request. It might still come to a court order, but Sebastian wasn't likely to find a judge willing to hear him out on Boxing Day; and, unless he wanted to find himself unemployed, he would have to consult Superintendent Lovell first and obtain his approval before approaching an officer of the court.

"Inspector, please believe me when I tell you that Amanda's mother has nothing to do with her death, so you're wasting both your time and mine," Matron Holcombe stated with an understanding smile and an air of exaggerated patience.

"How can you be certain that Amanda's family has nothing to do with what happened here?" Sebastian demanded.

"Because there were no strangers on the premises on Christmas Day. The doors were kept locked the entire day, and no one came in or out."

"Are there normally strangers on the premises?" Sebastian asked.

"There are daily deliveries of provisions, tours of the hospital conducted by committee members, and even occasional visits from politicians and journalists. The Foundling Hospital is a shining example of both industry and charity."

"Indeed," Sebastian replied without a hint of his usual sarcasm. He couldn't help but admire this woman, who held a position of great responsibility and respect. At the moment, she was walking a tightrope above a rocky gorge, and if she slipped she would never recover.

"What did the children do on Christmas Day?" Sebastian asked, deciding to focus on the practical.

"All classes and chores were suspended. That happens only

once a year, to honor the birth of our Lord," Matron explained sternly. "The children attended a morning prayer service that was followed by breakfast, then they took a walk on the grounds and were permitted an hour of free time until midday. After lunch, everyone moved to the chapel, where a Christmas service was followed by a holiday concert organized by Miss Parish and Mr. Simms. After dinner, the masters and mistresses escorted the children to their dormitories. They were allowed an hour of free time until bedtime."

"Was Amanda under the supervision of Mrs. Dixon the entire time?"

"Amanda performed in the concert. She had a lovely singing voice and delighted us with 'I Saw Three Ships.' One of my favorite carols," Matron added wistfully.

"I'm afraid I don't know that one."

Matron nodded. "Amanda had musical talent and rather admired Miss Parish, who encourages the children to express themselves through music. We have a number of gifted pupils."

"I would like a word with Miss Parish, but first, I would like to speak to Mrs. Dixon, then question Doris Dockett. Alone."

"Mrs. Dixon and Doris have already been questioned by your man. I see no reason to speak to them again, especially Doris. I will not permit you to intimidate a defenseless and grieving young girl."

"What makes you think I mean to intimidate her?" Sebastian asked.

"Because you intimidate me, Inspector, and I have considerably more experience with men of your ilk."

Sebastian didn't bother to ask her to explain what she meant. He had a fairly good idea.

"Is there anyone else you would like to speak to, Inspector?"

"You mentioned Mr. Simms."

"Mr. Simms is our chaplain."

"Would Mr. Simms have access to Amanda?"

Matron looked outraged at the very suggestion. "I assure you, Mr. Simms would have no reason to attack a young girl in the laundry."

"Nevertheless, does Mr. Simms have access to the girls?"

"Not individually, no."

"I would still like to speak to him."

"I'm sure that can be arranged. You may use the music room since it's empty just now. I will have Miss Parish brought to you, and Mr. Simms will be in the chapel. A porter will escort you once you're finished with Miss Parish. Now, if that is all, I really must get back to work."

"Thank you," Sebastian replied.

Matron had made it clear that he wouldn't be permitted to wander around the building, which meant he wouldn't be able to corner Doris or Mrs. Dixon for a private chat. He had little choice but to speak to the music teacher and the vicar and leave his investigation there for today. Then he'd wait for Gemma to finish her shift and escort her home. He had a feeling she might have something to share with him.

ELEVEN

The children weren't permitted to lounge on their beds during the day, so their free time was spent in a room designated for the purpose. Everything they did had to be constructive, so the girls were encouraged to read improving texts, do their homework, or work on their mending and needlework. Normally, the children went outside at least once a day, but given the day's happenings no one was permitted to leave the building, and the girls' fear and restlessness was palpable as they huddled in small groups or focused on their individual tasks.

Mrs. Dixon sat in the corner, her neck and shoulders tense, her gaze sharp in a nearly bloodless face. Gemma approached her first. Mrs. Dixon's eyes filled with tears and she looked at Gemma imploringly, allowing her guard to slip long enough to reveal a desperate need for sympathy and understanding. Now that the reality had set in and she had been questioned by the police, she likely feared the worst, and in Gemma's opinion her worries were not unfounded. She had witnessed this very thing in Crimea, when underlings would be blamed in order to spare their superiors embarrassment and show those in command that appropriate action had been taken.

"Are you all right, Mrs. Dixon?" she asked, even though the answer was obvious.

"I didn't do anything wrong," Mrs. Dixon moaned. "How could I have known that Amanda would go down to the laundry in the middle of the night?"

"You couldn't have," Gemma replied soothingly. "I'm sure no one blames you."

Mrs. Dixon shot Gemma an incredulous look. "The committee will want answers. Who do you think they'll blame?" she asked bitterly. "I will be accused of dereliction of duty and most likely dismissed without a character."

"Let's not jump ahead of ourselves," Gemma said. "We won't know anything for certain until the investigation is complete. Do you have any idea what Amanda might have been up to?"

Mrs. Dixon looked utterly helpless. "I honestly don't know anything. These girls are like vipers," she whispered. "They keep secrets and mock me behind my back. Sometimes I wish I had gone into service. I would have considerably more freedom as a nanny, and probably a better wage."

"Why did you take this job?" Gemma asked.

"I was orphaned when I was twelve. If not for my mother's widowed aunt, I would have wound up in an orphanage, or the workhouse. I felt it my duty to help those who genuinely need it," Mrs. Dixon explained. "I thought it my Christian duty. And now I will find myself out in the street."

Gemma hated to press her advantage, but this was the only way she could help both Sebastian and Mrs. Dixon. "Was Amanda particularly close with any of the other girls?"

Mrs. Dixon sighed heavily. "She was close with Doris Dockett and Ruby Marks. Amanda and Ruby were thick as thieves."

"Amanda's death is likely to haunt them for the rest of their lives, especially if they knew something that might have saved her. I think it's important that I speak to the girls, to be sure they're coping with the loss of their friend."

Mrs. Dixon nodded. "You are absolutely right, Miss Tate. The girls are not ill, but they're sick at heart over what happened. I don't believe that nursing should be restricted to the physical body."

"I couldn't agree more," Gemma said, glad that Mrs. Dixon wasn't raising objections to her request. "Where can I find them?"

Despite having just described the girls in rather unflattering terms, Mrs. Dixon clearly cared about her charges and worried about their emotional well-being. She scanned the room, presumably in search of Amanda's friends, and Gemma followed the trajectory of her gaze. There were two dozen girls spread out across the room, identical in their brown dresses with triangular white collars and three-quarter sleeves, white aprons, black stockings, and white caps. Mrs. Dixon was dressed in much the same fashion, except that her dress was black and had longer sleeves and a round collar. Like all the female employees, Gemma wore the same uniform when at work, but was currently permitted to wear a black pinafore and black lace cap over her hair on account of her bereavement. The children were not expected to go into mourning, not even if the deceased was a dear friend. By Gemma's calculations, they would never actually finish mourning, since a number of children passed away every year due to serious illness or tragic accidents.

Gemma hadn't been employed at the hospital long enough to know all of the girls by name. The only one she immediately recognized was Belinda Horton, who'd spent a few days in the infirmary several weeks ago with a nasty head cold.

"Doris is that one over there," Mrs. Dixon said, and discreetly pointed to a girl in the corner, who was sitting by herself and appeared to be staring into space. "Ruby is no longer with us."

"Is she dead?"

"No, she left us in September to go into service."

"Where is she employed?"

"Only Matron knows where the girls are placed," Mrs. Dixon replied.

"Thank you, Mrs. Dixon. You can always talk to me if you need a friend," Gemma said before she left the woman to her worrying. Mrs. Dixon nodded, but Gemma didn't think she'd be seeking her out.

Gemma made her way over to Doris and pulled up a chair. Doris was the same age as Amanda, but that was where the similarities ended. She was what Gemma's grandmother would have uncharitably referred to as peasant stock. Doris was big-boned and snub-nosed, with frizzy dark hair that stuck out from her cap and a sullen cast to her mouth. Although the girl was obviously in shock and grieving for her friend, there was something in her gaze that spoke to keeping secrets and gossiping behind closed doors. Gemma would have given her eyeteeth to speak to her privately, but Mrs. Dixon was watching and Gemma knew she only had a few minutes before she was asked to move on to other girls.

"I'm sorry for your loss, Doris," Gemma said.

"Thank you," Doris muttered.

"Doris, I know you feel honor-bound to protect your friend, but Amanda is not likely to get justice if Inspector Bell doesn't discover what she was up to. Will you tell me what you know?" Gemma asked, smiling at Doris in what she hoped was a reassuring manner.

"How will telling you help Amanda?"

"Inspector Bell is my very good friend," Gemma explained.

"Are you his mistress?" Doris asked, her apathy vanishing at the prospect of such juicy gossip.

Gemma felt heat rising in her face but didn't take the bait.

"I'm not, but Inspector Bell has asked for my opinion, and I would like to help him."

"A Scotland Yard detective has asked for your opinion?" Doris asked, her disbelief obvious.

"He wanted me to examine Amanda's remains."

That had the desired effect. Doris looked grief-stricken, and Gemma thought she also saw stirrings of guilt.

"Anything you tell me will remain between us," Gemma promised. "Mrs. Dixon and Matron don't have to know."

"They know everything," Doris said. "I will be shoveling nightsoil for a month if they think I knew something."

"Do you?"

Doris looked deeply conflicted, but guilt won out. "I saw Amanda slip out at ten o'clock."

"How do you know it was ten?"

"I heard the church bell strike the hour."

"Do you know where she went?"

Doris shook her head.

"Did anyone follow her?"

"No," Doris said, clearly surprised by the suggestion.

"Was this the first time Amanda had left the room after lights out?" Gemma inquired.

Doris sneaked a peek at Mrs. Dixon, but her attention was engaged by an argument that had broken out between two girls. Some part of Gemma wanted to demand that Doris tell her all she knew, but she had no right to demand anything and was overstepping her bounds by even speaking to the girl. She had to tread carefully.

"Doris, where did you think Amanda was going?" Gemma asked.

"She was going to meet someone," Doris said after a long pause.

"How do you know?"

"Because she put on her dressing gown. If she needed the toilet, she'd go in her nightdress."

The younger children used the chamber pots kept beneath their beds, but the older girls and the mistresses went to a cloakroom at the end of the corridor, where they could retreat behind a screen for privacy.

"Who do you think she was meeting?" Gemma tried again.

Doris shook her head. "I've known Mandy since we were both five. She wasn't a secretive person. She was trusting and kind, but this last year something had changed. She was different."

"In what way?" Gemma asked.

"She was excited, and hopeful. It was as if suddenly she had something to live for."

"Matron said Amanda had asked for domestic placement. Did she tell you that?"

Doris looked shocked. "No. She never said a word."

"Was there someone she didn't get on with?" Gemma asked. "Someone who might have meant her harm?"

"Mandy wasn't that sort of person. She was a peacemaker and never held a grudge, even when someone hurt her feelings."

"I think that's enough, Miss Tate," Mrs. Dixon interjected as she approached. "Doris has told you all she knows. You have ten minutes to check on the other girls, and then we must start on our afternoon chores."

Gemma nodded. She'd got as much as she was likely to from Doris, but she had one last question.

"Doris, was there anyone else Amanda was close with? Any truly special friends?"

"Just Ruby," Doris said. "She was sad when Ruby left. Said it was like losing a sister."

"Thank you."

Gemma made her rounds and asked her questions, but the other girls, although sad and frightened, did not claim to have a close friendship with Amanda and said they preferred not to dwell on what had happened. Gemma also kept an eye out for any evidence of a physical altercation, but didn't spot any scratches or bruises that could be the result of a fight with Amanda. That was as much as she could do, and it was time she went back to the infirmary. She hoped she would get a chance to speak to Sebastian and tell him about Ruby.

TWELVE

The music room was spacious and high-ceilinged, with a tall window that faced the courtyard and several paintings of pastoral scenes. There was a spinet with sheet music still on the stand, and a three-tiered wooden stand for the singers. Two hardback chairs flanked a small round table by the window. Sebastian assumed the table was there for a private audience, such as the matron or perhaps some of the benefactors who liked to see how their donations were used. A musical education wasn't necessary for an orphan who would go into the army or domestic service, but it was said that the benefactors liked to believe they were giving the children a well-rounded education and exposing them not only to hard work and basic skills but also to beauty.

Miss Parish had the air of a careworn angel, and, although no longer in the first flush of youth, she possessed that ethereal quality that instantly drew men in and brought out their protective instincts. Unlike Matron Holcombe and Mrs. Dixon, who were unmistakable representatives of their social class, Miss Parish appeared to be the victim of reduced circumstances and would have no doubt graced some man's parlor had life not taken an unexpected turn.

"Please, sit down, Miss Parish," Sebastian said, and she perched on the edge of the chair like a schoolgirl. "What is your full name?" he asked, his notebook at the ready.

"Faith. Faith Parish."

"I was told Amanda looked up to you."

Miss Parish smiled wistfully. "All any of these children dream about is a mother who'll love them. Since they have never met their own mothers, they feel drawn to any woman who shows them a bit of kindness."

Lucy's desperate attachment to Gemma sprang to mind, and Sebastian nodded his understanding. Were he an orphan, he felt sure he would feel drawn to Miss Parish, and Gemma as well, since they both possessed an air of gentleness and approachability that the other women Sebastian had met thus far so obviously lacked.

"Have you worked here long?"

"Nearly two years now," Miss Parish replied. "I was forced to seek employment when my father died. I'm afraid he did not leave me well provided for."

"I'm sorry," Sebastian said.

"I've been very happy here," Miss Parish replied with a radiant smile. "I enjoy the company of children."

"Is there anything you can tell me about Amanda?"

"She was a lovely girl, the sort you can't help but care for."

"Did she ever confide in you, Miss Parish?"

"Attachments of a personal nature are not encouraged, so I'm very careful about singling pupils out for special attention. I worry about losing my position."

"But surely you can't help but observe the children you teach. Did you happen to notice anything different about Amanda in recent weeks? A change in mood or perhaps a skittishness that wasn't there before?"

Miss Parish's eyes widened. "Why, no. Amanda was very much herself, Inspector. She seemed content. Happy even. I think she was excited about singing a solo at the Christmas concert. The children are not encouraged to seek attention for its own sake, but we all like to be noticed from time to time, don't we?"

This seemed a rhetorical question, so Sebastian continued, "Do you know if Amanda had any particular friends?"

"She mentioned Doris Dockett, I believe, only last week."

"In what context?"

Miss Parish shrugged. "Something about taking a walk in the grounds together."

"And did you teach Doris as well?" Sebastian asked.

"No," Miss Parish replied with a shake of the head. "Doris has no musical talent whatsoever, so I couldn't even use her in the choir, but she has other talents, I'm sure," she added charitably.

"And do you have any thoughts on Mrs. Dixon? Might she have overlooked something as Amanda's dormitory mistress?"

That was an unfair question, since Miss Parish would hardly know what went on in the dormitories, but it never hurt to ask. Perhaps she was privy to gossip and wouldn't be averse to sharing something she had heard.

Miss Parish's expression reflected her obvious discomfort. "I'm sorry, Inspector, but I know next to nothing about Mrs. Dixon. The only time we're in the same room together is during meals, and Mrs. Dixon prefers to sit with the other mistresses. I expect they have much to discuss."

Sebastian couldn't help but admire Miss Parish's delicacy, but he wasn't ready to give up just yet.

"Can you think of anyone who might have held a grudge against Amanda?"

Miss Parish shook her head. It was obvious she had nothing more to add and hoped Sebastian would leave.

"Do you have any idea why Amanda would have been in the laundry?" Sebastian asked, his desperation mounting. Thus far, he'd learned absolutely nothing that explained what Amanda had been up to or with whom.

"The laundry? Is that where her body...?" Miss Parish's voice trailed off and Sebastian thought she might succumb to tears. She stared down at her hands, her shoulders drooping with despair, and Sebastian was just about to offer her his handkerchief when Miss Parish inhaled deeply and looked up, meeting his gaze bravely.

"Forgive me. It's such a dreadful shock. The laundry, you said," Miss Parish repeated, her feathery brows furrowing with concentration as she considered Sebastian's question. "Perhaps Amanda needed to wash something," she said, suddenly blushing as if the very thought embarrassed her.

The possibility had never occurred to Sebastian, but it made an odd sort of sense. Perhaps Amanda had gone down to the laundry to wash an article of clothing or a sheet that might have been stained—with what? Menstrual blood? That would explain why there had been water in the tub. She might have filled it herself. Sebastian cast his mind back to the laundry. Had there been something in the room that Amanda might have washed? He didn't believe so, but he would ask to see the laundry one more time when he spoke to Matron.

"Thank you, Miss Parish."

"You're very welcome, Inspector," Miss Parish replied with a soft smile. "I only wish I could have been more help."

There was nothing outwardly inappropriate in Miss Parish's demeanor, but Sebastian was observant enough to notice when a woman took an interest. He supposed someone in Miss Parish's position didn't meet many eligible men, especially if she lived on the premises. In most workplaces, romantic relationships between members of staff usually resulted in immediate dismissal with no character, but Sebastian supposed he was fair game since he was an outsider.

"Good day," he said, and watched Miss Parish glide from the room.

A porter who introduced himself as Mr. Watts was waiting by the door to take Sebastian to the chapel. As he followed the man, he reflected that Matron was taking no chances in leaving him on his own.

The chaplain proved even less helpful than Miss Parish. He was a slight, balding man in his forties whose small, nearly lashless eyes betrayed his confusion at being questioned by a police detective. He had been the hospital chaplain for nearly three years but did not know any of the children by name and clearly paid little attention to their spiritual needs. He recalled a girl singing "I Saw Three Ships" but couldn't tell Sebastian anything about her or what had become of her once she'd resumed her seat. He had been informed of Amanda's death but had chalked up the incident to God's will and had nothing more to say on the subject.

Disappointed with his lack of progress, Sebastian asked Mr. Watts to take him down to the laundry. The man had to seek permission from the matron, but once it was granted he availed himself of a lantern and invited Sebastian to follow him down the stairs.

The laundry looked much as it had that morning. It was cold and dark, and smelled of damp wood and lye soap. It didn't take long to ascertain that no articles of clothing or bedlinens had been left either to soak or to dry on the rack. Whatever had brought Amanda to the laundry was not a desire to wash out bloodstains to avoid embarrassment, so the meeting with her killer couldn't have been accidental. Unfortunately, Sebastian was no closer to figuring out who Amanda had come to meet or why.

By the time he returned upstairs, Sebastian noted, the sun

had set and the temperature had dropped, both inside and out. The corridors were freezing, and still as eerily silent as they had been when he'd arrived. The children had been confined to the common rooms in order to contain the spread of panic and allow the police time to investigate, but soon they would be coming down to have their supper and then return upstairs to get ready for bed. Sebastian didn't expect to solve a murder in one day, but the last few hours had been particularly frustrating, the lack of clues maddening. He pulled out his pocket watch and consulted the time. All he could do now was wait for Gemma and walk her home, the only task he actually looked forward to before he returned to Mrs. Poole's boarding house and spent the evening with his cat Gustav.

Sebastian had at least half an hour before Gemma finished her shift, and he hoped he could remain indoors rather than stand in the cold. He was just about to inquire of a passing porter if there was a place he might wait when a ginger-haired young woman approached. She was dressed in a black gown and white cap and pinafore, so she was not one of the orphans. The woman pulled a folded scrap of paper from her pocket and handed it to him.

"Miss Tate asked me to give this to you, Inspector," she said and turned to leave.

"Is Miss Tate all right?" Sebastian called after her, wondering why Gemma hadn't sought him out in person.

The woman turned back and smiled. "She's rather busy in the infirmary at the moment, and I was on my way back to the kitchens anyhow."

"What is your name?" Sebastian asked, in case he might need to speak to the woman again at a later date.

"Ella Boone. I deliver meals to the infirmary, so I see Miss Tate quite often."

"Thank you, Miss Boone."

"My pleasure."

Sebastian unfolded the note as soon as Ella had gone, eager to learn what Gemma wanted him to know.

Amanda was close with Ruby Marks, who's now in service. Matron has the address.

Sebastian grinned, refolded the note, and pushed it into his pocket. Now all he had to do was obtain the address.

THIRTEEN

"I need an address for Ruby Marks," Sebastian said once he had knocked and was bidden to enter.

Matron Holcombe looked surprised, then shook her head. "Ruby has been in service for two months, Inspector. A visit from the police might predispose her employers against her."

"Her friend is dead," Sebastian snapped.

"What can she possibly know of what happened here last night?" the matron countered.

"Amanda might have confided in her. They were close."

"Much can change for an adolescent girl in two months' time, Inspector. Whatever Amanda told Ruby is no longer relevant. Isn't it time you were going?"

She made a point of looking at the ormolu clock that stood on the mantel. It was nearly five o'clock.

"I will be back tomorrow."

"I can't stop you coming back, but I can't see what more you think you can discover. You've spoken to everyone who might help and seem to have learned nothing."

"Are you suggesting I abandon the investigation?"

"I'm suggesting you tread carefully, Inspector. No employee

of the Foundling Hospital will speak to the press, since any breach will result in immediate dismissal and loss of wages. So, if the story appears in the papers, I will know that either you or your man were the leak. If that happens, I will see to it that your career with the police service is unexpectedly short-lived."

"Are you threatening me?" Sebastian ground out.

"I'm simply making you aware of what will happen, Inspector Bell. Some of our benefactors are men of considerable influence."

"Enough influence to make certain a murder is treated as an accident?"

"I want to see justice done as much as you do, but, unlike you, I'm looking at the bigger picture, which is the future of this institution and the well-being of the children who would end up in the gutter if the Foundling Hospital were to close its doors."

"And how does another murder figure into this picture?" Sebastian demanded, frustrated by the woman's refusal to see the danger everyone at the hospital was still in. "The killer is most likely within these very walls."

"I cannot worry about hypothetical crimes, Inspector Bell. I must deal with the situation at hand, and as of this moment we have only one murder and a potential scandal that could do untold damage to this institution. So I would thank you to stop your panic-mongering. Do we understand each other?"

"I believe we do," Sebastian replied, biting back the colorful retort that had sprung to his lips.

"Now, if you would be so kind as to leave the premises."

"Goodnight, Matron," Sebastian said, and tipped his hat.

"Goodnight, Inspector Bell," Matron said with the air of someone who'd just bested him in a contest of wills.

FOURTEEN

The night was bitterly cold, the sky clear and strewn with stars, and the moon nearly full. Black smoke billowed from the hospital chimneys, the exhalations carried off on the gusts of wind that tore at Sebastian's hat and managed to find its way inside his coat. The cobbles beneath his feet were icy and slick, and the courtyard and street beyond the gate were deserted, hospital business finished for the day, and anyone who did not reside on the premises on their way home or about to be.

Not wanting to draw attention to the fact that he was still there should someone see him and report back to the matron, Sebastian loitered a safe distance from the main gate. He spotted Gemma a few minutes later, her gait determined as she strode toward him, her bonnet tied securely beneath her chin. The wings of her cape flapped in the wind, and she shivered and wrapped her arms about her middle to keep in the heat. Even in mourning attire, Gemma was lovely, and, when the light of a nearby streetlamp cast a golden halo about her face, Sebastian was rewarded by a glimpse of an affectionate smile and an unmistakable warmth in her green eyes when she spotted him.

"Have you discovered anything?" Gemma asked without preamble as she gratefully accepted Sebastian's arm and walked carefully to keep the leather soles of her boots from sliding on the slippery stones.

"Amanda died by drowning, and her injuries support the theory that she was first slammed against the wall, then held underwater. How do you know about Ruby?" Sebastian asked.

"I spoke to Doris Dockett, who was a particular friend of Amanda's. She said that Amanda sneaked out from time to time, but Doris didn't know where she went or why. She did think Amanda was in good spirits, which tallies with what Matron told you."

"Gemma, you must be careful. Matron will not look kindly on you conducting an investigation of your own."

Gemma waved a dismissive hand. "Were you able to get the address?"

Sebastian shook his head. "Matron would not give it to me, nor would she tell me anything about Amanda's family. She was quick to warn me that she would see me sacked should the story make its way into the papers."

"Matron has much to lose should the newspapers start shouting about murder at the Foundling Hospital."

"I can understand her concerns, but it's almost as if she doesn't want to know the truth."

"Perhaps she doesn't," Gemma replied. "As long as she doesn't know who's responsible, she doesn't have to take any action or give the governors any reason to look into the running of the hospital more closely. Once the truth comes out, Matron will not be able to control what is said or who hears it."

"Surely she understands the killer must be within," Sebastian pointed out, the comment meant to remind Gemma once again that she needed to be more careful. Predictably, Gemma ignored him.

"Are you certain it couldn't be someone from the outside?" she asked.

"I can't say anything with one hundred percent certainty at this stage, but, given that whoever is responsible gained access to the laundry in the middle of the night, I think it's safe to say that the killer is either one of the children or a member of staff."

Gemma nodded. "A strong girl, someone like Doris Dockett, for example, could easily overpower Amanda and hold her down until she drowned, but I can't imagine what the motive for such a brutal act would be."

"Girls can be vicious. Surely you know that."

"I do, but what would they fight over? The children have nothing worth taking and are all given the same opportunities. What would be worth killing for?"

"So, you think it was a member of staff?" Sebastian inquired. When Gemma didn't immediately reply, he asked, "Gemma, I know the male teachers keep to the boys' wing, but have you noticed any men about recently?"

"I saw Mr. Frain several times last week."

"And who's he?"

"He teaches the boys carpentry, but he also sees to repairs. He replaced several balusters in the girls' wing staircase, and a few cots needed repairs, since the wood had cracked from prolonged use. There were also several drawers that were sticking, and loose floorboards. Matron decided to have everything done before Christmas."

"How long did it take Mr. Frain to complete the repairs?"

"About a fortnight."

"And what's your impression of this man?" Sebastian asked. If he looked anything like the vicar, it was highly doubtful that he could lead any young girl astray.

"He's a bit uncouth but seems to be of sound character," Gemma said. Sebastian could see her smile in the light of the streetlamp. "He's in his late twenties, handsome, and very rugged."

"How handsome?" Sebastian asked, romantic jealousy suddenly rearing its ugly head and making him feel ashamed. He was in the middle of a murder inquiry, and he was mooning over Gemma like an adolescent boy.

"Handsome enough to appeal to a lonely girl," Gemma replied.

Sebastian reached into his pocket and pulled out the funny little doll. "Colin found this in Amanda's hand. Could Mr. Frain have given it to her?"

Gemma took the dolly and held it up to the light, turning it over until she could see the face. "I suppose. Do you think Mr. Frain had singled Amanda out, and another girl killed her in a fit of jealousy?"

"That would explain the turned-out pockets. Maybe she was looking for this. Or maybe Amanda had taken it off another girl, and the girl wanted it back. Badly enough to kill for."

Gemma handed the doll back. "I daresay. I find it hard to believe that a painted peg would be a motive for murder, but I suppose people have killed for less."

"It might not have been premeditated, but things have a way of escalating when emotions are running high," Sebastian replied. "And I'm working under the assumption that Amanda went to the cellar willingly, which means she wasn't afraid of her assailant until things turned ugly."

"But why the cellar?" Gemma asked. "A number of rooms are empty during the night, and they're not nearly as frightening or as dark. I wouldn't care to go down to the cellar at night."

"It's a safe, quiet place where no one would catch them out."

Gemma stopped walking and faced him. "There's only one

reason I can think of that a girl would be willing to go down to the cellar at night."

"To meet a boy," Sebastian said. "Or a man."

Gemma nodded. "Any transgression would be punished, but if Amanda were caught in the midst of a romantic tryst, she would find herself in the street with no place to go or financial support to rely on. Was Colin able to tell..." Her cheeks colored slightly. Her voice trailed off, but Sebastian knew what she was asking.

"There is no evidence of sexual assault, but that doesn't mean Amanda wasn't a willing participant. How difficult would it be for an employee to gain access to the laundry at night?"

"Not too difficult, I should think."

"And how many men reside at the hospital?" Sebastian asked.

"I'm not sure about the porters, but a few unmarried male teachers live on-site."

"And how many of them besides Mr. Frain might appeal to a girl of fourteen?"

"Mr. Campbell comes to mind. He's the more recent hire. He's in his mid-twenties, and very handsome."

"Is he, now?" Sebastian asked, male insecurity rising in him once again. Just how many handsome men were employed by the Foundling Hospital and thrown into Gemma's path on a daily basis? Of course, it was just as likely that Gemma was being kind and these men were perfectly average and only stood out by virtue of their age. Sebastian decided to stick with the latter assumption but, unfortunately for him, Gemma had already noted his displeasure.

"You did ask," she teased, a smile tugging at the corners of her mouth.

"I did," Sebastian agreed and smiled back. "Anyone else come to mind?"

"There's also Mr. Clayton. He's a tailor."

"A tailor?"

"The boys are taught to make their own clothes. The hospital believes it's a useful skill. Mr. Clayton is closer to forty and not nearly as attractive as Mr. Campbell or Mr. Frain, but he does have a certain reassuring presence, which might appeal to a lonely girl."

"What about the doctor?"

"He's close to fifty and comes only when summoned."

"Was he there yesterday?" Sebastian asked.

"Not as far as I'm aware. However, there are a few porters who grew up at the hospital and chose to stay on."

"Would Amanda have come into contact with any of these men?"

"She would see them in chapel on Sundays."

"So she would have seen them on Christmas Day."

"Yes."

"Would it be possible for one of them to pass her a note?" Sebastian asked.

"Anything is possible, especially in a crowded space."

"Did you see any of these men today?"

"Mr. Campbell brought one of the boys to the infirmary," Gemma replied.

"And was the boy really ill?"

"He complained of headache and stomach pain and had vomited."

"So not a ruse, then?"

"I don't believe so. He returned to his dormitory before lunch. He was still a bit green about the gills, but there was no reason to keep him in the infirmary."

"I will speak to Mr. Campbell, Mr. Frain, and Mr. Clayton tomorrow—and anyone else you consider handsome or imposing," Sebastian added with a humorless smile. "I do need the address for Ruby Marks and the name of Amanda's birth mother, though."

"There's an outbreak of croup among the younger boys," Gemma said suddenly, her expression thoughtful.

"Is it life-threatening?" Sebastian asked. He didn't imagine the illness had anything to do with Amanda's death—it must just be on Gemma's mind since she had spent most of her day with children who were ill.

"No, but it's highly likely that there will be more cases. I think perhaps I should stay the night in case more boys are taken ill."

"Isn't there a night nurse?" Sebastian asked.

"There is, but she's not very experienced and will not undertake any treatment on her own initiative." Gemma stopped walking and looked up at Sebastian, her gaze alarmingly determined. "Will I see you tomorrow?" she asked.

"I expect so."

"Good evening, then." She turned on her heel and walked back toward the hospital.

"Gemma, please be careful," Sebastian called out as he took off after her.

"I will," Gemma promised. "Now, please go home, or you'll miss supper again. You need to eat properly, or you'll become ill."

"I can look after myself," Sebastian said, a tad too gruffly.

"And so can I. I will see you tomorrow."

Sebastian remained in place until Gemma was safely inside, then walked along until he came upon a street vendor. He purchased a smoked herring for Gustav and headed home to Clerkenwell.

Gustav seemed pleased to see him and weaved between Sebastian's ankles while he unwrapped the fishy-smelling newspaper and presented the cat with his offering. The newspaper bore a photograph of a Russian prince who had died in a railway accident in Austria nearly a month ago. Prince Sorokin's twelve-year-old grandson, Oleg, had survived the wreck but died of his injuries at a hospital in Vienna two days later. When Sebastian had read the article at the time of publication, it had gone on to praise Prince Sorokin's lifelong admiration of Great Britain and its sovereign, and expound on his well-documented opposition to Tsar Alexander II's support of the United States.

Queen Victoria herself had expressed sorrow at the prince's passing, which was the only reason the incident had even been mentioned, but, as with all news, the newspaper's only remaining use was to prevent the cleanly picked remains of Gustav's herring from soiling the floor. As Sebastian folded the paper and headed downstairs to dispose of the fishy rubbish, he wondered if Amanda would meet the same fate and be forgotten in a fortnight, the story of her life used to light a fire or line a litter box.

FIFTEEN

Matron Holcombe did not question Gemma's decision to stay the night.

"It's very good of you, Miss Tate. Very good, indeed. Miss Landry can benefit from your guidance, and we will all pray that no one else succumbs."

"You needn't thank me, ma'am," Gemma replied.

"I will see that Ella brings you some supper, and make sure you rest while the children are sleeping."

"I will."

Gemma returned to the infirmary, hung up her cape and bonnet, and went to check on the boys, who were having their supper. She felt conscience-stricken for using sick children as an excuse, but this was the only way she could help Sebastian and find out what had happened to Amanda, who was constantly on her mind. Gemma had never met Ruby Marks, but she knew something of adolescent girls. She'd been one herself. Nothing was quite real unless it was shared either with a trusted friend or with the pages of a diary. Unless it was something she couldn't tell a boy, Gemma had always confided in

Victor, whose counsel she still missed every day, and she wished she could share the details of her new life with him. She wasn't one for keeping a journal, not when she'd have to leave it at the boarding house while she was at work and take the risk of someone reading her most private thoughts.

Matron Holcombe didn't encourage keeping a diary. To her, it was a waste of paper and ink and an excuse for the girls to keep secrets; but Gemma suspected that the girls felt much like she did. To set something down on paper was to invite not only violation of privacy but possibly repercussions, but to talk to a friend was both heartening and safe. Few things could come between girls whose friendships had endured years of living in an institution and having their every move and thought monitored by individuals who might have their best interests at heart but didn't bother to forge an emotional connection. The girls had each other to rely on, and the only time they could speak frankly was after lights out. If Amanda had shared anything with Ruby, it was imperative that Sebastian discover what it was.

Gemma thought that Matron was probably right about Amanda's mother. The woman had given up her baby fourteen years ago. What relevance could that decision have to Amanda's death? Probably none, but Gemma trusted Sebastian's instinct. He was a seasoned detective, and, if he needed to see the register, he had his reasons. Gemma didn't think she could access the intake register, she didn't even know where it was kept, but she did know where Matron kept the employment book. It was in a locked drawer, and she had once seen Matron take a key from beneath the marble base of a cross that stood on the windowsill in her office, which was also kept locked.

Once the children had eaten and taken another dose of the balsam of honey to help them sleep, Gemma and Miss Landry ate the supper delivered by Ella Boone, then settled in for a long night. Miss Landry took out a book, which she read by the light of the oil lamp, while Gemma took the empty cot in the corner and lay down. It would be hours before she could set her plan into motion, and she could use the rest.

SIXTEEN

Try as she might, Gemma couldn't get to sleep. Her mind teemed with unanswered questions and half-baked theories that she evaluated and discarded one by one. Neither she nor Sebastian had found any evidence of animosity between Amanda and another orphan, and she didn't think a young girl could have had a physical altercation with Amanda and come out completely unscathed. She had not noticed any scratches or bruises on any of the other girls, and, according to Doris, no one had left the dormitory before or after Amanda. It was possible, of course, that the other girl was housed in one of the other dormitories and the meeting had been prearranged, but all the mistresses were on high alert and would have noticed if someone had turned up with injuries they hadn't had the night before.

One possibility Gemma kept returning to was an illicit love affair. Amanda had been a beautiful girl, the sort who might appeal to a lonely young man. And there were plenty of lonely young men at the Foundling Hospital, from older boys who were about to be sent into the army, an even stricter institution, to the teachers who were of an age when female companionship would be uppermost in their minds. Mr. Frain was one such man. Gemma had noticed Mrs. Baker smiling at him as he worked on the balusters, and she didn't think Miss Parish was immune to his charms. She'd overheard the music teacher offer to bring Mr. Frain a glass of water if he was thirsty. Mr. Campbell was handsome as well. His was a slightly more polished charm, and Gemma had never seen or heard the man say anything untoward, but he was young enough to develop an interest in an adolescent girl. Both the matron and Doris Dockett had said that Amanda had seemed happy, even excited. That didn't sound like a person who had something to fear. Amanda had been making plans, but no one seemed to have any inkling of what those plans were.

As the hospital grew quiet and dark and everyone had gone to sleep, including Miss Landry, who was now curled up on one of the cots and snoring softly, Gemma finally acknowledged the prodigious flaw in her plan. How on earth was she going to get into Matron's office? The only items she had to hand were a letter opener someone had left behind and a pair of scissors used to cut bandages. All she could hope to do with either was to damage the lock, and, as soon as Matron approached her office come morning, she would know someone had broken in and launch an investigation.

Sebastian would have something to say about that, and he would be absolutely correct. Gemma's plan was childish, ill-conceived, and doomed to fail. She was woman enough to admit that she had miscalculated rather badly, and the only sensible course of action now was to wait out the night and then leave tomorrow with her dignity intact. Gemma could have kicked herself for her lack of foresight, and she migrated to the chair by the window, since she didn't think she'd be able to sleep. The sky was clear, the moon bright enough to illuminate the street beyond the gates. A hansom rattled past, the driver hunched on his perch, his collar turned up against the cold. Two men

walked unhurriedly by, their gaits unsteady. They were probably the worse for drink. Gemma sighed deeply. This was going
to be a very long night, filled with self-recrimination and regret.

The only bright spot was the memory of the kiss she had
shared with Sebastian at Christmas. For a short while she had
felt hope for the future, but now Sebastian was in the midst of
another investigation, and whatever lay between them would
have to wait. Not that anything more *could* be decided. Gemma
was still in mourning for Victor, and Sebastian, although decid-
edly more in control of his emotions, was still in recovery from
his opium addiction and could easily relapse. Gemma was fairly
sure he hadn't given in to temptation these past few weeks, but
she knew the urge was still there, especially at times when he
permitted himself to grieve for his wife and son. It was only
natural that he should mourn the two people he had loved most
in the world, but Sebastian would never be ready to let go until
he forgave himself for the part he'd played in their deaths.

If Gemma was honest with herself, she didn't think Sebastian was capable of such an act of absolution. He still blamed
himself, and, as long as he did that, he would be too terrified to
start another family for fear of being the instrument of their
destruction. The stirrings of love were there, fragile, and beautiful in their most innocent expression, but they both needed
time to come to terms with their losses and feel truly ready to
take a step toward a future that at this point lay just beyond
their reach.

But Gemma had seen the light in Sebastian's eyes when
he'd spotted her walking toward him and had felt an answering
joy in her own soul. She felt deeply ashamed of thinking of her
own happiness when Amanda lay dead in Colin's cellar and
other children might be in danger, but such was the selfishness
of the human heart. It wanted what it wanted, and Gemma's
heart longed for Sebastian and the love and support only he
could provide. There were even moments when she felt threat-

ened by Louisa and the love Sebastian obviously still felt for her, but thankfully those moments were few and far between, and Gemma supposed it was natural to feel insecure when compared to someone whose memory shone so bright, all flaws long forgotten and forgiven.

Feeling unbearably alone, as one could only feel in the middle of the night in a place that wasn't home, Gemma stared up at the ceiling. Her gaze settled on the curtain rod above her head. The black curlicues in the ornate scrollwork reminded her of a story Sebastian had told her when she'd visited him during his convalescence. Gemma had asked him about some of his more memorable cases to distract him from the throbbing pain in his shoulder, and he'd told her about a spate of robberies that had stumped Scotland Yard since they had all involved the disappearance of food, mostly sausages. It had taken months to collar the thief, who had turned out to be a hungry ten-year-old girl handy with a hairpin. Gemma had voiced her disbelief that a lock could be so easily picked, and, although still in pain, Sebastian had asked her for two hairpins and had demonstrated his own skill.

Gemma took a shaky breath, her heart beating a little faster, as her hand went to her hair. She pulled out two pins and held them up to her face, the metal bright with moonlight. She had no notion how to pick a lock, but she had the tools. She shut her eyes and tried to recall what Sebastian had done. He'd bent one of the hairpins and inserted it into the lock, then carefully jiggled the straight hairpin until something inside had shifted.

Gemma stole a peek at Miss Landry, who was sound asleep, her mouth partially open, her arms folded across her abdomen. She didn't think Miss Landry would wake, but it wouldn't do to get caught trying to pick a lock. Gemma went next door, to a room that was used for overflow patients in case of a serious outbreak, and shut the door behind her, turning the key to lock the door from the inside. If Miss Landry woke and asked her where she'd been, she could always say she had needed to visit the cloakroom.

Gemma bent one of the hairpins and tried to recreate what Sebastian had done. Of course it didn't work, and the lock remained firmly shut. Taking a calming breath, she tried again. And again. And again. She tried to clear her mind and listen to the mechanism, but all she heard was ominous silence. She had been at it for about two hours when something inside the keyhole finally shifted and she was able to open the door.

Stifling a shout of triumph, Gemma locked the door and tried again. It didn't work the first time, but she got it open on the third try. By three o'clock in the morning, she was nearly as proficient as the Great Sausage Thief of Cheapside.

Making sure the children were settled, despite bouts of coughing, and Miss Landry was still insensible, Gemma removed her shoes, then slipped out and hurried along the corridor and down the stairs in her stockinged feet. The cold floor burned her soles, and the air outside the infirmary was as frigid as the winter night beyond since all the fires had gone out long ago. The tall ceilings and brick walls did little to keep in the warmth, and after hours of darkness and lack of heating the building was absolutely freezing.

The moonlight that shone through the windows was bright enough to see by, and Gemma found herself standing before Matron's office in no time at all. Her heart hammered in her chest and her breath came in jerky spasms, so she stepped into a darkened alcove and took a few moments to calm herself. She had one chance to get this right and couldn't afford to bungle her brazen attempt at amateur criminality.

Finally calm enough to proceed, Gemma left her hiding place and approached the door. All was quiet and calm, the silence terrifying in its sinister vastness. She unclenched her hand and looked down at the scratched hairpins.

"Don't fail me now," she begged as she inserted the first pin into the lock. She repeated exactly what she had done upstairs, but the lock failed to open. She tried again, but her hands were sweating and shaking, and she dropped a pin onto the floor. It seemed to make a terrifyingly loud noise in the silence. Gemma couldn't see the pin in the dark and had to get on her hands and knees and pat the floor next to the door until she finally found the narrow sliver of metal. She got to her feet, pressed her forehead to the cool wood of the door, and ordered herself to calm down.

Then she pushed the pins into the lock again. It gave on the sixth try, and she turned the knob, amazed that she had actually done it. Shutting the door behind her, Gemma tiptoed into the office. The moon shone onto the silver cross and the well-ordered desk. The room was just as she remembered it. Gemma lifted the cross, extracted the key, and unlocked the drawer. The ledger was there, a heavy book whose records went back decades. Many of the children whose departures from the hospital were recorded inside were now of middle age, some probably gone, lost to illness and possibly even old age.

Gemma opened the book to the last used page and ran her finger down the entries. They were organized by intake number and she didn't know Ruby's, but she did know that Ruby had been placed about two months ago, and there were only three entries recorded for that autumn. Gemma grabbed a sheet of paper and copied out all three numbers and addresses. She closed the inkwell, replaced the pen in the holder, then folded the paper and stuffed it into the pocket of her pinafore.

Just as she was closing the book, she noticed a sheet of paper that had been inserted into the front cover. It bore two numbers: 8412 and 8413. This wouldn't have meant anything to Gemma had she not seen both numbers only that morning.

Gemma replaced the ledger in the drawer, locked the desk, and returned the key to its hiding place. She then opened the door a crack, made certain the coast was clear, and hurried toward the stairs without bothering to lock the office door again. She wasn't that proficient and didn't want to waste precious time. She had to get back upstairs before Mr. Fletcher came up with his buckets of coal and began to light the fires that would allow the kitchen staff to start on breakfast and warm the arctic rooms before the children got up at six o'clock.

Once back in the infirmary, Gemma dove beneath the blanket and curled into a fetal position, her whole body shaking with nerves and the cold that had crept into her very bones and made her think she'd never be warm again. After a time, the shaking subsided, and the nervous energy turned to exhaustion.

A milky dawn was creeping across the sky when Miss Landry woke Gemma from a deep sleep. "Miss Tate, it's time to wake up," the night nurse's voice insisted. "Tommy is burning up with fever."

Gemma dragged her eyes open and instantly sat up, all her attention on the little boy who needed her, despite the bone-deep fatigue that pulled at her and begged her to lie down for a few more minutes.

"Start applying cold compresses to his forehead and neck, and I will go down to the kitchen and ask for some hot water to brew willow bark tea," she told Miss Landry.

Gemma's tongue felt thick in her mouth, and she was shivery and weak, but she had a job to do, and the little square of paper in her pocket reminded her that a few hours of lost sleep were a small price to pay for information that could prove very valuable indeed.

SEVENTEEN

MONDAY, DECEMBER 27

Sebastian was anxious to return to the Foundling Hospital, but before he did anything else he had to report to Lovell and apprise him of the situation. When he arrived at the Yard, Lovell was already in his office, wearing the pinched look of a man who was suffering from an acute bout of indigestion. Sebastian could only assume that he'd already heard the news, unless some other high-profile murder had taken place in the past few hours.

"Shut the door and sit down," Lovell growled when Sebastian knocked on the doorjamb.

Sebastian did as he was bid and took a seat across from the superintendent.

"Tell me everything," Lovell said, and Sebastian filled him in on the investigation to date.

"I have good news, and I have bad news. Which do you want first?" Lovell asked once Sebastian had finished.

"The good," Sebastian replied, needing a bit of a buffer before he was berated once again, his judgment questioned and his future at Scotland Yard threatened.

"Because you have recently solved two high-profile cases,

your stock with Sir David has risen in value and the commissioner thinks you're the man for this job. However, your
prospects are only as good as your most recent arrest, so don't
get too comfortable."

"What's the bad news?" Sebastian asked, not particularly
impressed with this backhanded compliment.

"As I'm sure you already know, the Foundling Hospital
relies on donations from wealthy benefactors. Has done since it
first opened its doors. Until the case is solved, the donations are
likely to be withheld. Sir David is under enormous pressure
since one of the hospital's patrons happens to be the Home
Secretary."

"I see. And I assume that the Home Secretary has already
been informed of Amanda Carter's death."

"You assume correctly. If this case makes it into the papers,
Mr. Walpole's reputation might suffer."

"Surely donating to an institution that sees to the welfare
and betterment of orphans' lives can only be seen as positive,"
Sebastian argued.

"No politician wants their name bandied about in connection with the murder of a child, Bell. I've already had a word
with Constable Bryant, and he has been warned as well. If I see
even a whiff of this story in the press, I will know whom to
blame," Lovell warned, echoing Matron Holcombe's warning.

"Do you not trust your men, sir?" Sebastian asked.

He bristled at the insinuation, but he knew that, as far as his
superiors were concerned, there was nothing more worthy of
protection than reputation and wealth, and the benefactors'
names might get dragged through the muck should an accusa-
tion of wrongdoing be leveled at hospital administration. It was
bad enough that a child had been murdered, but, if a member of
staff were implicated, the hospital and those who supported it
would have to weather a very damaging storm.

Superintendent Lovell sighed wearily. "My men are the

best policemen in London, but I do not set the pay scale, Bell. If the men can earn a little extra by selling stories to the press and splurge on a bit of extra coal or a few mutton chops, I can hardly fault them. Which is why you need to play this one close to your chest." Lovell suddenly looked old and tired. "If this goes the wrong way, my days with the police service might come to an abrupt end."

"Surely not," Sebastian replied. He couldn't see how one case could undermine Lovell's position to such a degree, but he was clearly not in the know.

Lovell glanced toward the door, then his gaze shifted back to Sebastian. "You wouldn't have heard, since the announcement is yet to be printed in *The Times*, but Inspector Ransome just became engaged to Laura Hawkins."

Sebastian knew of only one Hawkins, and it was the commissioner of police.

"Ransome is engaged to Sir David's daughter?" he exclaimed.

"He is indeed, and if he has his way he will be sitting in my chair before too long."

"Surely the superintendent of Scotland Yard should be chosen on merit," Sebastian protested.

"If not for your past troubles, I would gladly put your name forward, Sebastian, but I'm not ready to risk my reputation on a man who until a few months ago whiled away his time in an opium den. When asked, I told Sir David that John Ransome was qualified to take the helm should a replacement become necessary. I never imagined that Ransome would solidify his position by marrying Sir David's daughter. With this new familial connection, he will be unstoppable."

"You think Ransome is gunning for the commissioner's post?" Sebastian asked.

"John Ransome is an ambitious young man and will work this connection as far as he is able."

"I see."

"Please, don't let me down, Bell. I have considered retirement, I admit that, but then I realized that I'm not ready to face the twilight years of my life. I still have something to offer, and I would like to go out on my own terms."

"I understand, sir. I will not let you down."

"See that you don't," Lovell said, his expression solidifying into one of steely determination. "We still have work to do, you and I."

"We do, sir," Sebastian agreed.

"Then get to it, man."

There seemed nothing left to say, so Sebastian left Lovell's office and headed out into the frigid morning. He hailed a cab, settled on the icy seat, and instructed the cabbie to take him to the Foundling Hospital. Now that Christmas and Boxing Day had passed, Londoners were out in full force. Dray wagons and carriages thronged the streets and pedestrians hurried about their business, their heads pulled into their coats and shawls and their steps unsure on the icy cobbles as they risked life and limb to cross the road.

Maidservants carried shopping baskets, and men in woolen caps and well-worn coats hefted crates of produce and kegs of ale down the steps of bustling taverns. A bloodied side of beef was being delivered to the butcher, who was arranging fresh chops and hanging sausages in the window. Normally, the sight of such delicacies would rouse Sebastian's hunger, since he'd had nothing but porridge with butter and honey for his breakfast, but this morning his thoughts were on the conversation with Lovell.

He had to admit that what Lovell had told him had not come as a surprise. John Ransome had been hinting for some time that he was on the verge of a meteoric rise and, although Sebastian had not imagined that it might be facilitated by an engagement to Sir David's daughter, he had always known that

Ransome would not be happy to remain an underling for long. It simply wasn't in him to take orders.

Sebastian should have been thinking about the case and going over the questions he intended to put to those he meant to interview that morning, but he couldn't help but wonder how a change in leadership might affect not only Scotland Yard but his own prospects too. He liked and respected Superintendent Lovell, who had stood by him when he had been at his lowest right after Louisa's death and had made certain that Sebastian was assigned straightforward cases that had allowed him to continue to earn a wage. Without Lovell's support, he knew, he might have given up altogether and have wound up in a work-house or on the streets; but even Lovell's patience hadn't been infinite, and he had been more than willing to sacrifice Sebastian when a case that could have potentially embarrassed Scotland Yard had fallen into his lap.

When dealing with the commissioner, Home Secretary, and scandal-hungry newspaper editors, it always helped to have a ready scapegoat should things go horribly wrong. Sebastian didn't blame Lovell for choosing to protect Scotland Yard and by extension himself. Those were the sorts of decisions a competent leader was forced to make every day, and Sebastian did get the credit for solving the Highgate Cemetery murder, so he could hardly complain. But he would do well to remember that professional loyalty only went so far in men who had much to lose should their reputation come under fire, and he should look to his own interests.

Still, Sebastian thought it callous and disloyal of Sir David to attempt to force out a man who clearly wasn't ready to retire, even though there was a case to be made for promoting Ransome. The majority of the men at the Yard would probably support Ransome's appointment, since their loyalty to Lovell was conditional. Ransome was young and ambitious, a man who could introduce new procedures and hopefully convince Sir David to revisit the budget and increase the men's pay.

Also, the Yard needed more men. Not only experienced detectives, but bobbies to patrol the streets and seasoned constables who could provide backup during investigations and raids. Although Lovell was an experienced policeman who'd risen through the ranks, he was not as well versed in the nuances of governmental politics as Ransome and was wary of change, which was necessary if the police service were to thrive and continue to expand its authority.

The outcome of the current investigation would depend on Sebastian's abilities as a copper, but, whether he cracked the case or not, he didn't think his failure or success would influence the future of the Yard. Lovell had to suit up and fight his own battles if he hoped to keep his post, but, if Sebastian understood John Ransome as well as he thought he did, he was sure that the battle was already lost, and Lovell's carcass would be left on the field to be picked over as carrion as Ransome raised his banner. The only thing left to decide once that happened would be whether he would support Ransome wholeheartedly or allow his personal feelings to complicate their working relationship. Sebastian hoped he wouldn't have to choose sides for a while yet, but he was certain a departmental shakeup was in the offing.

EIGHTEEN

The first thing Sebastian did upon arriving at the Foundling Hospital was make certain that everyone had passed a peaceful night and, by extension, that Gemma was safe. He could hardly forbid her to stay the night or keep her from doing her duty, but he had been worried and had hoped she had locked the door to the infirmary and focused on her patients rather than devising ways to help him. He welcomed her input and thought she was one of the most courageous people he'd ever met, man or woman, but as an unmarried woman she was vulnerable, and her association with him did not work in her favor when it came to either reputation or employment prospects.

Londoners turned to the police—and demanded answers—in times of fear, but otherwise, despite their selfless service, coppers were generally viewed as no better than pigs and were called awful names and regarded with deep suspicion. Matron Holcombe had no choice but to defer to Sebastian if she hoped to retain her position, but when he was shown into her office her disdain for him was obvious and her reception frosty.

Sebastian splayed his hands on the desk and leaned

forward, towering over Matron Holcombe, who refused to be cowed.

"I require access to the register, madam."

"And I already told you that the information in the register is not relevant to your investigation."

Sebastian was quickly losing what was left of his patience, but he made a conscious effort to draw back and refrain from menacing the woman. Intimidation rarely worked, particularly on people of intelligence, and Matron Holcombe was not a woman to be trifled with in that regard. Knowing what he now knew, he was also acutely aware that she could demand to have him removed from the investigation and replaced by none other than John Ransome, who would take this opportunity to solidify his influence. If Sebastian hoped to keep his place on the police service, he had to tread softly. Kid gloves, as Ransome himself liked to say.

Sebastian moderated his tone and tried again. "Matron, can you be absolutely certain that Amanda's mother or some other relative did not make contact with the girl? And can you also be sure that Amanda did not unlock the door to the laundry and allow someone in?"

Seeing a flicker of doubt in the matron's dark eyes, he pressed his advantage. "Would it not look better for your institution, and by extension for you, if the killer came from the outside rather than turning out to be one of the employees you so carefully considered or the children you tried to mold into decent, God-fearing human beings?"

"Yes, I suppose it would," Matron Holcombe grudgingly agreed.

"I can't find a connection to the outside world without knowing who I'm looking for, now can I?" Sebastian continued, his voice now silky and cajoling.

Matron sighed heavily. "I will put your request to the

committee. With any luck, you should be permitted access to the register no later than tomorrow."

"Today would be better."

Matron gave him a look that suggested he shouldn't push his luck. "Surely there are other leads you can pursue in the meantime," she said.

"I would like to speak to several male teachers."

"Inspector Bell," Matron spluttered, but Sebastian wasn't finished.

"But first, I need to have a word with Miss Tate. I must consult with her regarding the results of the postmortem," he added to make certain his desire to see Gemma did not come off as a personal request.

"I will send one of the children to fetch Miss Tate. You may wait in the foyer," Matron announced imperiously. "Once you have finished with Miss Tate—whose role in this should have come to an end the moment the body was taken away—a porter will escort you over to the boys' wing so that you can speak to the teachers. But I assure you, Inspector, all the teachers came to us with impeccable references, both personal and professional."

"In my experience, it's the individuals you suspect least that turn out to be the most depraved," Sebastian replied.

"Yes, that is a sad truth we must all live with, but I sincerely hope I haven't misjudged anyone that badly."

Sebastian gave the matron a stiff nod and retreated to the foyer to wait for Gemma. When she finally came downstairs, she looked exhausted, the dark smudges beneath her eyes a testament to a sleepless night. Sebastian draped his coat over her shoulders and drew her outside. She needed a breath of air, and he needed to speak to her privately.

"Gemma, are you all right?" he asked as soon as they were out of earshot of the door and the windows.

Gemma nodded, her attention on a carriage that had just

pulled up. A well-dressed couple were in the process of alighting.

"What are they doing here?" Sebastian growled.

"Potential donors are given tours of the hospital," Gemma replied, her gaze on the woman, who was shaking out her voluminous skirts, her dark curls peeking from the sides of her spoon bonnet.

"Surely this is not the time to be giving tours."

"Matron can hardly put them off if the appointment was made before Amanda's death," Gemma replied. "As far as she's concerned, it's business as usual."

Sebastian shook his head. There were those who said that money didn't make the world go round, but they were wrong. Business never stopped, not for a second, and if Matron hoped for the continued support of the hospital she had to put on a brave face and pretend that nothing had happened. For a moment, Sebastian actually felt some sympathy for the woman; he could appreciate the difficult position she was in.

Gemma smiled, the grin lighting up her tired face. "I have something for you." Sebastian thought she looked very proud of herself. He watched as she withdrew a folded sheet of paper from the pocket of her pinafore and handed it to him. "One of these addresses is for Ruby Marks. I didn't know her number so couldn't be certain which one."

"How did you get this?" Sebastian asked, watching her closely.

Gemma's hand went to her hair and she patted it into place, smoothing the unruly waves that were loosely covered with a black cap. "I seem to be missing a few pins," she said, her eyes dancing with amusement. She looked deeply gratified when Sebastian's mouth fell open.

"Please, please tell me you didn't pick a lock," he implored her.

"How else was I supposed to get into the matron's office?"

"Gemma!"

"Can you never just say thank you, Inspector Bell?" Gemma replied, still looking like a cat that had got at the cream.

"Thank you," Sebastian said, and lowered his gaze so she wouldn't see the admiration that had to be shining from his eyes. It wouldn't do to encourage her.

"There is something else," Gemma said, keeping her voice low as the well-dressed couple made their way toward the front door.

"What?" His head snapped back up.

"There was a sheet of paper with two numbers. One belonged to Amanda. The other to Michael White, the boy who was sick yesterday."

"Was there anything written next to the numbers?" Sebastian asked.

"No."

"How old is Michael?"

"I think he's fourteen."

"Amanda was also fourteen, and she had recently asked for domestic employment. Is it possible that they were the next two children to leave the hospital and Matron was working on their placements?"

"Yes, it is, but what's odd is that their numbers are consecutive. 8213 and 8214."

"Might they have come to the hospital at around the same time?" Sebastian asked. That was the only reason he could think of that the numbers would follow one another.

"Yes, I suppose it is," Gemma replied. "I would say they came on the same day, or the same week at the very least."

"Do you think Amanda and Michael were related?"

"Yesterday morning, Michael had vomited and said his head hurt. He could barely keep his eyes open."

"Are you suggesting his condition was the result of severe distress?" Sebastian asked.

Gemma nodded. "I think it's a possibility."

"Could Michael and Amanda have been twins?" Sebastian asked. He hadn't seen Michael for himself, so couldn't come to any conclusions about the likelihood of a close familial relationship based on the boy's appearance.

"They didn't look alike, but that doesn't necessarily mean they weren't born of the same mother." Gemma fixed Sebastian with an intense stare. "Am I right in thinking that Michael is now your prime suspect?"

Sebastian shook his head. "Feeling ill is not evidence of a crime, but unless it's a coincidence I do think Michael might know something. I have told Matron that I'd like to speak to certain members of the male staff. I will speak to Michael afterwards. I trust he's not going anywhere?"

"I don't think so," Gemma said.

"Good. I will see you later, then," Sebastian said. "And good work, Nurse Tate. How many tries did it take to get the lock open?"

Gemma smiled smugly. "One or two," she replied coyly.

Sebastian highly doubted she was telling him the truth, but he wasn't about to question her. She deserved praise for her ingenuity and daring, even though deep down he wanted to wring her lovely neck for taking such an unnecessary risk.

"Well done," he said instead. "If this nursing thing doesn't work out, you can always turn to a life of crime."

"You think?" Gemma teased.

She shrugged off his coat and handed it back to him, and Sebastian watched her go back inside, her hips swaying in a way he suddenly found distracting.

NINETEEN

Sebastian didn't have to wait long before a middle-aged porter came for him. The man looked stern, and immediately rebuffed Sebastian's attempt at a friendly exchange while he escorted him to an outbuilding behind the west wing. The spacious shed was the domain of Mr. Frain, the hospital's carpentry teacher and repair man. There were several chairs, a table that didn't look quite level, and what looked like a kitchen dresser that needed a shelf replaced. The man himself was sanding a piece of wood but looked up, smiling in a friendly manner, when the porter and Sebastian walked in.

"Inspector Bell of Scotland Yard," the porter announced, as if Sebastian had just arrived for an audience with the Queen.

"Good morning, Inspector. To what do I owe the pleasure?" Mr. Frain asked. He appeared to be in his late twenties, and had a wiry build and a face that fell just short of handsome due to a nose that must have been broken once or twice and was now a little misshapen. The injury didn't take away from Mr. Frain's appeal, though. His dark blue eyes were large and expressive, and he had a warm smile that would probably charm a shy young girl.

"I'm investigating the murder of Amanda Carter," Sebastian said as he looked around the workshop.

"So, how can I help? I didn't know the girl."

"Are you sure?" Sebastian asked, watching the man for any sign of falsehood.

"Quite sure," Mr. Frain replied.

"I'm told you did some repairs in the girls' wing recently."

"I did. I'm asked to mend things all the time. That's my job. As a rule, I don't murder people while I'm at it."

"A girl's death is no laughing matter, Mr. Frain," Sebastian snapped.

"Who's laughing?"

"How long have you been employed at the hospital?"

"Nearly ten years now. I started here shortly after I finished my apprenticeship."

"Are you married?" Sebastian asked.

"Last I checked, having a wife wasn't a requirement for holding down respectable employment."

"Just answer the question," Sebastian replied. Mr. Frain was too cocky for his own good and had already managed to get on Sebastian's bad side with his irreverent attitude.

"I am married. Have been these four years. We have two boys and another child on the way. My wife is hoping for a girl. Is that better, Inspector?"

"Where were you on Christmas night?"

"Where any dutiful husband and father would be. At home."

"Can anyone vouch for you?"

"My wife, her parents, who joined us for Christmas dinner and stayed the night." Mr. Frain cocked his head to the side and studied Sebastian's irritated countenance. "Why did you single me out?"

"I'm speaking to a number of people."

"I bet you're not questioning that sour turd," Mr. Frain said, jutting his chin toward the porter, who stood outside the door. "What do you imagine my motive to be?"

"When it comes to a young girl, only one motive springs to mind when suspecting a young man."

The carpenter shrugged. "I'm very sorry Amanda is dead, but as I said, I never met her. At least not in person. She might have walked past me a hundred times, but that doesn't give me a motive to harm her."

Sebastian took out his notebook and flipped it open. "Christian name and address, please, Mr. Frain. I will be checking your alibi."

"Leo Frain, eight Gravel Lane, Houndsditch."

Sebastian made a note of the address, then returned the notebook to his pocket. "Do you paint as well as build and repair, Mr. Frain?"

"Of course. All the time."

"Where are your paint stores?"

Leo Frain appeared surprised by the question but led Sebastian toward the back of the shed, where several shelves held various instruments, rolled-up blueprints, and cans of paint. Sebastian examined each can closely but didn't find any matching the vivid red of the little dolly. He pulled it out of his waistcoat pocket and held it between thumb and forefinger.

"Ever seen one of these?"

Leo Frain peered at the little face. "No, but it would be easy enough to make."

"This was clutched in Amanda's hand. I would venture to say that it must have meant something to her if she wouldn't let it go even in death."

"What are you getting at?" Frain demanded.

"Might someone have made it in your workshop and given it to her as a gift?"

"That's not possible," Leo Frain replied, looking maddeningly calm.

"And how can you be so sure?"

"The boys are not permitted to make whatever they want. I set out projects for them and check on their work. Even if one of the boys managed to shape this peg and polish it, they would still need brushes and paints to decorate it." Leo Frain smiled at the little dolly. "I don't have brushes that fine, Inspector. I have no call to paint faces, do I?"

Sebastian had to concede that he hadn't found any brushes that could have been used to paint the dolly. "Do you have a theory regarding Amanda's murder?" he asked.

Leo Frain shook his head. "I don't, and I would rather not speculate."

"Thank you, Mr. Frain," Sebastian said, and turned to leave.

"I do hope you find whoever did this, Inspector. I wouldn't want any of my boys to go through life with a stain on their character. They're good lads, and they deserve a chance in life."

Sebastian nodded and shut the door behind him.

TWENTY

"Where to now?" the porter asked.

"Mr. Clayton, the tailor."

"As you wish."

The tailor's workshop was on the ground floor of the west wing, with tall windows allowing in bright December light that must make it easier to work. It was a large room with several tables covered with shears, patterns, and fabrics, and stools for the boys to sit on. Sebastian surmised that the children had been working on sewing shirts. He had to admit it was a useful skill, and wished his mother had taught him how to sew and mend his own clothes so he wouldn't have to rely on his landlady.

Mr. Clayton was a year or two shy of forty. With dark eyes, heavy brows, and a pencil moustache, he exuded a watchfulness that could be either reassuring or unnerving, depending on how much scrutiny one was comfortable with. The tailor's dark hair was parted in the middle and shone with pomade, and his clothes smelled of woodsy tobacco smoke, which wasn't unpleasant. He was a few inches shorter than Sebastian and rail thin in his well-cut black suit. When Clayton invited him to come inside and shut the door behind him, Sebastian noted that the man's movements were very precise.

"How can I help, Inspector?" the tailor asked once Sebastian had introduced himself and been directed to a seat.

"Do you teach the girls as well as the boys, Mr. Clayton?"

"The female staff generally see to the girls' education, but I do from time to time hold a class on cutting out patterns. It's a skill that requires not only precision but calculation and good sense."

"Why does it require good sense?" Sebastian asked.

Mr. Clayton smirked, then reached for a piece of linen and spread it on the table. "Let us say that a girl wants to make a handkerchief for her sweetheart. If she has no sense, she will cut out the square from the middle, therefore wasting all the fabric left over because it's no longer of use to anyone. However, if the girl has experience and knows something of domestic management, she will cut in a way that will create as little waste as possible, therefore making two handkerchiefs from this piece of fabric rather than one."

"I see," Sebastian said. "And did you ever have an occasion to instruct Amanda Carter?"

"I did, yes."

"And did she have sense?" Sebastian asked.

"I believe she did. She was a good pupil and had lovely manners."

"Interesting that you remember that."

Mr. Clayton smiled, and the smile transformed his face, making him appear more approachable. "Amanda thanked me at the end of class. That's not something many people do. I thought it was a polite thing to do."

"When was this?"

"About two years ago now. She would have been twelve."

"Have you seen her since?"

"I saw her from time to time, but I see everyone. That hardly makes me guilty of any wrongdoing."

"Do you reside on the premises, Mr. Clayton?"

"No, I do not. I keep a room at Mrs. McCreedy's boarding house in Clerkenwell. If you require an alibi, you may check with her."

"What makes you think I will need an alibi?" Sebastian asked, but he had to admire Mr. Clayton's cool.

"Why else would you be here? There were no classes on Christmas Day, so I wasn't expected at work. I spent the afternoon in my room, then joined the other lodgers for Christmas dinner. After that, I went back upstairs and read until it was time for bed. I breakfasted at seven on Boxing Day and arrived at the hospital by eight, as is my habit."

"Full name and address?" Sebastian said.

"Peter Clayton," the tailor said, then recited the address. "My brother, Henry, resides at the boarding house as well, so do be clear that you're asking for me."

"Very thoughtful of you, Mr. Clayton," Sebastian replied.

He couldn't imagine a world in which a fourteen-year-old girl would find Mr. Clayton appealing, but there was no accounting for taste, and in his years as a policeman he'd seen stranger pairings. He would have to ask Constable Bryant to verify Frain's and Clayton's whereabouts before they had a chance to forewarn their alibis that he'd be coming. Of course, if Amanda's murderer was clever, he or she would have done so already and made certain to cover their tracks.

Sebastian left the tailor's workshop and asked the porter to take him to see Mr. Campbell. Although it was still fairly early in the investigation, he suddenly felt a demoralizing sense of doom. It was more than twenty-four hours since Amanda's body had been discovered, but he had yet to unearth a single useful clue. He had theories but nothing to substantiate any of them, and, as he pulled the little dolly from his pocket and stared at it, he almost had the sense that the silly little grin was mocking him.

TWENTY-ONE

Mr. Campbell was in the middle of class, teaching mathematics to a group of older boys, who were all scribbling silently on their slates, and probably dreaming of being set free so they could go to lunch. Mr. Campbell sat behind a desk at the front of the classroom, his face a mask of saintly patience. Gemma had been right. Campbell was very handsome. He had liquid brown eyes that put one in mind of strong tea, and dark hair worn in natural waves. Like all the male teachers at the hospital, he wore a black suit, white shirt, and black cravat, but on him the somber suit looked dashing rather than funereal. When the porter entered the classroom and leaned down to deliver his message, he gave the man a friendly smile.

Campbell looked surprised by the porter's request, but didn't protest. He instructed the boys to continue working, then stepped into the corridor and held out his hand to Sebastian as if they were acquainted with each other and had met by accident on the street.

"Inspector Bell, a pleasure," he said.

"Is there somewhere we can speak privately?" Sebastian

asked. He didn't care to question the man in the corridor, where anyone could pass by and overhear.

"Ah, yes. There's an empty classroom just there." Mr. Campbell pointed to a room two doors down. "Perhaps Mr. Glass can keep an eye on my class," he said, addressing the porter.

"Of course, sir," Mr. Glass replied. "I would be happy to."

"Thank you," Mr. Campbell said politely, and led the way to the empty room.

Inside, it was like the classroom they'd just left, with a desk at the front and several narrow desks with hard chairs lined up in three rows. Sebastian appreciated the fact that Mr. Campbell did not take the desk at the front and leave him to either stand or take one of the pupil desks, thereby placing them on uneven footing for the duration of the conversation. Instead, Mr. Campbell approached the first row, pulled out a chair, and invited Sebastian to do the same. To sit at an adjacent desk would put them too close to each other and make it difficult for Sebastian to see Campbell's reactions, so he took a chair and brought it to face Campbell's desk, then sat down.

"I was very sorry to hear about Amanda's death," Mr. Campbell said. "I'm glad a bona fide detective was brought in to investigate the case."

"Who did you think would look into the matter?" Sebastian asked.

"I thought perhaps Matron would bring it to the governors, and they would assign someone."

"Is that what happened before?"

Mr. Campbell looked uncomfortable. "There haven't been any murders at the hospital as far as I know, but there was a boy who died in suspicious circumstances some years back. The governors dealt with it."

"What happened?"

"Some of the older boys were bullying the child and dared him to climb onto the roof to prove that he wasn't afraid. He fell."

"When was this?"

"About four years ago."

"Were you here then?" Sebastian asked.

"No. But I heard about it from some of my students who were here at the time."

"Are the boys who were responsible still here now?"

Mr. Campbell shook his head. "No, they were enlisted in an infantry regiment that was sent to Crimea. Last I heard, two of them were dead and the other two are still serving."

"And do you think it was a just punishment?" Sebastian asked.

He knew all about the horror that was the Crimean War, both from newspaper accounts and from Gemma, who'd been there and had survived conditions no human being should have to endure. It wasn't until he'd heard Gemma's descriptions of the senseless slaughter and appalling conditions at the hospital in Scutari that he had truly understood what it must have been like, and he didn't envy the poor sods who'd been sent there to die. Because die they had, by the thousands, torn apart by cannon fire, skewered by bayonets, run down by the cavalry, fired upon, and cut down by swords. There had been a time when he'd been so foolish as to consider a career in the army. Thankfully, common sense had won out—or maybe it was his inherent inability to deal with authority—but, dispirited as he sometimes got when dealing with his superiors in the police, Sebastian couldn't imagine a fate worse than that of a foot soldier.

Mr. Campbell sighed sadly. "Is there anything just in sending fourteen-year-olds to die, Inspector? Those boys deserved to be punished, and I'm sure if they had even a sliver of a conscience they would live with the guilt of their victim's death for the rest of their lives, but to send them to Crimea was cruel. Although I don't suppose the child's death really came into it. Those boys were of an age to leave the hospital, and chances are they would have wound up in the army regardless."

There was truth in what Campbell said, so Sebastian didn't bother to spend any more time on an incident that had happened four years ago. He had his own case to solve.

"Mr. Campbell, did you know Amanda?"

"Not personally, but I knew who she was."

"Why was that?"

"Miss Parish mentioned her."

"Miss Parish?"

The man colored slightly, and his gaze slid toward the window, giving him a moment to regroup. "Miss Parish and I are friends," he admitted at last.

"Friends?" Sebastian echoed, doing his best not to scoff. Miss Parish wasn't the sort of woman men wanted for a friend.

"I admire her greatly."

"I see," Sebastian said. "And are romantic relationships between members of staff permitted?"

"They are not, so I would appreciate it if you wouldn't divulge our secret." Campbell looked at Sebastian imploringly. "We're both unattached and have done nothing improper. We meet outside the hospital on our afternoons off and go for a walk and a cup of tea. Surely we're entitled to a life of our own outside these walls."

"How long have you two been involved?"

"Several months now."

"And do you have plans to marry?" Sebastian asked.

Mr. Campbell appeared flustered. "I did ask Faith to marry me, but she said she needs time."

"Time to do what?"

Miss Parish had to be around thirty, so time wasn't on her side, not if she hoped to have a family of her own. It wasn't for

Sebastian to judge—everyone had their own reasons and aspirations—but if he'd found himself living in an institution like this one he would have welcomed any sort of companionship, especially from a beautiful woman. Perhaps Miss Parish was worried that if they decided to marry, she and Matthew Campbell would have to find new employment and accommodation, which would be a drain on their finances.

"Marriage is a serious commitment, Inspector, and I think Faith has suffered a disappointment in the past. She wants to be sure, and I am happy to give her as much time as she needs to be certain of her feelings. I love her," Mr. Campbell said, his cheeks turning a violent shade of red. "I will never look at anyone else."

"Then I hope she accepts you, Mr. Campbell."

"Thank you. So do I."

"What did Miss Parish say about Amanda?" Sebastian asked once Mr. Campbell's face had returned to its natural hue.

"She said Amanda was a talented singer and one of Faith's more eager pupils."

"Did Amanda ever confide in Miss Parish?"

"Do I have your word that you will not be the cause of Miss Parish's dismissal?" Mr. Campbell asked.

Sebastian had no intention of making such a promise, but at the moment he needed to learn all he could. "I do not report to Matron Holcombe," he said instead.

That seemed to satisfy the man. It was clear he wanted to talk.

"Amanda told Faith that she wanted to leave the hospital. She didn't want to remain for two more years."

"Did she say why she wanted to leave?"

"Faith thought she had made plans with someone. Her guess was that Amanda might have connected with a family member."

"How would Amanda connect with someone from the outside?"

"The children are permitted to play outside every day. If someone happened to pass by the gates when they were outside, they could conceivably pass on a message."

"How would they know which child was theirs if they hadn't seen them since they were infants?"

"They would know their child's number, so they could ask whoever was closest to the gates to deliver the note to a child who'd been assigned that number. Since all the children are issued with a medallion when they're admitted to the hospital, it wouldn't be too difficult to find the right person."

"I see," Sebastian said. Once again the investigation had circled back to the numbers—and the register, which he had yet to see. "Do the mothers seek out their children often?"

"No, they don't. But it's not impossible that someone would try. I don't know anything about the circumstances of Amanda's birth."

"Might Amanda have been related to Michael White?" Sebastian asked, watching Mr. Campbell closely.

"Michael? Why on earth would you ask that, Inspector Bell?"

"It's come to my attention that their identification numbers are consecutive." There was no need to explain how he had come by that knowledge.

"Are they?" Campbell exclaimed. "I had no idea."

"So, are they related?" Sebastian pressed.

"I don't know, but it's my understanding that only one child per mother is permitted to be admitted to the Foundling Hospital."

"I thought that rule applied to women who give birth to more than one illegitimate child. Surely it doesn't apply in the case of twins," Sebastian replied.

"As far as I know, we don't have any twins, but perhaps the children have been kept in ignorance for a reason."

"And what reason would that be?"

"For one, to have a sibling among the orphans would offer an unfair advantage. For another, unless they were placed within the same household or regiment once they leave the hospital they would lose their only remaining family."

"Mr. Campbell, I was told that boys and girls are kept apart at all times, but would it be possible for them to find a way to meet?"

Mr. Campbell smiled sheepishly. "I grew up here at the hospital, Inspector. I was a foundling boy," he admitted. "Matron will tell you that there's no way around the rules, but there are always those who find a way. It's human nature. Some children never put a foot wrong, too fearful of the conse-quences, and others will do anything to get what they want. It makes them feel more human."

"Was Amanda someone who'd break the rules?"

"I wouldn't know."

"What about Michael?"

"Michael is a very well-behaved boy. I've never had reason to single him out."

"I understand he felt ill on the morning Amanda's body was found. Is he often unwell?" Sebastian inquired.

"No, but it does happen. I don't believe Michael's symp-toms had anything to do with what happened to Amanda. How would he even know?"

"He would know if he was the one who murdered her."

Campbell stared at Sebastian, his eyes growing wide with shock. "You think Michael murdered Amanda? Based on what? The poor boy had an upset stomach and a headache. Surely that's not a crime. Children get ill all the time."

"Can you be certain Michael White never left his dormitory on Christmas Day? You're in charge of the older boys, are you not?"

Mr. Campbell nodded. "I went to sleep around ten. I did not see or hear anything."

"But can you vouch for him?"

Campbell looked away. "I cannot vouch for any of the boys. I keep a bottle of brandy hidden at the back of a cupboard. I'm afraid I slept rather deeply that night."

Sebastian knew all about the benefits of sleep aids and didn't judge the man too harshly, but there was one more thing he needed to ask. He pulled out the little wooden dolly and set it on the desk before Mr. Campbell. The man looked surprised and stared at the object.

"Have you ever seen this?" Sebastian asked.

"No. What does it have to do with your investigation?"

"It was in Amanda's hand when she died. Where would she get such a thing?"

"I really couldn't say. I've never seen its like."

"Do you think Mr. Frain might have made it?" Sebastian pressed.

"Mr. Frain is a skilled craftsman, but I've never known him to make toys. Not even for the younger children."

Sebastian reached for the dolly and pushed it back into his pocket. "Thank you, Mr. Campbell."

The man looked anxious. "About what I asked before," he began.

"Your relationship with Miss Parish is of no interest to me, nor will I tell Matron about the brandy, but I strongly suggest you make that bottle disappear, and not in the way you're thinking."

"God bless you, Inspector. You have no idea what it's like to live one's life in an institution."

"You are no longer a foundling, Mr. Campbell. I expect you

probably have some say in where you live," Sebastian said, and took his leave.

He still wanted a word with Michael White, but the children would be going to lunch now, and Sebastian didn't want the lad to miss the meal since he'd probably have to go hungry until suppertime if he didn't turn up.

It was more pressing that he speak to Ruby Marks at her place of work, preferably before the cook began on the dinner preparations for the family and wasn't able to spare her.

TWENTY-TWO

After leaving Sebastian, Gemma checked on the children, then examined a twelve-year-old girl whom Mrs. Abbott, who was in charge of that age group, had brought in while Gemma had been outside with Sebastian. Helen, a thin, mousy-looking girl with pointed incisors, complained of stomach pains and tearfully told Gemma that she was going to die. Several carefully worded inquiries convinced Gemma that death was not imminent and Helen had just got her menses for the first time, something Mrs. Abbott should have prepared her for. Gemma patiently explained the situation and allowed Helen to rest for a while as she took it all in, then sent her off with instructions on how to deal with the situation in a way that wouldn't cause her any embarrassment.

Once Helen had been taken away by a shamefaced Mrs. Abbott, Gemma looked out the window, hoping to catch sight of Sebastian, but what she saw instead was Mr. Fletcher, his reddened hands holding tight to the reins as he guided the wagon through the gates and made his way toward the icehouse. Tears pricked Gemma's eyes when she saw Mr. Fletcher's cargo. There was no mistaking a body, even if it was discreetly covered and wrapped in several layers of sacking. Amanda was home, which meant the funeral would most likely be held in a few days.

As Gemma watched Mr. Fletcher stop the wagon and lumber inside the icehouse, probably to find a place to store the body until the burial, it occurred to her that Amanda would be laid to rest in her only dress, wearing her cap, pinafore, and worn shoes, since those were the only things she had owned in the world. Normally Gemma wouldn't see that as a problem, but, given that someone had turned out Amanda's pockets after she was dead, it was entirely possible that whatever they had been looking for was still at large. Might Amanda have hidden something in her dormitory, and had anyone checked her dress and shoes?

Or perhaps Amanda had gone down to the laundry that night because she'd hidden something in the room during the day. What if she had been contacted by her mother? Maybe that was the reason she had asked for early placement, so that she could establish a relationship with the woman who'd given her up. Maybe her mother had given her a gift, or maybe the gift had come from some other source. The only thing Gemma was sure of was that it was imperative to search Amanda's belongings before she was buried.

Gemma checked the time. The children would go to the dining hall in a few minutes, so the dormitories would be empty. Ella was sure to bring lunch to the infirmary for her and the sick children, but that wouldn't happen until the girl had finished serving and clearing up downstairs. Now would be the perfect time to nip to Amanda's dormitory and search her belongings. If anyone saw her, Gemma would say that she needed Amanda's things in order to prepare the body for burial, which could be true—someone would have to do it, and a nurse was the most likely candidate.

After making sure the children were comfortable and

Tommy's fever hadn't spiked, Gemma left the infirmary and made her way to the girls' dormitories. She could hear the clinking of cutlery and voices coming from the dining hall on the ground floor. Gemma reached the top-floor landing, made sure no one was about, then walked briskly down the corridor and pushed open the door to the older girls' dormitory.

She didn't know which cot was Amanda's, but it wasn't difficult to guess. One of the cots, located midway along the left side of the room, had been stripped. There were carefully folded clothes on a stool next to it, and worn shoes positioned beneath. All the other chairs were empty, and the cots were neatly made, identical blankets tucked in, and the pillows fluffed and centered. The girls' nightdresses lay folded beneath the pillows, and their serviceable dressing gowns hung over the footboards with slippers lined up underneath.

Gemma quickly checked under the bed but saw nothing, not even a layer of dust since one of the children's morning chores was to clean their dormitories from top to bottom several times a week. They wouldn't have done any cleaning on Christmas or Boxing Day, but Gemma was sure the floors had been swept and washed that morning; the wooden boards gleamed in the winter-bright light that streamed through the tall windows lining the opposite wall. Fresh sheets and pillowcases had been put on the beds, and, as the children changed their smallclothes twice a week, the laundry would be in use once again, probably as soon as that afternoon or tomorrow morning since as far as Gemma knew, Sebastian hadn't asked Matron to keep it off limits.

Gemma slid her hand beneath the mattress and ran it along the underside, checking every inch of the frame, then looked under the pillow, but if Amanda had left anything there, she thought, whoever had stripped the bed would have found it and either kept it or turned it over to Mrs. Dixon. Gemma ran her fingers along the back of the metal headboard, then checked whether there were any loose floorboards in the vicinity of Amanda's bed, but the floor was in excellent repair and not a single board so much as squeaked.

Amanda had been wearing her nightdress and dressing gown, which presumably had been returned with the body, but her dress, apron, stockings, cap, and shoes did not appear to have been touched since she had taken them off at bedtime on Christmas Day. Now that she saw the neat pile of Amanda's clothes, Gemma couldn't help but wonder if the girl might instead be buried in her nightdress or some sort of shroud. There had not been any funerals since Gemma took up her post in November, so she couldn't be certain, but Matron Holcombe wasn't the sort of woman to condone waste, and Amanda's things were still in perfectly good condition as far as Matron would be concerned. Waste not, want not, she always said.

Whatever was decided, the clothes wouldn't remain untouched for long. Gemma quickly checked the shoes, then set aside the cap and the stockings and reached for the apron. The pockets were empty. Amanda's dress was identical to all the others and still smelled of the girl who'd worn it, a scent Gemma had not picked up when examining the body since Amanda had lain in the water for hours prior to Mr. Fletcher's discovery. While she was folding the dress to replace Amanda's things on the chair, Gemma realized something—the dress was a little heavier than it should be. When she examined the garment more carefully, she noticed a small bump in the hem. Gemma closed her fingers around the spot and felt something hard within.

Having always been taught to mend rather than destroy, Gemma hated to tear the seam, but there had to be a reason Amanda had sewn something into the hem of her dress. It was the only place she could have hidden something of value, and done so without anyone noticing. If she had told Mrs. Dixon she had a torn hem, she would be expected to repair it, and no one would have any reason to question her for sewing the bottom of her dress.

Gemma grasped the material around the lump with both hands and pulled hard, tearing the seam enough to be able to unpick a few stitches and pull the fabric apart. As soon as the light penetrated the darkness of the little pocket, the object within glinted bright yellow. It was unmistakably made of metal.

Gemma extracted a gold ring and held it up to the light. She was shocked that Amanda would have had such a thing in her possession. The ring was too big for a child, or even a woman, the design distinctly masculine. The square top resembled a seal and was embossed with an image of a two-headed eagle and a crown suspended in midair between the outward-facing heads.

Gemma shoved the ring into the pocket of her pinafore, folded the hem of the dress back into place, and replaced Amanda's things on the stool. She had to find Sebastian, but first she had to get out undetected and return to the infirmary before anyone realized she'd been gone for the better part of a half hour.

Just as she returned, Ella arrived with a tray.

"Ella, do you know if Inspector Bell is still on the premises?" Gemma asked.

"He's not, miss. I saw him from the kitchen window just as the church bell went at noon. He was walking toward the gates."

"Thank you."

Gemma was in no doubt that Ella was correct. She might not have met Sebastian in person, but everyone knew everything that went on, and Sebastian's presence would not have gone unnoticed by the staff.

TWENTY-THREE

Having three possible addresses, none of which were nowhere near each other, Sebastian decided to spring for a cab. At the first house he called at in Kensington, the housekeeper had never heard of Ruby Marks. The same thing happened at the second address. Thankfully the third address proved to be the correct one, or Sebastian would have found himself back where he started when it came to locating Amanda's friend, which would have been a disappointing setback as well as a tremendous waste of time.

Ruby Marks had been placed with a family in Mayfair. The solid façade of their three-story brick building and the wrought-iron gates, erected to keep the riffraff out, were a testament to their wealth and place in London society. Sebastian couldn't help but wonder if Ruby's employer was one of the benefactors of the Foundling Hospital. It had to be the perfect place to find well-brought-up domestic servants who were pathetically grateful for the opportunity and probably terrified about losing their place and being cast out into a world they knew nothing about, having been isolated practically since birth and prepared only for life in domestic service or the army.

An endless supply of minions no one cared about or would miss.

Sebastian had been heartbroken and angry when he lost his mother at eighteen and his father had then passed a few years later, but only now did he understand how lucky he had been to have parents who had loved him and had done their best to prepare him for all the things they'd thought life might throw at him. He was almost glad they hadn't lived to see how things had turned out—their hearts would have broken for him—but perhaps he wouldn't have sunk to such depths of despair if he'd had someone to turn to who could offer him a safe place to bide until he felt strong enough to take tentative steps toward healing and forgiveness.

He had yet to write to his brother, Simian, who'd inherited the family farm and hadn't even bothered to come to Louisa's funeral, but Sebastian was ready to turn over a new leaf and had promised himself he would try to mend the relationship that had fractured when he'd decided to leave home and move to London to become a policeman. Simian was married now, to a girl they had both been sweet on as young men, and had two children Sebastian had yet to meet. Perhaps a visit was long overdue, he decided as he pushed open the gate and made his way toward the servants' entrance.

A boot boy of about eight opened the door, then called out to a footman. The man summoned the housekeeper, who introduced herself as Mrs. Beaton. She was a gaunt, stern-looking woman in her forties, with dark hair scraped into a severe bun beneath her lace cap and lips so thin they practically disappeared when she pressed them together in response to his inquiry. The family employed a very pompous butler as well, but, as domestic servants were the province of the housekeeper, the man saw no reason to bother with the likes of Sebastian and walked off without a word, his lips compressed almost as tightly as Mrs. Beaton's.

A policeman at the door, even the servants' entrance, never boded well, and the prevailing method of dealing with anyone who came calling was either to send them away or hide them in the bowels of the servants' quarters until they could be dealt with and sent packing, preferably before the master or mistress got a whiff of any hint of scandal.

"Why do you need to speak to Ruby, Inspector?" Mrs. Beaton demanded, her eyes narrowed in suspicion. "I was assured that she is a girl of unassailable character and would be a credit to the household, even though she didn't come with any references. Lord Littleton is a kind and generous man who likes to give those less fortunate a chance in life. It was his wish that I accept a girl from the Foundling Hospital."

It was obvious that Mrs. Beaton would have preferred to do her own choosing and would have hired a girl with impeccable references and years of experience, but clearly she had been overridden.

"Mrs. Beaton, Ruby has not done anything wrong, and my being here is not a mark on her character. I simply need to ask her a few questions regarding a girl she knew before she left the Foundling Hospital."

"What would a policeman want with a sixteen-year-old girl that's done nothing wrong?" Mrs. Beaton countered. "And who's this girl you're inquiring about? If their association was in any way unsuitable, I'll see that Ruby is sent right back where she came from."

"It's in relation to a case at the Foundling Hospital. Ruby knew the victim and might be able to help me identify her assailant."

"The victim?" Mrs. Beaton exclaimed, her unwarranted belligerence melting and draining away like pissed-on snow. "You mean a child?"

"A girl of fourteen. She was drowned in the laundry."

"Dear God! This just goes to show you that no place is safe for a young girl."

She had the air of someone who spoke from experience, but Sebastian decided not to ask.

He didn't need to. Mrs. Beaton's eyes misted. "My older sister was murdered when she was twelve. My mother sent her to the market, and someone tried to rob her on the way home. She must have put up a fight because they bashed her head against a stone wall and took her basket. She died for a handful of vegetables, Inspector Bell."

"I'm sorry."

"The world is a cruel place, especially to girls."

"Which is why I won't rest until I find out what happened. An orphan deserves justice as much as the daughter of a noble house."

"I do agree with you there," Mrs. Beaton said. "My sister's murder was never investigated, not that there was anyone to call on for help in those days. This was in 1830. The police service was hardly more than a few young lads with sticks. Didn't know their arse from their elbow, my mother said, and who could blame them? They didn't have any training or support. What could they do?"

"The police service has come a long way since 1830," Sebastian agreed. "There are still lads with sticks, but now there are also detectives." *And advantageously placed, self-serving lickspittles who turn policing into a game of political prowess and use their influence to back future sons-in-law rather than men who've dedicated their lives to the service and are vastly more deserving than a man who's barely thirty, capable though he might be,* he thought bitterly.

Mrs. Beaton permitted herself a small smile. "I daresay you look like someone who knows what he's about."

She took Sebastian past the servants' hall, where a lady's

maid was mending a lace collar, to a room along a narrow corridor that led deeper into the subterranean area of the house, where the servants dwelled. "You may use my parlor to speak to Ruby, but leave the door open. As long as she's employed here, her safety is my responsibility, and I won't have her left alone with a man."

"As you wish," Sebastian said. He'd long since stopped taking offense at the suggestion that he might abuse his power where a helpless female was concerned. He'd never touched a woman who wasn't willing, but there were plenty of men who might take advantage of a closed door and a frightened girl, some of them policemen.

Mrs. Beaton invited him to sit down, lit an oil lamp, and headed off, presumably to fetch Ruby. Sebastian took off his hat, shrugged off his coat, and settled in an armchair by the unlit hearth. The parlor was small but cozy, with embroidered anti-macassars, a shelf with several well-thumbed books, and a lace doily on an occasional table, which displayed a photograph of a young man in uniform. Since he bore no obvious resemblance to Mrs. Beaton, Sebastian could only assume he was Mr. Beaton— or perhaps a young man who hadn't lived long enough to marry. Housekeepers always went by the title of Mrs., but in reality most of them had never been married.

Ruby was tall and lean, with round dark eyes and chestnut hair parted in the middle and covered by a voluminous cap. She stood by the door, her worried gaze radiating apprehension at being suddenly summoned to be questioned by the police.

"Please, sit down, Ruby," Sebastian said.

He pulled out his warrant card and held it up for the girl to see. She came closer, studied it for a moment, then perched on the edge of a chair, her back ramrod straight, her shoulders tense.

"I've done nothing wrong," she whispered. "Smithson

found Lady Littleton's earring. Just ask her. It'd rolled beneath the vanity table. I never even went in that room. I don't go upstairs. I'm the kitchen maid."

"I'm not here about a missing earring, and I know you've done nothing wrong," Sebastian said, keeping his voice calm and friendly. "I'm afraid there's been a death at the Foundling Hospital."

Ruby paled. "Who's dead?"

"Amanda Carter."

"No," Ruby cried, her hand going to her bosom. Her eyes filled with tears that she angrily wiped away. "You wouldn't be here for a mere death," she said.

"I believe Amanda was murdered."

"Who would do such a thing?"

"That's what I need to find out."

"How did she die?" Ruby asked, visibly bracing herself for his answer.

"She was hit on the head, then drowned in a laundry tub."

Ruby bowed her head, and Sebastian saw tears drip onto the bib of her pinafore. He took out his handkerchief and held it out to her, but she waved it away and used her apron to wipe her eyes.

"I hated leaving her. Mandy was the closest thing I ever had to family. And now she's gone too," she said softly.

"Ruby, did Amanda have any enemies?" Sebastian asked, his notepad at the ready.

Ruby shook her head. "No, she didn't. She was the sort of person others tended to overlook."

"Why?"

"Because she was quiet and serious, but also really sweet. She didn't talk a lot, but when she did she always meant what she said." Ruby bowed her head again, probably to hide her distress.

"Did Amanda ever sneak out during the night?"

Ruby didn't look up, but her head went up and down.

"Where did she go?"

Ruby finally met his gaze, her eyes red from crying. "She said she was going to get married."

"Married? At fourteen?"

"They were going to wait until she was sixteen, but she said she was betrothed. She was so happy," Ruby added.

"To whom was she betrothed?" Sebastian asked. Was it possible that one of the men he'd spoken to had decided to take a teenage bride?

Ruby sniffled. "She wouldn't tell me, but I thought it might have been one of the teachers."

"Why did you think that?"

"Because only a teacher would be able to move about freely during the night. He'd have keys, you see."

"So, you think a teacher entered the girls' wing and met Amanda down in the laundry?"

Ruby nodded. "Amanda said he loved her, and they would have a wonderful life together. They would get married and have a family, and she'd never be alone again."

"How long ago did Amanda tell you this?" Sebastian asked.

"Just before I left. She said she'd come and find me once she was out, and we'd meet for a cup of tea like grownups and talk about our lives."

"Do you know if this man tried to coerce her into having intimate relations with him?" Sebastian asked. Perhaps Amanda's suitor had grown tired of waiting and things had turned ugly when she refused him again.

"I don't think so. Mandy said that no child of hers would ever end up in an orphanage, so lying with a man before marriage was never an option."

"Things can change when two people are in love."

Ruby looked scandalized. "Not for Mandy. I told you, she

always meant what she said. She wouldn't go back on her word."

Sebastian pulled the dolly out of his pocket. "Have you ever seen this?"

Ruby's face crumpled, and she dissolved into tears. Then she nodded. "It was Mandy's."

"Where did she get it?"

"He gave it to her. She said it was a baby doll and it represented the family they were going to have someday."

"Ruby, is there anything at all you can think of that might help me to identify this man?" Sebastian asked. It seemed Amanda had been exceptionally good at keeping secrets and, even when she'd confided in her friend, had told her precious little.

"His Christian name starts with A."

"How do you know that?"

"Amanda said she was going to embroider a handkerchief for him and put an A in opposite corners. One for him and one for her."

"Thank you, Ruby," Sebastian said, and stood to leave. "Take care of yourself, and don't go out on your own until this case is solved."

"Do you think I'm in danger?" Ruby exclaimed. She clearly hadn't thought that far.

"You were Amanda's closest friend, so whoever killed her might think you know more than you do."

"I won't leave the house, Inspector Bell," Ruby cried. "Not until I know it's safe."

"Good."

Sebastian left Ruby to compose herself and stepped out of the housekeeper's parlor, and directly into Mrs. Beaton's path.

"Was Ruby able to help?"

"She was. Mrs. Beaton, please keep an eye on her."

"I understand, Inspector. Nothing will happen to Ruby on

my watch," Mrs. Beaton promised, and drew herself up to her full height as though heading into battle. She couldn't save her sister, but it seemed she meant to protect Ruby with everything she had at her disposal.

Sebastian thanked her for her assistance and left.

TWENTY-FOUR

It was close to five o'clock by the time Sebastian emerged from Lord Littleton's house. The sky was dark, the moon and stars obliterated by thick clouds that had rolled in while he was indoors and hung ominously close to the chimney pots that belched black coal smoke into the night. Although not windy, it was cold and damp and a soupy fog was beginning to creep in and wrap the world around him in a yellowish haze that swallowed the light from the streetlamps. The muted glow from curtained windows was too dim to light pedestrians' way, the long stretches of darkness leaving them vulnerable to mischief.

It was too late in the day to question anyone else, and Sebastian saw no reason to return to Scotland Yard. He had nothing to report and didn't care for Lovell to see his anger and frustration. What he really wanted was to speak to Gemma, but he couldn't call on her at the boarding house, not after the last time, when he'd pushed his way in and demanded the use of the parlor and a bottle of brandy. He'd had good reason: Gemma's friend had been found murdered, and he could hardly break the news on the doorstep; but Mrs. Bass didn't care about any of that. She didn't care to deal with a troublesome tenant, nor did she want a policeman hanging about her establishment. It gave the wrong impression and cast Gemma in an unfavorable light.

Sebastian would never forgive himself if Gemma were to be evicted because of him, so he'd have to wait until tomorrow and speak to her at the Foundling Hospital, where he also had to be careful not to single her out at her place of employment for fear of endangering her position. It was difficult to find respectable places to meet, especially at the end of December, when the city was cold and dark when Gemma left the hospital in the evenings.

By the time Sebastian reached his own front door, yellow tendrils of mist swirled around lampposts and hovered above the ground, the fog muffling the sounds and making him feel as if he were in a dense bubble. Sebastian hated the fog. It made him feel deaf and blind, two conditions that were crippling for a man in his profession, but he had to admit that even if the night were clear and bright he'd feel much the same, since he couldn't make heads nor tails of this case.

As soon as he entered the narrow entryway, Sebastian was confronted by an enraged Mrs. Poole, who was clad in a gown of mauve and beige and resembled a quivering mound of liver and tongue in aspic. She planted her hands on her ample hips and glared at Sebastian in a way that suggested he might be sent to his room without supper, which suddenly didn't seem like an unwelcome prospect.

"What seems to be the problem, Mrs. Poole?" he asked, glaring back. After the day he'd had, he really wasn't in the mood for one of his landlady's emotional outbursts.

She had become snippier with him over the past few weeks, her feminine pride wounded by his relentless rejection. He'd never said anything to her outright, but his evasive behavior, his refusal to acknowledge her less-than-subtle hints that she was interested in him, and his friendship with Gemma, had left her feeling vulnerable, more so during the holidays, when she no doubt felt more alone than ever and only wanted a little attention.

"You have a visitor, Inspector Bell," Mrs. Poole hissed.

"Has my visitor done something to upset you, Mrs. Poole?"

"Other than being female, you mean? No women allowed. What part of that do you find difficult to understand? I bent the rules for you when you were convalescing, but I highly doubt Miss Tate is here in her professional capacity. I want her out!"

"Then why did you let her in?" Sebastian asked, his spirits instantly lifting at the thought of seeing Gemma.

"Because I would not have it on my conscience if I left her to wait on the doorstep and she fell afoul of some ruffian who saw fit to accost a defenseless woman."

"You're the soul of kindness, Mrs. Poole," Sebastian said, and meant it.

Mrs. Poole wasn't a bad sort. She'd simply had the misfortune of becoming widowed at a young age and setting her sights on the wrong man, one who could never appreciate what she had to offer. Sebastian was sure that sooner or later a lodger would come along, possibly a man of mature years, who would see Mrs. Poole as the answer to all his prayers. Unless, of course, his prayer strayed to a desire for good food. Mrs. Poole was an appalling cook whose culinary creations were limited to boiled fowl, boiled beef, and boiled cod.

"You have five minutes, Inspector."

Sebastian found Gemma in the parlor. She was sitting by the fire, her head turned away from the door and her mourning bonnet forming a shield around her face. Her hands were demurely clasped in her lap, her feet together, the tips of her boots pointing outward like arrowheads. When she realized she was no longer alone, Gemma's head whipped around.

"I'm so sorry," she said, and sprang to her feet.

"You heard that?"

Gemma nodded. "I know I shouldn't have come. Mrs. Poole is right to be upset, but I urgently needed to speak to you."

"We can't talk here," Sebastian said, and handed Gemma her cape. "Let's find somewhere more private, and then I will escort you home."

"There's really no need," Gemma protested.

"There's every need. Come now."

Mrs. Poole's eyes fired daggers of jealousy at Gemma as she walked past her, but Gemma didn't seem to notice. The thought of Mrs. Poole as a rival had probably never occurred to her.

"Don't expect me to hold your supper for you," the landlady snarled at Sebastian.

"I don't expect any special treatment, Mrs. Poole," Sebastian replied.

The landlady harrumphed but said nothing as the door closed behind Gemma and Sebastian. They found a hansom and headed to Camden Town so they could remain close to Gemma's boarding house in Birkenhead Street. If Gemma missed curfew, Mrs. Bass would lock her out and she would be left with no place to spend the night. There was a passable chophouse just down the street that Gemma and Sebastian had eaten at before, so they went there. The proprietor, who had erroneously assumed that they were husband and wife when he saw them last, greeted them effusively.

"Welcome back," he exclaimed as he beamed at the two of them. "A pleasure to see you again. Table by the window?"

"We'd prefer the corner," Sebastian replied.

It was best if Gemma wasn't seen out with a man if one of her fellow lodgers happened to pass by. They were sure to report back to Mrs. Bass, who would welcome more ammunition should she wish to cast Gemma out of her establishment.

"Of course. Right this way," the proprietor said.

The chophouse wasn't crowded, but a few tables were occupied, mostly by men who sat either on their own or in pairs.

There was only one other woman, who sat with her back to the dining room and was dining with an older gentleman with florid cheeks and bushy muttonchop whiskers. The two sat in silence, the man eating with relish, the woman picking at her food. Everything in her posture cried defeat.

Once they were seated and had placed their order, Sebastian fixed his attention on Gemma, whose skin glowed pale against the black satin of her bonnet. She had assured him that she was in no danger and had only wanted to speak to him privately, but Sebastian knew she wouldn't risk coming to a gentleman's boarding house in the evening unless she had something urgent to say. And the fact that she had wasted money on a cab—because even Gemma wouldn't be courageous enough to brave the streets at night—convinced him that whatever she had to tell him was more important than she had initially let on and not information she cared to mention at the Foundling Hospital, where they might be overheard.

It was maddening that there was no place they could meet in private, but it was probably for the best. Not only would meeting him compromise Gemma's reputation, it would also lead to temptation, at least for him. Having kissed her once, he longed to do it again, and again, and, although he would rather die than hurt Gemma in any way, he was human and male, and had been terribly lonely for far too long. These were dangerous thoughts, and Sebastian dragged his mind away from enticing romantic possibilities and focused all his attention on Gemma, who unclasped her reticule, withdrew a lace-trimmed handkerchief, and unfolded it to reveal a gold ring.

"Whose ring is that?"

"I found it sewn into the hem of Amanda's dress."

Sebastian didn't bother to ask Gemma what had compelled her to examine Amanda's things. In fact, her industry only served to remind him that he should have thought of it himself and checked Amanda's clothes before they were either used to bury her in or given to another girl. He wanted to compliment Gemma on her cleverness, but didn't want to encourage her snooping. He'd never forgive himself if anything happened to her as a result of his negligence, but Gemma had reminded him time and time again that she was her own woman and didn't need his permission to do anything. He was neither her husband, brother, nor employer. All he could do was ask her— no, beg her—not to do anything reckless, but clearly she had ignored his advice, as usual. So instead he picked up the ring and studied it, trying to examine the insignia in the dim light of the wall sconce that was too far away to let him see the design clearly. He ran his finger over the embossed image, then weighed the ring in his hand. It was heavy. Solid gold.

"How would Amanda come by such a thing?" Gemma asked, lowering her voice as a waiter passed, carrying two plates.

Sebastian slid the ring onto his bare ring finger. It fit perfectly and glinted in the light.

"This is a man's ring," Gemma observed, giving voice to what he was thinking. "And it looks valuable."

"Thanks to you, I was able to find Ruby Marks," Sebastian said as he pulled off the ring. It had felt strange on his finger, as if he had just tried on another man's personality for size. He slid the ring into the pocket of his waistcoat, next to the peculiar little dolly.

"What did she say?" Gemma asked, her gaze bright with curiosity.

"She said Amanda was betrothed and had planned to marry when she turned sixteen."

"Did she tell you who the man was?" Gemma asked. She didn't look particularly surprised by Sebastian's news. Having already known about the ring, she had probably come to a similar conclusion, and a few about the man in question as well.

"Amanda never told her anything about him except that his Christian name begins with A. He must have given her this ring as a token of his promise. Can you think of anyone whose name begins with A?" Sebastian asked.

"The only person I can think of is Alf Timmins. He works as a porter and has been married for thirty-two years. He has three children and twelve grandchildren. I seriously doubt Amanda was planning to marry him."

"What about the teachers?"

"As far as I'm aware, no other teacher or porter has a name that starts with A," Gemma replied, looking perplexed.

"It's easily enough checked. I can ask Matron."

"It had to have been an adult," Gemma mused, "since no boy of fourteen could have given Amanda a solid gold ring."

"Unless he stole it," Sebastian said. He could feel the edge of the ring pressing against his side, as if it were nudging him to figure this out. "It's the only possibility that makes sense if Amanda was in love with a fellow foundling, but how would a boy who's never permitted off the premises steal such a valuable item, and from whom? The crest looks foreign."

"It's Russian," Gemma announced, taking Sebastian by surprise.

"How do you know that?"

"Because I've seen that insignia before. In Scutari. It's the coat of arms of Imperial Russia."

"Did you treat Russian soldiers at the hospital?" Sebastian asked, surprised.

Russians had been the enemy, so he had assumed they would have their own doctors and hospitals and not expect to be treated by British doctors and nurses, who'd barely had enough hands or supplies to spare for their own wounded. He supposed that, in the confusion that had reigned after each battle, it was possible that some Russians had made it onto the transport ships that carried the men to the hospital in Turkey.

Gemma shook her head. "No, the Russian soldiers, at least those deemed worthy of saving, were tended to by their own medics. Many were simply left to die where they fell. Not a fate I would wish on anyone, particularly since it would have taken some men days to die."

"That seems awfully cruel, even for Russians," Sebastian quipped.

Gemma nodded. "I never went anywhere near a battlefield, but I heard stories, especially from patients who were on the mend and needed to talk. Many suffered from horrible night-mares, reliving what they had witnessed night after night. Some felt pity for the Russian soldiers and only wanted the war to end."

"Why would they pity the enemy?"

Every time they spoke about the Crimean War, Sebastian realized just how little he understood of what had actually tran-spired and the extent of what Gemma had seen and heard. Perhaps he would be better informed if he had bothered to read the endless accounts in the papers, but he had been fighting his own war at that time, just trying to survive after his life had been brutally torn apart, his sanity hanging by a thread as he sought oblivion rather than claw his way to sobriety at a time when neither his mind nor his heart could handle the truth. Had he not lost himself in days-long opium dreams, he probably would have blown his brains out just to stop the pain. The only thing that had stopped him from pulling the trigger was the sure knowledge that if he committed suicide he would never be reunited with Louisa and their boy, so he had clung on.

"British soldiers are whipped into obedience by the officers, who operate according to their own code of honor. The foot soldiers' every move is scheduled, monitored, and judged. Not so in the Russian Army. Many soldiers who were herded onto the battlefields to face the enemy were nothing more than peasant conscripts, and the professional soldiers were no better. Not only were they not trained for combat, but, from what I was told by numerous patients, they were so drunk, they could barely keep their feet."

"Drunk?" Sebastian exclaimed, ignoring the waiter, who'd placed their meals before them, bowed, and made himself scarce.

"Russian soldiers, including the officers, were allocated something like two cupfuls of vodka per day, along with their rations of bread and meat. It was said that on the day of the Battle of the Alma River, the soldiers were denied their rations and were forced to obtain liquor by other means, since they couldn't bear to go into battle sober. They were able to get drunk on stores they got from nearby towns and sympathetic officers, but drinking on an empty stomach left them virtually incapable of fighting and the Russians suffered a resounding defeat."

Gemma smiled sadly as she recalled that time. "Russian commander-in-chief Prince Menshikov was so certain of victory, he invited a party of local ladies to watch the battle from a nearby hillside. The ladies were treated to a sight they'll probably never forget. It was said that they fled in terror, leaving all their possessions behind."

Sebastian withdrew the ring and stared at it once again. "This is not something a peasant or a foot soldier would own."

"This ring would belong to an officer, someone who was likely a scion of some noble family."

Sebastian blew out his breath in exasperation. "How? How did Amanda come by this ring?" he demanded, not really expecting an answer. "There's no one that's Russian at the Foundling Hospital."

"No," Gemma agreed, "there isn't."

They were silent for a few minutes, each lost in their thoughts and suppositions, then Sebastian shook his head, having come up empty. "We need to go back to the beginning."

"You mean you intend to reinterview everyone?" Gemma asked.

"No, further back than that. I need to know where Amanda came from. Who were her people?"

"Amanda was born long before the war in Crimea," Gemma reminded him.

"Yes, she was, but what if she was approached by her father? Or brother?"

"And you think they would present her with this ring as a token of their affection?" Gemma asked, sounding dubious. Sebastian had to admit the theory was far-fetched, but it wasn't completely unrealistic.

"Perhaps they wanted to give her something that would ensure her survival should things become difficult once she left the hospital. This ring was obviously stolen, but Amanda could always fence it."

"All right, let us say that Amanda's male relative was in Crimea and took this ring off a dead Russian officer. The man managed to smuggle it back to England without anyone realizing he was in possession of a small fortune and then selflessly gave it to Amanda. But that doesn't explain Amanda's supposed engagement."

"Perhaps the ring has nothing to do with her betrothal and we're dealing with two separate individuals," Sebastian replied, thinking out loud.

"So, how will you find the man who gave Amanda the ring?" Gemma asked.

"I'm going to speak to Matron and demand to see the register tomorrow. I need the name of Amanda's mother and the token she left for her daughter. I have no plan beyond that, but hopefully it will throw up some leads."

Gemma nodded. Her cheeks were turning a rosy pink now that she was warm. She smiled contritely. "I'm sorry I came to the boarding house. I seem to have made an enemy of Mrs. Poole."

"Never mind about Mrs. Poole. I'll deal with her later," Sebastian promised. "Now eat your supper before it gets cold."

Gemma had barely made a dent in her chop. She obediently picked up her knife and fork.

Sebastian returned to his cooling beefsteak. The food was heavenly compared to what he would have been likely to get at Mrs. Poole's this evening. As he cut into his meat, he realized that his shoulder ached. He shouldn't have lifted Amanda's body, but he'd forgotten all about his injury in the face of such savagery.

"You're in pain," Gemma said, watching him closely.

"It's nothing."

Gemma didn't look like she believed him, but didn't bother to lecture him on the need to look after himself, for which Sebastian was grateful. He knew he was pushing himself too hard, but he'd rest once the case was solved and he could enjoy a few slow days before another brutal murder was committed and his expertise was once again called for.

They talked of other things as they finished their meal and even decided to split a pudding before navigating through the thick fog toward Gemma's boarding house. The street was nearly deserted, but Sebastian walked Gemma to the door, then waited by the lamppost until she was safely inside and he could begin the long trek home.

TWENTY-FIVE

TUESDAY DECEMBER 28

Tuesday morning found Sebastian in Matron Holcombe's office once again. She didn't seem overly pleased to see him, and drew herself up as if preparing for a physical assault. Sebastian had his doubts about sharing his findings with the woman, but he needed answers and hoped she might be able to supply at least a few. He drew the ring out of his pocket and held it in front of her face. The gold glowed a pale yellow in the light streaming through the office window.

"What's this?" Matron demanded.

"This was sewn into the hem of Amanda's dress."

Matron's shock was evident, but she instantly went on the offensive. "And how do you come to have it, Inspector Bell? I don't recall allowing you access to the girls' dormitories."

"How I come to have it is not really the issue, is it? What was a foundling girl doing with a solid gold ring that had clearly belonged to some Russian nobleman?"

Matron blanched. "What makes you think this belonged to a Russian nobleman?"

"Because this is the insignia of Imperial Russia. I doubt a peasant, or some lowly craftsman, would own such a thing."

"It's clearly stolen."

"Indeed it might be, but how did it come to be in the hem of Amanda's dress? Is there anyone here who has ties to Russia, no matter how tenuous?"

Matron seemed to sink deeper into her chair, her expression one of complete puzzlement. "No," she said at last. "No one."

"Let me rephrase that," Sebastian countered. "Is there anyone here who served in Crimea?"

"Crimea?"

"Someone might have taken this ring off a dead or wounded Russian officer."

Understanding seemed to dawn, and Matron nodded. "Matthew Campbell was in Crimea. He came back to work at the Foundling Hospital after he was released from the army."

"Now we're getting somewhere," Sebastian said.

"Matthew Campbell is an honorable man, Inspector."

"So you would stake your reputation on vouching for him?"

Matron went quiet, then shook her head. "I wouldn't vouch for anyone's character, Inspector. People have a way of disappointing one, don't they?"

"They do," Sebastian agreed. "Has anyone else served in Crimea?"

"No. No one."

"I'll see that register now, or should I come back with a warrant?"

Matron Holcombe sighed, then stood and walked over to a discreet cabinet at the back of the room. She flipped through more than a dozen of the keys on her keyring until she found the one she was searching for, then bent down and unlocked the bottom drawer. She extracted a thick leather-bound volume that looked like some antique manuscript and carried it over to her desk. The dates 1800–1850 were embossed on the cover in gold lettering. Given the bulkiness of the register, it seemed a lot of children had been left at the hospital over the course of fifty years.

Matron laid the volume on the desk, then carefully leafed through it until she reached the appropriate year. Amanda would have been born in 1844, so Matron started with January and ran her finger down the list of admissions as she searched for Amanda's number. There was a detailed entry for each child and a token affixed to the page with the aid of thread or adhesive.

"Here we are," Matron said at last. Sebastian thought she might refuse to show him the page and only tell him what he needed to know, but she turned the register around and allowed him to see for himself. Sebastian reached for his notebook with the intention of copying out the information. Amanda's entry wasn't as long as some of the others. It said:

Mother, Mary Skelton, aged nineteen, surrendered female infant, no name given, to the care of the Foundling Hospital on June 16, 1844. The infant was said to be born on June 2, 1844. Mother unmarried. No known father. Token left: drawing of a heart pierced by five swords, and silver band.

The drawing of the heart was folded and affixed to the page. Sebastian carefully pried it off and unfolded the paper, which bore a plum-sized depiction of a red, bleeding heart, the swords poking out of the plump organ. There was also a very thin silver band etched with snaking ivy. Sebastian held up the band and studied it. There was nothing telling about the sliver of silver. Perhaps Mary Skelton had left the ring for her daughter so that she would have something precious once she finally came of age. If Amanda sold the ring, she wouldn't get much, but it was probably the only thing of any value Mary had owned, and she had left it to show that she had loved the child she'd been forced to give up.

"I need to take these," Sebastian told Matron.

"You cannot remove tokens from the register," Matron countered. "It's against the rules."

"Amanda is dead," Sebastian said. "She will never have need of these tokens more than she does now. These things are the only connection to her mother, who will recognize the mementos she left for her child."

Matron sighed. "Fine. You may take them. But this is all the information I am able to provide."

"There's something else I need to see."

Matron looked startled. "Which is?"

"Show me the entry for Michael White."

"Why?"

"Because Michael's number is 8413 and Amanda's number is 8412. I need to know if they were related."

"I can assure you they weren't," Matron said. "Michael White was simply the next child to be registered with the hospital. There's no significance to the closeness in numbers."

"Are you certain?" Sebastian asked.

"I am. If a child was registered today as number one, then the next child would be number two, and so forth. That doesn't mean one and two are related. I'm sworn to protect this information and keep it confidential, and, unless you have evidence that proves Amanda and Michael were somehow connected, I'm unable to help you. You have what you came for, Inspector."

"Are there any male employees whose Christian names start with A?" Sebastian asked.

"Why on earth do you need to know that?" Matron asked.

"Just answer the question, please."

Matron shut the register, locked it up, then took another register from a shelf and brought it back to her desk. She opened it to the last written-on page and showed it to Sebastian. It was a list of employees and the wages they would receive on 31 December 1858, payment for the final quarter of the current year.

Sebastian scanned the entries but, except for Alfred (Alf)
Timmins, no one's Christian name began with A. The only
other person who came close was Matthew Campbell, whose
second name was Aaron, and who was certainly both young and
handsome enough to arouse the passions of a young, innocent
girl.

"What about the boys? Are there any of the older boys
whose names begin with A?"

"Well, of course there are," Matron exclaimed, clearly exasperated by the question. "What's this about, Inspector Bell?"

"According to a friend, Amanda talked of marrying
someone whose name begins with an A. If she wasn't involved
in an inappropriate relationship with one of the employees, it
had to be one of the boys."

"That's not possible. Social interaction between girls and
boys is not permitted. Amanda could not have had a relationship with anyone, foundling or teacher. Someone would have
noticed if anything untoward was going on," Matron protested.

"And yet she told her friend that she did, and had two items
in her possession that she couldn't have obtained within the
walls of this institution."

"Two items?" Matron asked warily.

Sebastian showed her the dolly. "Have you ever seen this
before?"

"No. Was this also in the hem of her dress?"

"No. Amanda was clutching it in her hand when she died."

"It's an odd little thing," Matron said. "But harmless
enough, I should think."

"Amanda's plan to marry would explain her desire to leave
the hospital earlier than necessary. She would be free to meet
with her intended on her afternoons off and start earning a
wage, which would help the couple once they were ready to
begin their life together."

"Inspector," Matron said with what was obviously the last

reserve of her patience, "orphans crave love. They long for family and a future in which someone is waiting for them. Amanda could have made up this boy. He's a fantasy."

"How do you explain the ring then, and the dolly?"

"Gentlemen of quality come to the hospital all the time. They are given a tour and introduced to some of the children. It is possible that someone lost the items and Amanda found them and pocketed the loot."

"So you're proposing that some random gentleman just happened to lose a gold ring with a Russian Imperial crest."

"Need I remind you, Inspector Bell, that Her Royal Highness Queen Victoria has ties to the Russian royal family? Perhaps the gentleman was a guest at the palace."

Sebastian sighed. If he were honest, Matron's theory wasn't any more far-fetched than his own suggestion that a male relative had stolen valuables from the dead, sought out Amanda, and gifted her a valuable ring. Sadly, that was the best he had at the moment, and the only other possibility was that Matthew Aaron Campbell was the man Sebastian was searching for.

"I will take a list of boys whose names start with A," Sebastian said.

"Shall I include boys as young as twelve, or will thirteen and fourteen do?" Matron asked, not bothering to hide her irritation.

"I'll start with the older group," Sebastian said, but he had to agree with Matron that it was probably futile. To interview a dozen or more boys whose names had not come up during the investigation thus far was likely a waste of time and would only distract him from focusing on someone who had a motive and the means to murder Amanda.

"Very well. I will have the list for you by the end of the day," Matron replied.

"Can I rely on you to keep what we discussed confidential?" Sebastian asked. The last thing he needed was for the culprit to leg it if he got wind that he was being investigated in connection with the murder.

"Of course. Now, if you will excuse me, I have a hospital to run."

Sebastian gave Matron a stiff bow and left her office. He paused in the foyer to consider his options. He was faced with several choices. He could try to find Amanda's mother, which could prove to be a wild goose chase and eat up not only the rest of the day but possibly several days and still leave him empty-handed. He could also confront Matthew Campbell, who'd already denied any involvement in Amanda's death and wasn't likely to change his story.

When cornered, Campbell might put up a fight. Normally, Sebastian wouldn't think twice about taking on a man of Campbell's size and age, but his aching shoulder reminded him what was at stake and that he could lose his quarry due to his injury. The wisest course of action was to return to Scotland Yard and come back with backup. Constable Bryant was ten years younger and strong as a bull. He could tackle Campbell if it came to it and bring him back to the Yard.

The station was relatively quiet so early in the morning. Sergeant Woodward was reading a newspaper, Constable Meadows was taking a statement from a shopkeeper who'd come in to report a burglary, Superintendent Lovell was in with Inspector Ransome, a meeting that had to be fraught with tension if not outright animosity, and Constable Yates was attempting to subdue a thrashing lad of about twelve who was trying to bite the constable's hand in order to make his escape. Constable Forrest came to the rescue, and together they were able to drag the boy down the stairs toward the cells, where he would presumably be given time to calm down and reflect on whatever it was he'd done.

"All right, Seb?" Sergeant Woodward asked Sebastian.

"I need assistance."

"Constable Bryant has yet to grace us with his presence this morning, so you'll have to settle for Constable Forrest."

"I need a more experienced man," Sebastian replied. He couldn't take the chance of Constable Forrest cocking things up. "Give me Meadows or Yates."

Sergeant Woodward nodded. "Take Yates, then."

"Thanks, Albert."

"Don't mention it," Sergeant Woodward said. "Are you close to making an arrest?"

"I think I am, but the evidence is circumstantial at best."

"If I know you, you'll soon find irrefutable proof," Sergeant Woodward replied.

Sergeant Woodward hadn't had much confidence in Sebastian a few short months ago, not when he'd had to come to find him in Mr. Wu's opium den and bodily drag him out into the light to keep Sebastian from losing his place with the Yard. The fact that he was so supportive now could mean only one thing: Sebastian's tarnished reputation was starting to recover from the blow it had been dealt. But given the current climate, he could either become the Yard's new darling or a convenient scapegoat. The current investigation could prove to be the deciding factor in his future, since he now had to consider Ransome's goodwill as well as Lovell's if he hoped to retain his position.

Constable Yates had just returned to the duty room, and Sebastian beckoned to him. "Constable, I need you to bring in Matthew Campbell. You will find him at the Foundling Hospital. He's one of the teachers there and might be of a mind to put up a fight."

"Don't worry, Inspector Bell," Yates replied, smiling to reveal tobacco-stained teeth. "I'll have your man trussed up and waiting for you when you return."

"Take Constable Forrest with you," Sergeant Woodward said. "You heard Inspector Bell. The cove might put up a fight."

"I can manage to arrest a man on my own," Yates protested.

"No doubt you can, but Forrest needs to see how these things are done, and he can only learn by watching an experienced man."

Constable Yates looked thoroughly annoyed, but had no choice but to acquiesce and go to fetch reinforcements.

"Where're you off to, then?" Sergeant Woodward asked Sebastian.

"I'm going to look for Amanda Carter's mother."

"Do you know where to find her?"

"I have a fairly good idea," Sebastian replied, but did not elaborate.

Sergeant Woodward nodded, his expression grave. "Imagine not seeing your sprat for fourteen years and then learning she's been murdered. Not news any mother would like to receive, even an absent one."

This observation didn't really warrant a reply, so Sebastian bid Sergeant Woodward a good day and set off.

TWENTY-SIX

Back when Sebastian had been a young bobby, spending his days patrolling the streets of London and walking from place to place because he couldn't afford to spend money on cabs, he had thought that one day he might appreciate the knowledge he'd gleaned from traversing the city. He'd always been curious and liked to learn about the history of various landmarks and the stories behind the more colorful names. He supposed he'd got that from his father, who loved history and would tell Sebastian and Simian stories about epic battles, clever alliances, and disastrous royal marriages. Simian had been bored out of his mind and used to whine endlessly, but Sebastian had loved all that intrigue and adventure. He realized now that his father had left out the more gruesome parts, of which there were many, and played up the heroics to make the stories more appealing to two small boys who had the attention span of a gnat. Sebastian could trace his desire to become a policeman back to those stories, told by the fire on cold winter nights. And perhaps it was those stories that had kindled Simian's need to live a life in which nothing changed but the seasons.

As he left the Yard, Mary Skelton's drawing in hand, Sebastian knew precisely where he was headed. Had Mary drawn a treasure map and used an X to mark the spot she could not have been clearer. There was only one place in London that sprang to mind—Bleeding Heart Yard. The yard was just off Greville Street and was thought to have been named after an inn that had been located in nearby Charles Street in the days before the Reformation. There had been nothing notable about the inn, except the ancient wooden sign that hung above the entrance and depicted the bleeding heart of the Virgin Mary skewered by five swords.

The inn was long gone, and so was the sign, but the name had stuck because the cobbled yard that still bore the name had played a role in another colorful legend. While walking the beat in Holborn his second year in London, Sebastian had heard the story of Lady Elizabeth Hatton, whose body had been found in Bleeding Heart Yard some two hundred years before, her limbs torn asunder, her heart still pumping blood, and her skull bashed against the pump that stood near the entrance to the yard. The murder had never been solved—the culprit had melted into the night—and although Lady Elizabeth had got a fine burial, like all unexplained happenings, the tale had taken on a life of its own over the years and been embellished in the telling.

The story had evolved to accuse Lady Hatton of witchcraft, the storytellers talking of a bargain that had been struck with the Devil to expand her power. But Lady Elizabeth had grown too ambitious and hadn't wanted to mind her master anymore. Never had a mortal been able to outwit the Devil, for such was his power that he always knew what was in his opponent's mind, and Elizabeth Hatton had gone the way of all such fools.

Sebastian didn't believe in witchcraft any more than he believed in the Devil, especially since Sergeant Roberts of Division E, where Sebastian had been a constable at the time, had assured him that neither story was true. Lady Elizabeth Hatton had lived to a great age and had died of natural causes. Still, the name had stuck, and Mary Skelton had obviously been a clever girl blessed with her fair share of good sense. Not enough sense to keep from getting with child out of wedlock, but enough to bring her daughter back to her should Amanda go in search of her birth mother once she came of age.

Sebastian caught a ride with a farmer headed for Smithfield Market, then walked the rest of the way. The yard hadn't changed much since he'd last seen it some years back. Surrounded on three sides by three-storied brick buildings, it had the air of a neighborhood that had come down in the world, but not so low as to think of itself as a slum. The windows were mostly glazed, and the cobbles were well worn. The famous pump was still there, after all this time, the iron rusted and flaking in places. Two small boys played with a hoop and stick despite the cold, a girl of about fifteen walked past with a basket slung over her arm, a vendor pushed a wheelbarrow laden with pots and pans and called out that he also sharpened knives, and an old man sat on an upturned crate, sucking on a pipe. Sebastian didn't bother with the children or the vendor, who might or might not live in one of the buildings. Instead, he went for the old-timer.

"Good morning," he said to the man, and smiled in a friendly manner.

"Mornin' yerself."

"Have you lived here long?"

"Most of me life. What's it to ye, son?" the man asked, eyeing Sebastian warily.

"I'm looking for someone."

"And who might that be?"

"Mary Skelton."

The man stared up at Sebastian, surprise evident in his rheumy gaze. "Then I'd say ye're a few years too late, mister."

"Did she die?"

"Aye, she did at that."

"Did she have any family?" Sebastian asked.

The man studied Sebastian for a moment, no doubt wondering if he should volunteer the information.

"I don't mean them any harm," Sebastian said. "I only need to speak to someone who knew Mary."

"Are ye a copper?" the old man asked.

"Inspector Bell of Scotland Yard."

"And what would an inspector of Scotland Yard want with Mary's kin?"

"Mary's daughter died at Christmas. I thought someone should know."

The man stared at Sebastian as if he had said something very strange, then shrugged with indifference. "Kind of ye, to be sure, but not necessary."

"What makes you say that?"

The man shrugged. "What good will it do to cause pain?"

"Would you not want to know if your child had died?"

The man's expression said it all. "Me children are dead already, Inspector. Son slaughtered in Crimea, daughter dead of consumption at fifteen. And let me tell ye, Inspector, I'd rather not know they're gone and finish out me days believing they'll come back one day."

"I'm sorry for your loss," Sebastian said. "But I'd still like to speak to Mary's kin."

"Suit yerself." The man used his pipe to point toward the building opposite. "Second floor. Door on the right."

"Thank you."

The man nodded, his attention already on an elderly woman who was coming toward him, a brown woolen shawl wrapped about her shoulders.

"Come inside, ye old coot," she chided. "Ye'll catch yer death out here."

"I like it here," the man protested.

"And who'll take care of ye when ye get ill?" the woman demanded. "I've enough to be getting on with."

"Quit yer blathering, woman," the old man snapped, but pushed to his feet, his limbs creaking like an old cart.

Sebastian crossed the yard and entered the building the old man had indicated. The stairwell was lost in shadow, and there was the usual stench of dried urine, mouse droppings, and boiled cabbage that seemed to haunt buildings in the poorer areas. The staircase was missing several balusters, and the treads were worn, the wood creaking beneath Sebastian's weight. He climbed to the second floor and looked around. There were three doors on the landing, all black, the paint crisscrossed with a web of small cracks and peeling in places. The landing had been cleanly swept, and there were no cobwebs in the corners. Whoever lived here took pride in their home and probably wasn't on the brink of poverty, but any change in circumstance might be all it took to catapult them into a fight for survival.

Sebastian approached the door on the right and listened. He didn't hear anything and hoped he hadn't had a wasted journey. He rapped on the door and waited. A few moments later, a woman of about fifty responded to his knock. She wore a gray shawl, a gown of unrelieved black, and a black cap over hair that was more gray than brown. Her bright blue eyes immediately put Sebastian in mind of Amanda. The woman clutched at her shawl, her gaze fearful when she realized she had opened the door to a stranger.

"What do you want?" she asked.

Sebastian held up his warrant card, but wasn't sure the woman was able to read it. "I'm Inspector Bell of Scotland Yard. I'm looking for Mary Skelton's family."

"Why?" the woman asked, her fear palpable.

"Because I have questions."

"What about?"

"Are you Mrs. Skelton?" Sebastian asked.

The woman nodded. "Mary was my daughter. She passed three years ago. So whatever answers you seek died with her."

"Mrs. Skelton, Mary left her child at the Foundling Hospital."

Mrs. Skelton's surprise at that pronouncement was evident, and she took an involuntary step back, revealing the room behind her and the girl Sebastian had seen earlier walking with the basket. It wasn't immediately clear if she was shocked to learn that her daughter had given up her child or astonished that Sebastian was aware of that sad event in her family's history.

"How did you find us?" she asked, keeping her voice low.

"Mary left this for the intake register." Sebastian showed Mrs. Skelton the drawing.

She nodded. "Mary drew that. I recognize her hand."

"There was also this."

Mrs. Skelton paled at the sight of the ring. "How do you come to have it?"

"Who gave it to her?" Sebastian asked, not quite ready to offer an explanation.

Mrs. Skelton smiled sadly. "I did, on her sixteenth birthday. It belonged to my mother, and her mother before her. A family heirloom, ye might say." She scoffed. "That was all I had left of them."

Sebastian held out the ring to the woman. "Then perhaps you should have it back."

"Shouldn't you give it to Mary's child?" When Sebastian didn't answer right away, she sighed in understanding, accepted the ring, and slid it on her finger. "You'd better come in."

She stepped aside to let Sebastian in, shut the door behind him, and threw the bolt. The girl hadn't moved, her dark eyes watching him fearfully, as if he might pounce on her at any moment. The Skeltons probably didn't get many visitors, especially strangers, and the bolt spoke to fear and a need for greater safety. Perhaps someone had tried to break in before, or maybe it was natural for a household made up entirely of women to seek reassurance from a piece of metal.

The room beyond was well proportioned but crammed with too much furniture. There was a square table surrounded by four chairs, a peeling blue dresser filled with mismatched crockery, and a round iron stove positioned near a door that led to another room, presumably a bedroom. There was a good fire going, and the stove gave off a fair amount of heat, probably enough to warm both rooms. A neatly made cot stood in the corner, with a well-loved cloth doll on the pillow.

Sebastian couldn't help but notice that the floor was clean and well maintained, the table shone with polish, and a pretty watercolor hung above the bed, depicting a lone boat floating down a wide river, possibly the Thames.

"Mary painted that," Mrs. Skelton said when she saw him looking at the picture. "She liked to paint the river."

"It's very good," Sebastian replied.

Mrs. Skelton turned to face the girl. "Take a walk, Eva," she said.

The girl raised her chin defiantly. "Where am I meant to go? It's cold, Gran."

Mrs. Skelton reached for a small jar on the top shelf, drew out a coin, and thrust it at the girl. "Get a loaf of bread from the baker. See if you can get one of yesterday's for cheaper." She pulled off her shawl and handed it to Eva. "Take my shawl. It's warmer."

Eva accepted the shawl, wrapped it about her shoulders, and tucked the ends into her apron to keep it in place, then cast another worried look in Sebastian's direction and left.

Mrs. Skelton pointed to a chair and took a seat herself. She looked thinner without the thick shawl, her shoulders narrow and stooped.

"What is it that ye want?" she asked as she laid her work-reddened hands on the table.

"I want to talk to you about Mary, and her daughter."

Mrs. Skelton's eyes filled with tears. "It weren't a peaceful death, were it?"

"No."

"What happened to her?"

"Amanda was murdered, Mrs. Skelton, and I'm going to find out who's responsible."

"So ye don't know?"

Sebastian shook his head. "That's why I need to ask you some questions."

"And what can I possibly tell ye? I haven't seen the girl since she were two weeks old."

"I thought Amanda might have reconnected with her kin," Sebastian said.

"Ye thought wrong, then."

"Are you certain?"

Mrs. Skelton squared her shoulders and fixed Sebastian with an anxious gaze. "How did she die, the poor lamb? Amanda," she added softly, as if trying the name on for size.

"She drowned," Sebastian said. He decided to spare Mrs. Skelton the gruesome details. What was the point of upsetting her further? "It was probably quick."

Mrs. Skelton nodded. "Were she interfered with?"

"I don't believe so."

"Well, that's something, I reckon," Mrs. Skelton said. "At least she didn't have to suffer through that."

"Is that what happened to Mary?" Sebastian asked carefully.

Mrs. Skelton shook her head. "That's what happened to me. When I were in service. My employer's son were Mary's father, but he never saw his girl. I were sacked as soon as my condition became obvious. Tossed into the street without so much as a farthing of compensation or a character. They said it were my fault. Too pretty by half. Led the poor boy astray," she said bitterly. "Mary and I would have died in a workhouse had a good man not taken pity on us. Mr. Skelton, God rest his soul, he were a good husband and a loving father to Mary, but not strict enough. And she were willful, my girl. And stubborn."

Mrs. Skelton sighed heavily, as if all the old arguments were suddenly playing out in her head and Mary was still a young girl with her life ahead of her.

"Mary could have had a comfortable life, but she wanted more for herself than days filled with drudgery and a marriage built on obligation. I told her, 'Ye be careful. Look what happened to me,' but young girls don't listen to what their mothers have to say, not until it's too late."

Sebastian didn't interrupt. Mrs. Skelton seemed eager to talk. Perhaps hearing about a granddaughter she hadn't seen in fourteen years or had agreed to give up had brought up feelings of regret and she needed to explain herself to a stranger to absolve herself of guilt.

"Mary were a barmaid at a public house near Hatton Garden. The publican were a kind man, and well off. He'd lost his wife in childbirth the year before and had a soft spot for my Mary. He were older, and no one would accuse him of being handsome, but we all have to make sacrifices in life, don't we, Inspector? If I could have talked any sense into that girl, she'd have been set for life, even if she'd have three stepchildren to raise. But Mary fell in love with an ostler as worked in a livery not far from here. He were a fine-looking boy, Gareth, I'll give him that, but he were seventeen and didn't have a pot to piss in. And it all ended much as you'd expect," Mrs. Skelton said angrily. "Mary got with child, and Gareth went and did a runner. Took the Queen's shilling and died on some foreign battlefield, the foolish boy."

"Are you certain Gareth is dead?" Sebastian asked.

"Oh, yes. His father told Mary as much, and no one's seen hide nor hair of him since he left."

"And Mary?" Sebastian asked. He didn't want to ask about Eva outright and hoped Mrs. Skelton would get to her eventually.

"Well, Mary had lost her place at the pub, and no one would give her the time of day, not when she were unmarried and with a child on the way. So I took in sewing, charred for half a dozen families, and kept us going until the girls were born."

"Girls?" Sebastian asked. He'd already surmised that Eva was Amanda's sister, but it hadn't occurred to him that the girls might be twins.

"That's right," Mrs. Skelton said. "Eva came first, and then the other one, nearly an hour later. I delivered them myself. Couldn't spare the coin for a midwife."

"The other one?"

Mrs. Skelton nodded sadly. "Mary never named her. Couldn't bring herself to claim the child as her own." She blinked away tears and let out a shaky breath, and Sebastian could see what it had cost her to tell him the truth. "We couldn't manage two children. We couldn't even manage one, but Mary begged me. She cried and pleaded and said she'd harm herself if she had to give both babies away. So it were decided that Eva would stay, and the other one would go. Mary were heartbroken, but she were glad when they accepted the girl at the Foundling Hospital. 'She'll be looked after, Mam,' she said. 'She'll have a future.' And that were that, Inspector. We never saw her again, and I hadn't heard of her until today."

"Does Eva know she had a twin sister?" Sebastian asked.

"No. Mary never told her. Couldn't bear to admit to the cruelty of separating the girls, even though it were never her fault."

"Mrs. Skelton, is there anyone who knew that Amanda had

been given to the Foundling Hospital and would have any reason to harm her?"

"If they did, I know naught about that, Inspector Bell. I reckon no one even knew Mary had twins."

"What will you tell Eva?" Sebastian asked.

"I'll tell her ye'd come asking after another girl. No use breaking her heart, is there? She's already lost her mother. Life's hard enough for the poor girl."

Sebastian didn't question Mrs. Skelton's decision. It was her choice what Eva was told, since it seemed she was Eva's only family, and he thought it was probably kinder not to tell her the truth. He did wonder about the Skeltons, however. Mrs. Skelton had led him to believe that she and Eva were barely getting by, counting every farthing, and buying stale bread, but the coal hod was full, the furniture looked sturdy, and Mary had clearly been able to afford watercolors, paper, and brushes, not items a poverty-stricken woman would waste her hard-earned money on. Perhaps things had changed for the better once Mary had been able to work again, but Sebastian's copper's nose told him something didn't smell quite right, and Mrs. Skelton might not have told him the whole truth.

"Do you know Gareth's surname?" he asked.

"Gareth Wilson. His father, Graham Wilson, owns the livery over on Greville Street."

"Thank you, Mrs. Skelton."

"Will she get a proper burial, Amanda?" Mrs. Skelton asked, her eyes brimming with tears. "Will she have a stone?"

"She will be properly buried," Sebastian promised. "I don't know about a stone. A cross, maybe."

The Foundling Hospital had its own cemetery, where dozens of children had been buried over the years. Sebastian hadn't visited it, but he imagined it was neat and well kept, with graves that were evenly spaced and lined the paths the way the children's cots were lined up in the dormitories. Order had to be maintained, even in death, and funds had to be carefully administered and not spent unnecessarily. Mr. Frain, as well as undertaking repairs in the Hospital building, probably also made crosses for the children that had passed; the wood and his labor would be much cheaper than the services and products of a mason, who'd charge so much more for a headstone.

The children who slept in those lonely graves had earned a marker to commemorate their brief lives, but the markers bore names that weren't quite theirs, and there was no one to mourn the dead once their friends left the hospital to make lives outside the institution. Their graves were probably also forgotten, unless they had managed to build families of their own.

Mrs. Skelton said, "I hope Amanda had a good life at that hospital."

Sebastian thought she might have had a better life with her mother and sister, no matter how poor the Skeltons were, but it wasn't his place to judge either Mrs. Skelton or Mary. He'd seen babies left on the side of the road to die because their mothers couldn't care for them, and he'd seen infants and toddlers fished out of the river or washed up on the riverbank by the tide. At least Amanda had been given a chance and would have had a future, had someone not decided to end her life.

"I think she did," Sebastian said, his mind going to Ruby, who'd seemed such a solid presence. "She had friends."

"Thank the Lord for that," Mrs. Skelton said. "I always did wonder."

Not enough to find out, Sebastian thought as he stood to leave. The Skeltons could have taken Amanda back at any time, but they'd left her there and had never made contact, if Mrs. Skelton could be believed. They'd simply erased her from their lives and chosen to love Eva instead.

TWENTY-SEVEN

Sebastian left Bleeding Heart Yard and walked the short distance to Greville Street. Wilson's Livery wasn't hard to find, nor was the man Sebastian was in search of. Graham Wilson was a thick-set fellow with bushy, curling gray hair, deep-set dark eyes, and stubbled cheeks. He greeted Sebastian affably, assuming he was in need of a horse, but the smile of welcome faded when Sebastian introduced himself and showed the man his warrant card.

"How can I help, Inspector?" he asked warily.

Sebastian explained the situation and watched the man's face transform, first with shock, then sorrow. His lower lip trembled, and he looked away, presumably to hide his grief. Sebastian gave him a moment, then asked, "Did you know there was a twin?"

Mr. Wilson shook his head. "Mary never said. And neither did Jane Skelton." He looked distraught. "I would have helped. I tried to, but Mary was a proud girl. Can't say as I blame her. She were hurt by what Gareth did."

"What did he do?" Sebastian asked. He'd heard Jane Skelton's version of events, but perhaps Graham Wilson's would offer differing insight into the situation.

"Gareth took off in the night as soon as he found out Mary was with child," Mr. Wilson said, and Sebastian could see the shame in his eyes. "I finally received a letter, three weeks later, telling me he'd joined the army and was going out to India with his regiment. He sounded excited and proud. Not a word of remorse about leaving that poor girl in the lurch."

"What happened to Gareth?"

"My son died somewhere near Punjab during the war against the Sikhs in 1845. It breaks my heart to know that his bones lie in foreign soil, and no one will ever visit his grave."

"Was Gareth your only child?"

Mr. Wilson nodded. "He was, and if the lad didn't favor me I'd think he was some other man's spawn."

"Why was that?"

Mr. Wilson laid his hand on a horse's neck, as if the contact could bring him comfort in the face of his loss.

"Obstinate as a mule, that boy. Would never listen to reason, not even when he was a child. His mother spoiled him something rotten, and he was always popular with the girls. The silly hens see a pretty face and all reason goes out the window," Graham said with a wistful smile. "When he told me about Mary, I told him he should do right by her. Marry the girl, look to his family. But he refused. Said he wasn't ready and just wanted to have a bit of fun before he settled down," Graham Wilson went on with disgust. "Mary loved him, and he threw it all away. And now his dear child is dead, and I never even met her."

"So you've met Eva, then?" Sebastian asked.

"I have, but she didn't know she was my granddaughter until about a year ago. Mary didn't want me hanging about. She blamed me for not stopping Gareth from leaving. I finally convinced Jane to let me see the girl, and I mean to leave Eva everything when it's my time. I owe her that much."

"How do Jane Skelton and Eva manage on their own?"

"I help out. Jane wouldn't take anything from me at first. She was always proud, that one. Where do you think Mary got her airs and graces from? But Jane came to see the wisdom of accepting my help once the nights grew cold and the larder was empty, but she won't take a farthing more than she absolutely has to. She'd rather eat stale bread and ration the coal than admit she needs my help."

"Does Eva know she's going to inherit?"

"I never told her as much, but Jane knows. I wanted her to know I mean to do right by my family." Graham shook his head again. "That wily old fox. She never told me Mary had twins. I could have kept Amanda out of the Foundling Hospital. I don't care what they call it. It's an orphanage all the same." He sighed heavily. "To have to choose between your children. That's a whole other level of hell."

"I imagine it must be," Sebastian said, but his mind was no longer on Mary. He fixed his gaze on Graham Wilson. "Mr. Wilson, how long ago did you tell Jane that Eva was going to inherit your estate?"

"Just before Christmas. I called around to see Jane and Eva. Brought them a bag of coal and some supplies to get them through the end of the year. I told Jane when Eva went to lie down in the bedroom. She was under the weather," Graham explained.

"Might Eva have overheard you?"

"I suppose she could have. What are you suggesting, Inspector, that Eva would murder her own sister to make sure she got it all?"

"According to Mrs. Skelton, Eva doesn't know she had a sister. But someone else might have known."

"Who?"

"Someone who might profit from Eva's inheritance when the time comes."

Sebastian studied Mr. Wilson's worried expression and took stock of the man. He appeared to be in reasonable health, his age notwithstanding, so it would probably be years yet before Eva got to enjoy her windfall; but if money was at the root of this murder, then Graham Wilson's life might be in danger.

"Mr. Wilson, have you made out a last will and testament?" Sebastian asked.

"I have. That's what I went to tell Jane about. I wanted her to know. The will was drawn up by a lawyer in Charles Street. Mr. Reddit. And he will see to all the necessary arrangements."

"Who'll get the lot if something happens to Eva?" Sebastian inquired.

"My brother's boy. Archie."

"And where might I find Archie? I'd like a word."

"He will be back in a few minutes. He went to buy us some oyster stew from the public house on the corner."

"So Archie works here with you, in the livery?"

"That's right. Has done since he was a boy. He's been a great help to me."

"And does your nephew know that he will not inherit the business he helped to build?"

Graham shook his shaggy head. "I haven't told him, if that's what you're asking, but Archie will profit just the same."

"How so?"

Graham smiled. "Archie is sweet on Eva. Always has been. If they marry, Archie will still get the livery, and the girl besides."

"I see," Sebastian said as the pieces began to rearrange themselves in his mind.

TWENTY-EIGHT

Archie Wilson returned a few minutes later, as promised, with a crock of stew and a loaf of bread. He smiled at Sebastian in a friendly manner, clearly assuming he was a customer, as his uncle had done. Sebastian was in no hurry to disabuse him of that notion, and took stock of the lad. He set some store by first impressions. They weren't always correct, and the person always revealed more of themselves on further acquaintance, but there were certain characteristics that usually jumped out on first meeting someone, and they weren't to be dismissed because they went a good way toward understanding a person.

Archie was a good-looking lad of about twenty. He had thickly lashed brown eyes, light brown hair that curled gently around a fine-boned face, and a generous mouth. He was also tall and solidly built. Like his uncle, he wore clothes that were serviceable and could be easily cleaned if they became covered in muck, but the difference was that Archie wore a paisley waistcoat beneath the navy blue peacoat he had on to keep warm. That little bit of flair would be enough to attract Sebastian's attention, but there was one more thing of note about Archie's appearance. The top of his left ear, which he seemed to have tried to cover up by wearing his hair longer than was the norm, was missing.

"What happened to your ear?" Sebastian asked when Archie noticed him looking. His hand immediately went to the spot, his fingers covering the ear as if he could hide the deformity. Sebastian hadn't meant to embarrass the lad, but the explanation might be important.

"Got shot. In Crimea," Archie added.

"You were in Crimea?" Sebastian asked. Archie would have been very young, but no one much cared about the age or fitness of foot soldiers. They took them as young as fourteen.

"Forty-Fourth Regiment of Foot," Archie said proudly. "This here saved my life." He touched the ear again, this time affectionately. "A smidgeon to the right and I'd be dead, my head split like a melon. Couldn't hear nothing out of this side for a long while."

"And now?"

"I reckon it's as good as it's going to get," Archie said. "A bit muffled, but enough to make out what folk are saying."

"You got lucky," Sebastian said.

"Don't I know it!" Archie replied with a sad smile. "Luckier than some. Half the lads in my regiment are still over there, rotting in mass graves."

"You bring back any souvenirs?"

"Souvenirs?" Archie looked confused.

"You know, from the war. Maybe something you picked up on the battlefield."

"Like what?"

"Like maybe a dagger or a ring you took off a dead soldier."

Archie stared at him with obvious disdain. "You've never been in the army, have you, mister? Stealing from the dead is a criminal offense, punishable by death."

"Punishable by death? Really?" Sebastian asked, feigning shock.

"The powers that be would court-martial an officer, but someone of no account, like me, they wouldn't even bother. They'd probably just shoot me and leave my carcass where it fell. I'd have to be really daft to risk my life for a bit of scrap."

"But others must have taken things. When it's all confusion and smoke and corpses littering the ground, who'd even know, right?" Sebastian said with a shrug.

"Why are you asking me this?" Archie demanded. "What's it to you who did what?"

Graham Wilson looked distinctly uncomfortable, probably having realized that he should have warned his nephew that he was speaking to a detective of the police and not just an inquisitive customer.

"I'm Inspector Bell of Scotland Yard," Sebastian said. "And I'm asking because I'm investigating the murder of Amanda Carter."

"And who's Amanda Carter?" Archie asked, looking nonplussed.

"Amanda Carter was the twin sister of Eva Skelton."

"Wha'?" Archie muttered, his gaze going to his uncle. "Eva had a sister?"

"I just found out myself, Archie lad," Graham said. "Seems Mary didn't tell no one she bore twins."

"And she was murdered, this Amanda?" Archie sounded incredulous.

"She was. On Christmas night. Where were you, Archie?"

"I was at home, with my parents and Uncle Graham. I never left."

"Surely everyone went to sleep at some point," Sebastian said.

"My mam had a toothache, so I made cold compresses for her throughout the night. She kept my da up too with her moaning. They both saw me," Archie exclaimed, now clearly nervous that he would be fitted up for a crime he hadn't committed.

"You can ask her. She went to the barber surgeon first thing in the morning and begged him to pull her tooth. He was closed for Boxing Day, but he made an exception for her, on account she was so desperate."

Archie's face became even more tense as he recalled the earlier questions Sebastian had so casually asked. "Why did you ask about Crimea? What's that got to do with anything?"

"You ever see this before?" Sebastian asked as he took the ring Gemma had found from his pocket and showed it to Archie.

"No, but that's Russian, that is," he said. "I've seen the double-headed eagle in Crimea." Archie stared at him. "Where'd you get it?"

"Amanda kept it hidden. I expect someone gave it to her."

Archie shook his head. "Well, it wasn't me."

"No, I don't believe it was," Sebastian said. "But I will check your alibi."

Archie shot him a belligerent look. "Even if I knew about this Amanda, why would I murder her?"

"This is a nice livery. Profitable, I expect."

"So?" Archie asked, clearly not following Sebastian's train of thought.

"So it would be worth killing for."

"I don't understand," Archie said. "What's he talking about, Uncle Graham?"

Graham glared at Sebastian, probably cursing him for revealing his plans at such an inopportune moment, but he owed his nephew an answer, particularly if Archie could be held liable for a crime that could be tied to the ownership of the livery.

"I mean to leave the livery to Eva when I go," Graham said. His discomfort was obvious, and it was plain to see that he hadn't shared his intentions, or indeed his connection to Eva, with his family.

"To Eva?" Archie cried. "Why would you leave the livery to Eva?"

"'Cause she's my granddaughter, Archie. Eva is Gareth's girl."

Archie looked like he'd been slapped. Hard. He took his cap off a nail in the corner, put it on, and pulled the brim down low, then walked out without another word.

"Where does your brother live?" Sebastian asked Graham.

Graham gave him the address and turned away, signaling that their conversation was at an end. Sebastian couldn't blame the man for being angry, but he hadn't had much of a choice when questioning Archie, not when the lad had been in Crimea and his name started with A. Sebastian was investigating the murder of a child, and other people's sensibilities didn't come into it.

Sebastian left the livery and stopped by the Wilsons' home, where he confirmed Archie's alibi by speaking to his mother, whose cheek was still swollen after the extraction. He also spoke to the barber surgeon, who said he'd pulled Mrs. Wilson's tooth on Boxing Day and went on to describe her acute suffering. Sebastian filed away the information, but he wasn't ready to discount Archie Wilson completely. Alibis were useful when trying to prove one's innocence in court, but everyone knew they could be fabricated, and Archie would have a plausible motive if it turned out that he had in fact been aware of Amanda's existence.

TWENTY-NINE

Superintendent Lovell appeared to be ill at ease when Sebastian returned to Scotland Yard after speaking with the Wilsons. Although nothing specific was said outright, Sebastian got the impression that Lovell was sorry he'd confided in him about Ransome's prospects and wished he could take that conversation back. Sebastian could understand how sharing such news had made Lovell feel vulnerable and embarrassed in front of a man he'd been ready to sack for giving in to his own vulnerability only a few months ago. Loyalty was a fragile thing that was all too easy to lose, and Lovell was probably wondering who would support him at a time when he was facing what had to be the greatest challenge of his career.

"I hear you got your man," Lovell said by way of greeting.

"I'm not ready to charge Campbell, I don't have any physical evidence, I just thought it was time to speak to him in a more formal setting."

"So, find the evidence," Lovell said. "I have a meeting with the commissioner tomorrow, and I intend to bring him news of an arrest."

Sebastian watched as Lovell, having delivered his decree,

stalked away. It almost sounded like he was willing to charge anyone as long as he could look good in front of Sir David. Many a man had gone to the gallows on trumped-up evidence and false witness, but it wouldn't happen on Sebastian's watch. He would gladly charge Campbell and be done with it, but he didn't want to punish the man if he wasn't guilty, and Sebastian wasn't convinced, especially now that he'd spoken to Jane Skelton and the Wilsons. Perhaps what he'd learned had nothing to do with Amanda's death, or maybe it had everything to do with it. Only uncovering further evidence would tell.

Sebastian walked back to the duty room and approached Sergeant Woodward, who looked at him expectantly. "Sergeant, please have Mr. Campbell brought to interview room one," he said. Once the sergeant dispatched Constable Hammond to fetch Campbell, Sebastian made his way to the interview room and took a seat at the table.

When Matthew Campbell entered the room, he looked absolutely bewildered. "Why am I here, Inspector Bell? I have answered all your questions." He looked at Sebastian imploringly. "If word of my arrest gets out, I could lose my position."

Sebastian settled more comfortably and faced the man. "You will not lose your position if you've done nothing wrong, Mr. Campbell."

"Have I done something wrong?" Campbell replied, his expression one of wounded innocence.

"Mr. Campbell, you were a foundling boy," Sebastian said. "Where did you go when you left the hospital?"

"I went into the army, like many other boys."

"Were you sent to Crimea?"

"Yes. But what does this have to do with Amanda's death?" Matthew Campbell looked utterly perplexed.

Sebastian took out the gold ring and laid it on the table between them. "Ever see this ring before?"

"No."

"But you recognize the insignia."

"Yes, but so would many other people. What of it?"

"Mr. Campbell, this ring was found hidden in the hem of Amanda's dress. She told her friend Ruby Marks that she was betrothed. I can only assume her intended gave her this ring as a token of his love. As far as I'm aware, you're the only employee of the Foundling Hospital who was in Crimea, fighting in a war against Imperial Russia."

"And that automatically makes me guilty?" Campbell demanded, his voice rising in anger.

"This is a man's ring. Most likely an officer's ring, since no peasant could afford something so fine. I have no doubt that many things could be found on a field in the aftermath of a battle, and that, if someone happened to help themselves, no one would be any the wiser. This is solid gold," Sebastian added. "If fenced, it would fetch a tidy sum."

"And you think that I stole a ring, managed to keep it hidden when discovery would have meant certain death, brought it back to England, and gave it to a fourteen-year-old girl as a token of my affection? You have quite an imagination, Inspector Bell."

"I don't rely on imagination. I rely on facts. And the fact is that you're the only person who came into contact with Amanda who also has a connection to Imperial Russia, no matter how trivial. You have access to keys that would allow you to move about unchecked, and, by your own admission, you know the ins and outs of the hospital and have said that those with a will can always find a way to get about unnoticed. Likewise, you wouldn't be the first man to pursue a young girl and make promises to secure her love."

"I assure you, Inspector Bell, I have never seen that ring before, nor have I had any dealings with Amanda Carter. You will not find a single person willing to impugn my character because I answer to my conscience, and my conscience is clear. What you are suggesting is pure conjecture."

"I agree," Sebastian said. "It's a theory. But as an investigator, I must start with conjecture and work my way toward a provable case."

"Charge me or let me go, Inspector. You have my word of honor that I will not flee. I will return to the Foundling Hospital and resume my duties. If you find evidence against me, I will come willingly and address whatever accusations you make."

"I'm afraid I can't do that, Mr. Campbell. If you are innocent, then you have nothing to fear. I have no intention of fitting you up for a crime you didn't commit. However, until I can either prove or disprove your guilt, you will remain our guest here at Scotland Yard."

Matthew Campbell looked like he was about to cry with frustration, but he nodded curtly and stood. He had been a soldier, and he understood not only protocol but taking orders. His only hope was that, if he was innocent, justice would prevail.

Sebastian left Campbell to Sergeant Woodward and headed to Blackfriars. He needed to speak to Colin Ramsey, since he could hardly hold Campbell for much longer without a shred of physical proof.

THIRTY

When Mabel let him in, Sebastian made his way down to the cellar and pushed open the door. He immediately regretted his rashness. The stench was eye-watering, the corpse on the table in such an advanced state of decomposition that Sebastian's stomach did a somersault and threatened to empty itself right there on the floor. Colin kept a sawdust-filled box beneath the dissecting table to absorb bodily fluids that dripped through a hole in the table, and currently the sawdust was soggy with something noxiously putrid.

Grabbing for his handkerchief, Sebastian held it over his nose and mouth while choking out, "Dear God, Colin! That's lethal."

"This one's been dead for several weeks, but I can never pass up an opportunity to learn from a body. Cancer of the stomach," Colin announced triumphantly, as if the cadaver on the table were in any position to care or to benefit from his diagnosis.

Sebastian made a mental note to leave instructions that his grave be equipped with a metal grille to prevent resurrection men from stealing his corpse. The thought of winding up on someone's dissection table, even someone as respectful of the dead as Colin, made him feel ill. He didn't fear death, but he dreaded this, and the thought of lying naked and split open like a rotting gourd, his organs extracted one by one, and his brain measured, left him not only queasy but suddenly angry.

Science was a valuable tool for the police and helped the detectives understand not only the cause of death but what had taken place immediately before, but surely the dead deserved to be left in peace, their remains treated as holy. Sebastian could still remember how Louisa had looked in her coffin, her face so white, so still, her fair hair neatly arranged, and her lashes brushing against her cheeks as if she were asleep. Colin had put her back together so that Sebastian could remember her as she had been, not as she had looked the day her life had ended. And he had cleaned up their little boy and had wrapped him in muslin, so that he looked like the newborn he'd never be when Sebastian said his goodbyes. Sebastian would have eviscerated anyone who'd dared to desecrate Louisa's remains and would have slept on her grave until it was safe to leave—had he been in any condition to make that decision; he couldn't remember much about the days that followed the funeral, lost as he had been in an opium dream. But Colin had made certain Louisa's final resting place had not been disturbed.

Surely the poor specimen who now graced Colin's table deserved the same respect. As did Amanda, whose remains were nowhere to be seen. Colin pulled a sheet over the open body, then flung open the door to the alley to allow some fresh air to dispel the miasma of rotting flesh.

"How can I help?" he asked, seemingly oblivious to the extent of the horror.

"Has Amanda's body been collected?" Sebastian asked.

"Yes. Why?"

"I needed to make certain she wasn't with child, now you've done a full postmortem."

"Why do you think she might have been?" Colin asked. He enjoyed going over the evidence and sometimes offered helpful observations and medical insights.

"There was definitely a man. Gemma found a gold ring hidden in the hem of Amanda's dress." Sebastian held up his hand before Colin could chastise him. "I know, Colin. I told her time and time again not to do anything foolish, but there's no stopping her once she gets an idea in her head. Stubborn as a mule, and just as determined."

"An unfortunate affliction that plagues mainly unmarried women," Colin replied, and Sebastian would have taken him seriously had his friend managed to keep from smiling. "She wants to help you."

"I don't need help. I need to know that Gemma is safe."

Colin nodded. "She did find the ring, though, didn't she?"

"She did. And it changes everything."

"May I see it?"

Sebastian showed Colin the ring, and Colin reached out, took it from him, and held up the insignia to the light. He let out a low whistle. "Where on earth would Amanda get a thing like that?"

"My guess, from a man who'd served in Crimea."

"And do you have many of those in your sights?"

"Two. One is a teacher at the hospital, and the other fancies Amanda's twin sister and might inherit his uncle's livery if he marries the girl."

Colin looked gobsmacked. "Amanda had a twin sister? And why would this man inherit his uncle's livery if he marries her?"

"Because Archie's uncle just happens to be Amanda and Eva's grandfather and has decided to leave the lot to his son's daughter. However, he didn't know Amanda existed until today."

"Are you suggesting that this Archie knew about Amanda?" Colin asked.

"I don't know, do I?" Sebastian replied, feeling inordinately frustrated and wishing he could kick something to ease his suffering. "According to Amanda's grandmother, no one knew about Amanda, but what if they did? If Graham Wilson had got wind of a second granddaughter, he would most likely have divided the inheritance between the two girls. That would cut Eva's portion in half, and by extension Archie's if he planned to make things legal. This would make Amanda an impediment, unless Archie had other plans. Maybe marry Amanda and somehow cut out Eva instead. Archie served in Crimea, and his name starts with A, which, according to Amanda's friend, was the first letter of Amanda's beau's Christian name."

"You think Archie found a way to woo Amanda, then killed her?" Colin mused.

"I don't believe this murder was premeditated. I think Amanda had a row with whoever she met in the laundry and things got out of hand. Whether that someone was Archie is impossible to tell. It just so happens that Matthew Campbell's second name also begins with A. Perhaps Amanda called him Aaron instead of Matthew. But if Amanda was with child, that would certainly give her killer a motive, whichever of the two it was."

"But why would Matthew Campbell need to murder Amanda?" Colin asked, his expression pensive. He wasn't devious enough to see how such a revelation might affect the man's prospects.

"If the child was Campbell's, he'd lose his position if it came out that he'd had relations with one of the orphans and had given her a ring he'd most likely stolen from a dead Russian officer," Sebastian explained. "If either Campbell or Wilson was involved with Amanda and suspected the child wasn't his, that would give them both motive for murder. But that theory applies only if Amanda was pregnant."

Colin shrugged apologetically. "If she was further along, I

would have discovered evidence of a pregnancy during the post-mortem, and I didn't. If she was very recently pregnant, as you know, it's impossible to tell for certain. I'm sorry, Sebastian, but I can't offer you a definitive answer."

Sebastian felt like he was suffocating from the stink of the corpse. He strode toward the open door and took a few gulps of fresh air, then a few more, until the odor didn't feel as if it were trapped in his nose and mouth. Then he was able to think more clearly. He was missing something vital but, no matter what angle he came at this case from, he couldn't see it, and it was driving him mad.

Colin looked preoccupied, staring into space as he seemed to ponder something Sebastian had said. "Here's the thing," he said at last. "Whether Amanda was with child or not is not really the point."

"What is?"

"If this man *believed* she was with child, he'd still have a motive."

"You think Amanda might have lied in order to force his hand?" Sebastian asked.

"She wouldn't be the first."

"Amanda's friend Ruby said that Amanda was planning to marry when she turned sixteen," Sebastian said. "I wonder if that was just a ruse."

"Perhaps Amanda didn't want to wait that long and devised a scheme to bring the marriage forward, not realizing that the man she'd pinned her hopes on was capable of murder," Colin suggested.

"That would certainly explain the secret engagement and Amanda's sudden desire to leave the Foundling Hospital," Sebastian agreed.

"But if a teacher were to suddenly announce that he was marrying one of the girls, there'd be a terrible scandal that would reflect badly on the governors and administrators of the hospital."

"Especially if the story made it into the newspapers," Sebastian added. "The governors and donors would not take kindly to someone tarnishing their reputations and undermining their commitment to charitable works. To have a man they'd trusted seduce one of the girls would invite the public to question the integrity of the institution and the moral fitness of the individuals who are entrusted with the welfare of the children."

Colin nodded. "Precisely. If the man in question found himself backed against the wall, he would be likely to lash out and try to extricate himself from a situation that could go very badly for him. That seems to be the only theory that fits the facts."

"The problem is that I can't prove any of this," Sebastian said with a frustrated sigh. "We don't know if Amanda was with child, only that she had a relationship with someone who gave her that ring and supposedly promised to marry her."

"Well, you can be sure a fellow foundling didn't give her the ring," Colin replied. "How would a child come by such a thing?"

"Which brings me back to Matthew Campbell and Archie Wilson, who both served in Crimea and have names that start with A. There are a few other male teachers at the hospital, and several porters, but there isn't a shred of evidence that ties them to Amanda."

Colin was just about to reply when the door to the cellar burst open and a wild-eyed Mabel came flying down the steps, her breath coming in short gasps of panic.

"Mabel, what's happened?" Colin asked.

Mabel sucked in a steadying breath before she wailed, "Mrs. Ramsey is gone."

THIRTY-ONE

Colin stared at Mabel in confusion. Anne Ramsey had not gone anywhere on her own in months, possibly years. She was easily confused and likely to forget where she was going, an affliction she might not acknowledge aloud but seemed aware of on some deeper level, and she clung to the two people who looked to her safety. Sebastian had noticed that she had grown worse over the past few months, her mind struggling to recall names, details, and connections between the people she had known in happier days. She had seemed docile, though, sitting in her favorite chair in the parlor whenever Sebastian came by and asking questions about a woman who was long gone but in Anne's mind still alive and expecting their first child. It was strange how some things remained while others drained away like water through a sieve.

"What do you mean, gone?" Colin exclaimed when Mabel failed to elaborate and just stood there on the bottom step, looking at him expectantly.

"I helped Mrs. Ramsey up to her room after luncheon. She was going to have a rest while I got started on dinner. I went to check on her in an hour, the way I always do, to see if she was ready to come downstairs and have a cup of tea, but she wasn't there."

Colin stood still, his mouth slightly open as he tried to process what Mabel had just said. "But where could she have gone?" he muttered. "There are not that many rooms, and she didn't come down here."

"I think she went outside," Mabel replied. "She's left the house, Mr. Ramsey."

"Oh, dear," Colin cried, now that he finally understood why Mabel was so distraught.

"Let's go," Sebastian said. "She couldn't have gone far."

The three of them hurried up the stairs and trooped into the foyer. Colin hastily put on his coat, while Mabel grabbed her cape and pulled on her bonnet, ready to join in the search. Colin closed the front door behind them and hastened down the steps, but came to a stop once he reached Mabel and Sebastian, who were waiting for him in the street.

"We should split up," Colin said as he peered into the distance, looking in both directions to see if he could spot his mother. There was no sign of her.

"Mrs. Ramsey is not wearing a coat. Or shoes," Mabel cried. "She's still in her nightdress."

Even in a coat and hat, and wearing a muffler and gloves, Sebastian was cold and the ground beneath his feet icy enough to seep through the soles of his leather boots. If Mrs. Ramsey was wearing nothing but a nightdress and was barefoot, she'd catch her death if she was outdoors longer than a few minutes.

"I'm going toward the river," Colin declared. "Mabel, check Queen Victoria Street. Let's all meet back at the house."

Colin and Mabel took off at a run, while Sebastian hastened toward St. Paul's Cathedral. He wasn't sure why, but his gut instinct seemed to point in its direction. The area grew busier as he neared the church, both pedestrian and road traffic choking the streets. Everyone had returned to work after the holiday, and the shops were doing a brisk trade. Dray wagons rattled past, a cart loaded with casks pulled into an alleyway adjacent to a tavern, and several sleek private carriages went past, the drivers navigating the congestion without having to slow down.

Several well-dressed pedestrians strolled past, one man stopping to leaf through piles of used books displayed on a rickety table outside a bookshop. A young girl walked past with a half-empty tray of oranges slung over her shoulders, half-heartedly calling out her wares. Another vendor stood near the statue of Queen Anne, ladling soup from a huge vat into enamel mugs. Several men stood nearby, their work-roughened hands wrapped around the mugs for a bit of warmth as they gulped down the soup before returning to work. Several beggars sat on the steps leading up to the grand entrance of the cathedral, rattling their cups in the hope that someone would toss them a coin, but most people just walked past without a second glance. Several boys darted past Sebastian, probably pickpockets, their lips blue with cold and their ankles bare and pallid beneath the hems of trousers they'd outgrown years ago. There was nothing even remotely unusual about the scene, and no sign of Anne Ramsey.

Despite the number of people out in the street, Sebastian didn't think anyone would notice an elderly woman clad in nothing but her nightdress. Most people learned early on to look through those who needed help, their suffering of no concern to anyone. He'd lost count of how many children he'd come across who'd either died of starvation or frozen to death on the streets of London. It broke his heart and made him angry at the same time. England was the greatest country in the world, a military superpower that was at the heart of a vast and prosperous empire, but the government did nothing to take care of its most vulnerable citizens and left countless people to die agonizing deaths that could easily be avoided by implementing basic social reforms. The dead houses were overflowing, especially in the winter, and the streets in the poorer neighborhoods teemed with crippled men who'd fought for their country in various foreign wars but were no longer of use since returning home, especially if they'd been maimed and could no longer do a day's work.

Same went for the nurses who'd returned from Crimea to be met with derision, suspicion, and slights on their character; those who would discredit them routinely accused them of loose morals and lewd behavior with both male doctors and male patients. Nurses who had no families to return to were forced to accept menial jobs in infirmaries, overcrowded hospitals, and prisons, where their experience and practical knowledge were ignored and sometimes ridiculed by the male doctors, who didn't think a woman's brain was biologically suited to absorbing even the most basic medical facts.

The nurses were expected to take out chamber pots, roll bandages, and spoon-feed those who couldn't feed themselves. Their wages reflected their reduced status. Gemma had been lucky to find the position with the Foundling Hospital after her brother died and left her on her own.

Sebastian fervently hoped that he hadn't compromised her situation by singling her out and asking her to examine Amanda's remains when he should have allowed Matron to believe that their relationship did not go beyond a casual acquaintanceship.

He turned into St. Paul's Churchyard and hurried toward the west entrance of the cathedral. He took the steps two at a time, ignoring the beggars who called out to him and maniacally rattled their cups, and yanked open the door. The interior was virtually empty, only a few people seated in the pews, their heads bowed in prayer. They paid him no mind, so Sebastian strode up the nave, looking to the left and right, but saw no sign of Mrs. Ramsey. His footsteps echoed in the silence, and he suddenly felt dwarfed by the sheer magnitude of the cathedral and unsure how to proceed. He didn't want to call out, but the interior was vast, with a number of chapels, aisles, the north and south transepts and quires, galleries, and a sizable crypt. It would take him at least an hour to search the cathedral, and if Anne Ramsey wasn't there he'd be wasting precious time, during which he could have been checking the nearby streets and alleyways. Still, something told him to stay and perform at least a cursory search.

Sebastian stopped beneath the dome and looked from side to side, then turned toward the south transept and walked along, but he didn't see anyone besides a young man who appeared too dazed to be of any help. Sebastian must have been searching the cathedral for a quarter of an hour at least when he spotted a lone figure standing quite still in front of the John Donne memorial, a white piece of linen draped over their head blending with a white chasuble. At first he thought he was looking at a member of the clergy, but, when the person turned their head slightly to the side, Sebastian realized he was looking at Anne Ramsey, who wore a veil over her hair and whose flowing white nightdress resembled a clerical robe.

The similarity between the statue and the woman was almost uncanny, the poet's face chalk-white, the masterfully executed stone shroud draping his head and body and pooling at his feet, which were positioned atop an urn. Anne's face was as pale as Donne's, and the folds of her veil echoed those of the marble shroud. If not for John Donne's sculpted beard, the two could have been mirror images of each other, two individuals who had once been full of humor and wit but were now frozen in time. Anne Ramsey's feet were marble-white, the veins like blue rivers on milky skin. Her lips were moving, as if in prayer, and she seemed oblivious to everything but the statue, her gaze fixed on the stone effigy with an expression of exaltation.

"Mrs. Ramsey," Sebastian said softly. He didn't want to

startle her, but he had to get her attention. She didn't turn around, but she had heard him.

"Isn't it beautiful?" she replied rapturously. "It's such a good likeness."

Since the poet had died more than two hundred years ago, Sebastian wasn't about to ask if Mrs. Ramsey had known the man, but she seemed to gaze upon him with the worshipful expression of someone who was in love.

"I always said Colin favored his father," Anne said. "Can you see the likeness, Mr.... erm?" She looked to Sebastian for help.

She had previously referred to Sebastian as Mr. Melville, but even that name seemed to escape her now. She was lost in her own mind, clearly mistaking John Donne for the man she'd loved for more than thirty years and had lost not so long ago.

"Bell. Sebastian Bell," Sebastian reminded her gently. "I'm Colin's friend."

"I don't think I've had the pleasure, Mr. Bell."

"Mrs. Ramsey, you'll catch your death in here. Please, let me take you home."

"Home?"

"Colin and Mabel are frantic. They're looking for you."

"Nonsense," Anne Ramsey exclaimed, sounding stronger now. "Colin is in Edinburgh. He's going to be a world-famous surgeon. You wait and see. And who's this Mabel?"

"He's a surgeon already, Mrs. Ramsey, and he lives with you, in your family home. And Mabel is your maidservant. She looks after you when Colin is working. Please, let me take you home."

Sebastian shrugged off his coat and draped it over Anne Ramsey's shoulders, then held out his hand. Anne accepted it reluctantly, gazing at Sebastian with mistrust as he escorted her toward the exit. He asked her to wait by the door, where it was slightly warmer, while he sprinted toward the street and hailed a passing cab. He then returned to Anne Ramsey and swept her into his arms despite her protests. A sharp pain in his shoulder demanded that he set her down immediately, but he could hardly allow the woman to walk to the cab barefoot. Her skin felt icy to the touch, and further exposure to the cold just might kill her.

Inside the cab, Sebastian drew a worn, shaggy rug provided for the purpose over her to keep her warm and wrapped his arm about her to supplement the rug with his own body heat. Mrs. Ramsey initially appeared scandalized by such uninvited intimacy, but then slumped against his shoulder and looked up at him, her expression suddenly coy, as if she were a young girl.

"I must admit, you're rather handsome, Mr.... er, Dell, but what my dear mama would call 'a bit of rough.' I daresay no woman is safe in your presence," she added with a suggestive smile.

"I assure you, Mrs. Ramsey, you're quite safe with me."

Anne Ramsey looked momentarily disappointed, then shut her eyes and appeared to fall into a deep sleep. The ride took less than ten minutes, but it felt much longer. Sebastian kept his fingers on Mrs. Ramsey's pulse to make certain she was still with him. As soon as the cab pulled up in front of the house, he shook Mrs. Ramsey awake, then jumped down and helped her alight. He had to practically drag her inside the house, since she didn't seem to recognize her own home and thought he was taking her somewhere against her will.

Settling Anne before the hearth in the parlor, Sebastian covered her with his coat, then added more coal to a fire that was close to dying and called out to Colin, but no one seemed to be at home. Torn between going to look for Colin and Mabel and keeping watch over Mrs. Ramsey, Sebastian decided to stay put. He left the parlor and shut the door behind him, propping a chair against it in case Mrs. Ramsey should try to abscond, then went to the kitchen, where he filled the kettle from the pump and set it on the range, which was still hot since Mabel had been in the process of making dinner.

Afraid to leave Mrs. Ramsey alone for too long, he checked that the parlor door was still closed and the chair in place, then found a tin of tea, the sugar bowl, and a jug of milk that Mabel had left in the larder. He also found some biscuits, which he arranged on a plate.

Once the kettle finally boiled, Sebastian made a pot of tea, set it on a tray with two cups, and added sugar, milk, and the plate of biscuits. He then brought the tray into the parlor. Not an easy feat since he had to move the chair out of the way with his foot and then open the door without upending the tray.

Anne looked up in surprise, her feathery brows lifting unnaturally high when Sebastian set down the tray. "Why, Mr. Melville, how very kind of you. I do hope you didn't go to too much trouble. Did your wife make the biscuits?" she asked as she reached for one and shoved it in her mouth whole.

Sebastian poured Mrs. Ramsey a cup of tea, added milk and sugar, and handed it to her. "Please, be careful. It's hot," he said, and made sure that she was holding on to the saucer securely before letting go.

"Well, of course it's hot. It's tea," Mrs. Ramsey said reproachfully. She took a sip and sighed with contentment. "You do make a good cup of tea. Strong, just the way I like it."

"Thank you."

Sebastian poured himself a cup of tea as well, then positioned himself by the window in case Colin or Mabel passed by.

"What are you looking at? It's bad manners to drink tea standing up," Mrs. Ramsey admonished him.

"I'm looking for Colin," Sebastian explained.

"I think he's out with his nursemaid. They love to go to the park, even in winter."

Mrs. Ramsey did not have a chance to reminisce further about Colin's childhood, since just then the adult Colin burst into the room, looking like he'd been dragged through a hedge backwards.

"Mother, thank God," he cried, and wrapped his arms around the stunned woman.

"Colin, what on earth is the matter?" Mrs. Ramsey asked crossly.

Colin let out a deep sigh and sank into a chair without bothering to take off his coat. "Any tea left in the pot?" he asked. "I'm frozen through."

Sebastian nodded and went to fetch two more cups. By the time he returned, Mabel, who'd also come back and had already divested herself of her bonnet and cape, was fussing over Mrs. Ramsey and urging her to get back to bed and under the covers.

"Where did you find her?" Colin asked.

"She was standing in front of the John Donne memorial in St. Paul's. I got the impression she thought it was a memorial to your father."

Colin let out a humorless laugh, then his face crumpled, and he looked like he was about to cry. "What am I going to do, Sebastian? She seems to get worse every day."

"You're going to have to hire a nurse. Mrs. Ramsey is too much for Mabel to manage on her own."

Colin nodded. "Perhaps Miss Tate can recommend a reputable nurse of her acquaintance. I would hate to entrust Mother to someone who might be unkind to her."

"I'll ask Miss Tate today. I'm going to the hospital now."

"Sebastian, have you eaten?" Colin asked, giving him a stern look.

Sebastian shook his head. "No, but I don't have time to stop. I can't hold Campbell forever, and if he is responsible for Amanda's murder I need to find the proof."

"Thank you for your help," Colin said, his emotions all there in his eyes. "It wouldn't have occurred to me to look in

St. Paul's, and Lord knows where she would have gone once she grew tired of looking at John Donne. For a moment, I thought she might have walked into the river."

Sebastian nodded. The same thought had occurred to him. "I'm sorry, but I really must be on my way. I hope Mrs. Ramsey doesn't suffer any ill effects."

Colin nodded. He seemed too drained to stand, so, with a comforting clasp of his friend's shoulder, Sebastian left him to his tea and took off.

THIRTY-TWO

Back at the Foundling Hospital, Sebastian was once again escorted to Matron Holcombe's office. The woman seemed even less pleased to see him than before, if such a thing were possible. She glared at him from behind her desk.

"How can I help, Inspector Bell?"

"I need to speak to Michael White and check the backgrounds on both him and Matthew Campbell," Sebastian said.

"To what end?" Matron demanded haughtily.

"Mr. Campbell was a foundling, so you must have information on his mother and whatever token she left for him. And Michael's name keeps cropping up in connection with this case."

That was all the explanation Sebastian was willing to offer. He didn't need the woman's approval, only her cooperation. Matron Holcombe sighed with the weariness of someone who'd just been asked to fetch the moon.

"I will allow you to speak to Michael, if you think that is somehow relevant, but you may not see the register, Inspector. Matthew Campbell's details are private and have no bearing on your case. How could they?"

"I won't know until I look," Sebastian retorted.

"What do you think you're going to find in a notation that was made more than twenty-five years ago?" Matron countered. "It's absurd."

"So you can wholeheartedly vouch for Matthew Campbell, then?" Sebastian challenged her.

Matron Holcombe couldn't have known him very long if Campbell had been hired after returning from Crimea, unless... It hadn't occurred to Sebastian before, but the hospital did have a history of employing its own, so it wasn't beyond the realm of possibility.

"Matron, did you grow up at the hospital?" Sebastian asked. If she had, that would explain her fierce protectiveness toward the secrets the register held and her desire to safeguard not only her own position but that of another foundling and the hospital itself. The Foundling Hospital would be the one thing that had stood between her and possible death on the streets of London.

Matron appeared stunned by the question, but Sebastian could see the answer there in her eyes.

"I did. What of it?"

"So you must have seen your own details, no?" Sebastian asked.

She shook her head. "I never looked."

"Why not?"

"I take it that, despite your pugnacious demeanor, you were born into a loving family, Inspector Bell?"

"Yes, I was," Sebastian replied softly, long-buried grief twisting his insides at the thought of his parents. He was one of the lucky ones, a child whose parents had lived long enough for him to reach adulthood, but losing them hadn't hurt any less. Possibly more, because he had known them and loved them and had felt supported by them, and then suddenly they were gone, and he was left with Simian, who possessed all the warmth of a frozen turd, at least toward his younger brother.

"For an orphan, the question of where they come from can become an obsession, Inspector Bell," Matron said. "That deep-seated need to know, to understand, can ruin a child's life and prevent them from working toward their future. That's why we keep the information locked away. As long as they don't know, they can imagine anything they like. A loving mother who wept inconsolably as she left her precious child. A father who was killed on a battlefield or in some work accident, rather than a scoundrel who ran off, leaving the woman he'd seduced without a backward glance. Maybe they have siblings out there, people who they imagine belong to them, but the only people they truly have are here. This is their family, and we are their parents. And yes, I can vouch for Matthew Campbell, Inspector. I simply don't believe he's capable of murder. He was always one of the good ones."

"So you will have no objection to me searching his room?" Sebastian countered.

Matron's face registered shock, but she recovered in record time. "I will not permit you to search Matthew Campbell's room without a warrant, Inspector," she replied, and it was clear from her demeanor that she would not budge from her stance. "And I have serious objections to your methods, which appear to be just this side of legal and border on bullying."

"I can certainly understand your reservations, Matron, but this is a murder investigation, not simply a stroll down memory lane for sentimentality's sake. Amanda Carter was a twin," Sebastian announced. "Did you know that?"

"No, I didn't, but I don't see how that changes anything."

"Don't you?"

"Unless Amanda was murdered by said twin, I don't see the relevance."

Sebastian didn't bother to explain about Eva's inheritance or Archie Wilson's possible stake in her future. It was pointless. "I would like to speak to the head of the committee."

"I'm afraid that's not possible."

"Not possible or not convenient?"

Matron stood and placed her hands on top of her desk, her back straight and her chin lifted in defiance. "Amanda will be buried tomorrow. Once she is laid to rest, I will request that the investigation is closed."

"Don't you care who killed her?" Sebastian demanded.

"I care more about maintaining order and moving on from this horrible tragedy."

"So you're willing to take the chance that the killer will strike again?"

"They won't."

"How can you be so sure?" Sebastian felt an overwhelming urge to grab the woman by the shoulders and shake some sense into her, but he could hardly give in to his anger. He had to remain calm and objective.

"You said yourself that Amanda and whoever she met that night had a relationship that had turned sour. This was personal, not some random act of evil that's likely to happen again. Whoever is responsible has no reason to harm anyone else."

"Sure, are you?"

"Inspector, children die all the time. The cemetery is full of graves of orphans who didn't live long enough to leave the walls of this institution. Amanda was simply another child whose life came to an untimely end. It's unfortunate but not unusual. Your investigation is distressing for the children and is undermining the authority of the staff. How do you think his pupils will feel about Mr. Campbell when he returns? He will never be able to regain their respect, not after he's seen the inside of a police cell."

Sebastian let out a slow, deliberate breath. They were going in circles and wasting valuable time. Perhaps he could find a way to circumvent Matron's authority. In the meantime, he had to speak to Michael.

THIRTY-THREE

As Sebastian walked into the music room and settled at the table, he reflected that something about the space was soothing. Perhaps it was the tall windows that let in the radiant December light, or maybe the presence of musical instruments. He associated music with happy occasions, and realized it had been far too long since he'd listened to music—not since he'd attended a concert with Louisa a few months before her death. Perhaps once Gemma was out of mourning they could go to a concert or even the opera. Sebastian had never been to the latter, but he would welcome the experience.

His reverie was interrupted by the arrival of Michael, who looked at him with obvious fear.

"Hello, Michael," Sebastian said, and pointed toward the other chair. "Please, sit."

Michael sat down and interlaced his fingers on the table before him. He was a good-looking boy with thick fair hair, dark blue eyes, and the expression of a biblical saint. There was something refined about his features and his long, elegant fingers, which looked well suited to playing a musical instrument.

"Why do you wish to speak to me?" Michael asked when Sebastian failed to speak.

"Because I think you can help me. Did you know Amanda?"

Michael looked deeply conflicted and his gaze slid toward the window as he tried to settle on a suitable answer.

"Michael, you're not in any trouble," Sebastian said. "I only want to know if you knew Amanda. That doesn't mean I'm accusing you of anything."

"Boys and girls are not supposed to know each other," Michael replied. "So if I say I knew her, I'll be in trouble with Matron."

"This conversation will remain strictly between the two of us," Sebastian promised. He could see that Michael needed a gentle push to admit to a past association.

Michael nodded, then said, his voice very low, "I knew her."

"How did you come to know Amanda if you weren't allowed to interact?"

Michael sucked in a shuddering breath, his eyes reflecting the magnitude of his loss. He hadn't just known Amanda; he'd loved her. That was obvious.

"Mandy and I were left at the hospital the same week, even though our birthdays were months apart. We were sent to foster with the same family, the Carters," Michael explained. "We spent our first five years together."

"So why do you have different surnames?"

Michael's expression was wistful. "The Carters were told to give me a different name so Mandy and I wouldn't think we were related. Mrs. Carter told me that before we were taken back. She chose White because I had such light hair."

That sounded plausible based on what Sebastian had learned from Matron. Since surnames were assigned, the Carters or the hospital could choose any name, and he could see why two children that had been reared together would be discouraged from believing they had a claim on each other.

"But you were returned to the hospital when you were five, and now you're fourteen. Did you find a way to remain friends with Amanda all this time?"

Michael nodded again. "We weren't allowed to see each other once we came back. Not ever," he said. He looked unbearably sad. "We were taken from the only family we'd ever known and not permitted to speak to each other after spending each day together before that," he exclaimed, his anguish there in his eyes. "You can't imagine the loneliness, the grief."

Sebastian thought he could understand how these poor, helpless children must have felt, but at the moment, he was more concerned with the logistics of Michael and Amanda's scheme.

"How did you get around the rules?" he asked, watching Michael carefully for any hint of subterfuge; but, now that Michael had admitted to his relationship with Amanda, he seemed proud and eager to explain.

"The only time we saw the girls was in chapel on Sundays, but we weren't allowed to speak to them or make eye contact. Looking around and fidgeting could result in being sent upstairs while everyone went to Sunday lunch."

"So, how did you make contact?" Sebastian asked. He could picture it all too well, having sat through long, tedious sermons himself when he was a boy and still having found ways to entertain himself despite his mother's admonitions.

"We sit in the same pews every week and follow the same routine when coming in and leaving the chapel. Mandy sat on the end," Michael said, smiling for the first time, and Sebastian could see the child within, a sensitive and lonely boy who had never got over the loss of his first friend. "Amanda smiled at me when no one was watching," he went on, and Sebastian thought the poor lad might cry at the sweet memory of that unexpected connection. "Once I learned to write, I wrote Mandy a note and managed to press it into her hand as we were being led out of the chapel. I told her how much I missed her."

"And she wrote back," Sebastian concluded.

"We found a way to exchange notes without anyone noticing. It's easy to fall out of step when there are several hundred children walking toward the door."

"How long did this go on?"

"Until Christmas. That was the last time I saw Mandy alive."

"Were you and Mandy making plans?" Sebastian asked gently.

Michael nodded. "We were going to get married once we turned sixteen. Mandy was going to go into service at fourteen, so that she could start earning a wage, and I would be apprenticed. I didn't want to go into the army. I wanted to learn a trade. We'd find a way to meet on our afternoons off and then pool our resources once we were of age."

"Did you and Mandy ever find a way to meet in secret?"

"No. We only exchanged notes."

"Did Mandy ever tell you if someone was bothering her or if she communicated with anyone else?"

"Like whom?" Michael demanded, clearly upset by the possibility that Amanda might have been stringing him along.

"Like Mr. Campbell, perhaps."

"What would Mr. Campbell want with Mandy?"

"What do men generally want with pretty young girls?" Sebastian countered.

"Mr. Campbell is a good man, Inspector. He cares about us because he was one of us once. He'd never abuse his position."

"You seem very sure of that."

"I am," Michael said. "Mr. Campbell helped me when I was in trouble." He blushed furiously, and Sebastian knew the boy had just revealed something he'd never meant to.

"What sort of trouble were you in?" Sebastian asked softly.

Michael looked like he was about to cry and bowed his head, staring at his feet beneath the table. He shook his head. "I can't talk about it," he whispered.

"Michael, Mr. Campbell is a suspect in Amanda's murder. If there's anything you know that might exonerate him, you must tell me."

"Mr. Campbell would never hurt Mandy," Michael cried, his head shooting upward and his eyes blazing with anger. "He's a kind man."

"How did he help you, Michael?"

Michael's eyes filled with tears, and he looked away again, his face pale in the weak sunshine. "He had a word with Mr. Frain."

"And what did Mr. Frain do that required Mr. Campbell to speak to him?"

"Mr. Frain was unkind to me," Michael choked out. "He called me names."

"What sort of names?"

"He said I was useless and better suited to women's work."

"Why was that?" Sebastian asked.

"I don't excel at woodworking," Michael explained. "And I didn't want to hurt my hands. It would prevent me from playing the spinet."

The boy's gaze slid toward the instrument in the corner, and Sebastian thought he could see his longing to play.

"Miss Parish says I have musical talent, and playing makes me happy. For a few minutes, I can create something beautiful," Michael said softly.

"So, how did Mr. Campbell know that Mr. Frain was bullying you?"

"He found me hiding in his classroom one day after the woodworking lesson. I just needed a moment to calm myself. Mr. Campbell asked me what was wrong, so I told him."

"And has Mr. Frain changed his behavior towards you?" Sebastian asked.

"I saw him sneering, and I'm sure he would have liked to say something cruel, but he didn't. He left me alone after that. Mr. Frain respects Mr. Campbell. I think they're friends, from when they were foundling boys."

Sebastian nodded, not particularly surprised to learn that Mr. Frain had also grown up at the Foundling Hospital.

He studied Michael, and it wasn't difficult to see the toll Amanda's death had taken on him. Sebastian had planned to show the boy the ring and the little dolly, but now he changed his mind. There was no way Michael could have made the dolly or given Amanda the ring, and to tell him that someone else had would break the boy's heart. It was kinder to allow him to remember his Mandy as she had been, the girl who'd loved him and wanted to build a life with him.

"What will you do now that Mandy is gone?" Sebastian asked.

Michael shrugged. "Go into the army, I suppose. No reason to remain in London."

"What about playing the spinet?"

"I don't feel much like playing these days."

"I'm sorry, Michael," Sebastian said. "I know how difficult this must be for you, especially since you can't talk to anyone about your loss."

"I can talk to Miss Parish," Michael said, his face brightening. "She always listens. She's kind to everyone but feels sad when the children leave the hospital. She gets attached, so she understands." Michael looked at Sebastian imploringly. "Can I go now?" he asked. "Please."

"Go on."

Sebastian sighed heavily once Michael had gone. He felt desperately sorry for the boy and could understand all too easily how heartbreaking it was to lose the one person you loved. He hoped that Michael would change his mind again about going into the army, and that in time he would meet someone who would fill the empty space Amanda had left.

Sebastian opened the door to the music room and hailed a porter who was walking down the corridor. "I need a word with Nurse Tate."

"You'll need to ask Matron's permission," the man said.

"I don't answer to Matron, and Nurse Tate is a grown woman, not one of the children in Matron's care. Kindly fetch her to me right now."

The porter looked like he was about to refuse, then nodded and headed toward the stairs.

THIRTY-FOUR

Gemma looked worn out when she joined Sebastian in the music room a few minutes later. Sebastian thought she'd even lost weight in the past few days. Not surprising since she'd probably had no time to eat, what with the multiple cases of croup and the investigation into Amanda's murder.

Gemma shut the door behind her and slid into the chair, her gaze searching Sebastian's face for clues. "Have you discovered something?"

"Yes. But I'm still woefully short on evidence."

"What have you learned since last time?"

Sebastian recounted everything that had happened since speaking with her last, leaving his conversation with Michael for the end.

"Michael White and Amanda Carter were placed with the same foster family and managed to maintain a personal relationship in spite of regulations. According to Michael, they planned to leave the Foundling Hospital this year, with Amanda going into service and Michael starting an apprenticeship so that he could remain in London. They planned to marry when they turned sixteen."

"But you're not convinced Michael is responsible," Gemma stated, instantly picking up on Sebastian's doubt.

"Michael says he and Amanda never sneaked out, which could be a lie. But even if they did find a way to meet after everyone had gone to bed, he couldn't have given her the ring. Where would he get something so valuable and obviously foreign? The ring points toward a grown man, a former soldier who served in Crimea, and a teacher who would have the sort of access a child wouldn't."

"So you still believe the killer is Matthew Campbell?"

"Campbell ticks all the boxes, but I don't have any physical evidence to tie him to the crime. Matron will not permit me to search Campbell's room without a warrant, but, even if I were able to obtain one during a week that most highly placed government officials take off work, I very much doubt I would find anything incriminating. Matthew Campbell is too clever to leave evidence lying about, especially if he's guilty of murder and would prefer to keep his neck out of the noose."

"Yes, I tend to agree with you there. Is there anyone else you suspect?" Gemma asked, her expression thoughtful.

Sebastian filled her in on his visit to Bleeding Heart Yard and the revelations that had followed. Gemma looked stunned.

"A twin?"

Sebastian nodded.

"Were they identical?"

"No, they weren't, but there was a resemblance."

"This case just gets sadder and sadder," Gemma said with a heavy sigh. "I'm almost glad Amanda never learned the truth. It would have broken her heart to learn that Eva had been allowed to stay while she had been given away without so much as a name to call her own. I know I have no right to judge Mary Skelton, but I don't think I would have been able to do what she did."

Sebastian was tempted to ask Gemma what she would have

done in Mary's situation, but he already knew. Gemma would have found a way to keep both children, and if she had to go begging to Graham Wilson she would have done so, because her pride would be the least of her worries. She would have put those girls first, at any cost, and would have loved them both.

"Do you really think there might be a connection?" she asked, her expression thoughtful.

"Archie Wilson stands to inherit his uncle's livery if he marries Eva. Archie was in Crimea and could have pocketed a gold ring that he'd either found or stolen in the aftermath of a battle, but there's nothing to suggest that he ever came in contact with Amanda or even knew of her existence."

Gemma made a dismissive gesture. "Even if Archie Wilson had somehow found out about Amanda and come here, I can't see how he would find her among the hundreds of girls who are housed here, even if he knew precisely whom he was looking for, which presumably he didn't since the sisters weren't identical twins. But on the off-chance that he had found her, how would he have managed to forge a relationship with her?" she asked.

"When a theory is too far-fetched, it's usually not the correct one," Sebastian agreed. "But I'm missing something, Gemma, and time is running out."

"What do you mean, time is running out?"

"Amanda is to be buried tomorrow. After that, Matron will petition Lovell to close the case."

"But the killer is still out there," Gemma protested.

"Matron is more interested in moving forward and reestablishing control and routine."

"A child is dead. How can the superintendent ignore that and agree to close the case?"

"It would benefit those who hold the purse strings to both the police service and the Foundling Hospital, so he may very well agree. Besides, Lovell has his own battles to fight just now."

"What sort of battles?"

"The sort where one is not ready to be put out to pasture but has outlived one's usefulness."

"That's a hard truth to swallow," Gemma said. "Who would take his place?"

She shot him a quizzical look, but Sebastian shook his head. "No. I'm not even in the running."

"You're the best detective the Yard has," Gemma argued with touching loyalty. "You should be the one to step into Lovell's shoes."

"Thank you for the vote of confidence, but I don't want the job."

"Whyever not?"

"Because Lovell is a paper-pusher. He hasn't worked a case in years. I'm not sure he even remembers how. I have no desire to spend my days in an office, watching other men do a job I know I'm good at. Or was good at," Sebastian added morosely.

"Self-pity doesn't become you," Gemma said. "And what's wrong with your shoulder?" Sebastian stared at her, and she gave him an appraising look. "You keep shifting position and rolling your shoulder, presumably to alleviate discomfort."

"It's nothing. Must be the weather."

"Are you really going to try to fob me off?" Gemma demanded. "What have you done? Please tell me you didn't dig up a grave."

"I lifted Anne Ramsey and carried her to a cab."

"What? Why?"

"Long story that's best left for another time. Anne is fine," he added when he realized Gemma was genuinely concerned. "Colin will need to hire a trained nurse, though, so if someone comes to mind do ask them if they might be looking for a new situation."

"I'll ask around," Gemma promised. She looked at him expectantly.

Then, just as she made to rise, Sebastian said, "Perhaps I'm wrong about Michael."

"Go on," Gemma invited him.

"Just because he couldn't have given Amanda the ring doesn't mean he didn't kill her."

Gemma fixed her tired gaze on him, waiting for him to elaborate on this new theory.

"Michael believed he and Amanda had a future together, but what if Amanda changed her mind? Or what if she was making plans with someone else and Michael found out? He is an emotional boy who doesn't respond well to embarrassment or rejection."

"How do you know that?" Gemma asked.

"He was very upset when Mr. Frain ridiculed him in front of the other boys. Campbell had to have a word with Frain to ask him to back off."

"Did Mr. Frain say something truly hurtful?"

"Just the sort of thing some men say without thinking to shame someone into trying harder. Unkind, yes. The sort of thing that would require intervention from another teacher, I'm not so sure."

"So, you're suggesting that Michael felt betrayed and lost control?"

"It's possible. Perhaps he realized that the other man had given Amanda something of great value, which would explain the turned-out pockets. He might have wanted to see what it was, get rid of it, or use it as leverage against his rival." Sebastian sighed. "I would still like to know more about Michael's background, and also Campbell's and Frain's. Turns out Frain was a foundling as well. Matron might be right and I'm grasping at straws, or maybe there is something in their past that can help me figure this out. Unfortunately, Matron guards the register like some mythical dragon."

"The register is the only record of these children's lives,"

Gemma said. "And it protects not only their privacy but the privacy of their mothers."

"This is a murder inquiry. Privacy comes second."

"I agree. What will you do?"

"Normally, I would obtain a court order signed by a judge, but I don't think Lovell will agree. He's not in a position to ruffle influential feathers just now. And I don't think it would be wise to go above his head. I won't solve this case if I lose my job."

Gemma pushed to her feet, and Sebastian stood as well. The light beyond the window had grown lavender, the night quickly closing in.

"May I walk you home?" he asked.

"Matron asked me to stay at the infirmary for a few nights, due to the croup outbreak. There's been another case."

"I'll speak to you tomorrow, then."

"I'll look forward to it. Give Gustav a cuddle for me."

Sebastian chuckled. "I will, if he lets me."

The parted ways, and Sebastian headed toward the exit, then turned back and walked toward Matron's office. He wasn't going to give up so easily, and he had one more trick up his sleeve.

THIRTY-FIVE

"It's four o'clock," Sebastian announced as he walked into Matron's office, eliciting a look that warned him that her forbearance was at an end.

"So it is," Matron replied. "What of it?"

"I reckon I have enough time to get to the offices of the *Daily Telegraph* before the editor-in-chief, with whom I'm personally acquainted, leaves for the day. I wager Mr. Lawrence would give his eyeteeth to hear what I have to say."

"Are you threatening me, Inspector?" Matron replied, her voice rising despite her best efforts to remain calm.

"I am." It was clearly not the answer she'd been expecting, and so much the better. "Who do you think will get the blame when the public hears that the Foundling Hospital petitioned to close an investigation into the murder of a child in order to appease those whose deep pockets buy them infinite protection from prosecution?"

Matron Holcombe's already bloodless face paled as she no doubt envisioned a future in which she lost her position and her professional reputation was left in tatters. She was too intelligent a woman not to realize that the governors would need a scapegoat should the hospital come under attack in the press, and it would, if Marshall Lawrence had anything to say about it. Sebastian knew from experience that he was an indifferent man who cared only about profit. The fate of the orphans or the future of the Foundling Hospital would be of no interest to him, only the shock value the story would garner and the possible increased circulation of the paper.

"What would you have me do?" Matron asked, more amenable now that her back was to the wall.

"Provide me with the information I need, and I will leave quietly. No one has to know," Sebastian added.

"But they will know if you find something incriminating," Matron replied.

"If I find something incriminating, they will have more pressing concerns."

Matron Holcombe nodded. "You leave me no choice, Inspector."

"You can comfort yourself with the knowledge that you did the right thing."

Matron scoffed. "The right thing? The right thing is to protect this institution and my place in it. Contrary to what the Gospel of John teaches us, the truth rarely sets anyone free."

Sebastian chuckled. "Some would call that blasphemy, madam."

"No doubt they would, but not you, Inspector, because you know it to be true. In the real world, it's money and influence that set you free, not piety or good intentions."

"I'm a little short on piety, but I do have good intentions, and seeing justice done is the closest I've come in a long time to feeling free."

Matron gave him a sour look that said *good for you*, then pushed to her feet, shut the door to her office, and walked toward the cabinet that held the register. She unlocked it and lifted out the ledger Sebastian had seen before. Since it covered the first fifty years of the century, it had to include the entries for Matthew Campbell and Leo Frain.

"I will need the registration numbers for Mr. Campbell and Mr. Frain," Sebastian said.

He hoped Matron Holcombe wouldn't try to trick him and give him random numbers that would leave him none the wiser, but she nodded, returned to her desk, and extracted the employment register. She consulted the records and showed him the entries that corresponded to Matthew Campbell and Leo Frain and the registration numbers entered in the appropriate column. It seemed the foundlings never lost their identification number, not even if they returned to the hospital as adults. They were marked for life.

Matron wrote out the numbers, handed Sebastian the sheet, then put away the employment ledger and invited him to sit at her desk. Sebastian had half-hoped that she would leave him on his own, but clearly Matron would never trust him with the register. Instead, she settled in the guest chair, obviously intending to watch over his every move.

As Matron had predicted, the entries for Campbell and Frain failed to reveal any great secrets. Matthew Campbell had been born 6 July 1832, to one Glynis Campbell, aged sixteen. Matthew Campbell was his real name, a fact he likely wasn't aware of unless he'd seen the entry. The token Glynis had left for her son was a strip of faded blue and green tartan with a red line running through it. Either Campbell's father had been a Scot or, the more likely explanation, given her surname, was that Glynis had Scottish roots. At a remove of twenty-six years, Sebastian didn't think he'd be able to track down Glynis Campbell, nor did he think Campbell's background had bearing on the case.

"Has Mr. Campbell seen this?" Sebastian asked.

"Yes, he would have seen the token when he came of age."

"Was he not permitted to take it?"

"He told me he didn't want it," Matron replied, and Sebastian could see that she shared Matthew Campbell's sentiments. What good would a piece of tartan do him at this stage?

Sebastian then leafed through the register until he found Leo Frain's number. Leo had been born 19 November 1827, to Frances Pike, aged eighteen, who had died in childbirth. The boy had been left with the Foundling Hospital by Frances's mother, Deborah Pike. The token was a faded ink drawing of a pretty young woman who had to be Frances. Leo bore little resemblance to his mother, whose features were delicate, her expression that of a gentle fawn. Sebastian was surprised that the drawing was still in the register; he would have thought Leo Frain might want to hold on to the only reminder of his mother. Perhaps he had no use for it, or found it too painful.

As Sebastian turned the pages forward to get to Michael's birth year, he could sense Matron's mounting satisfaction. Everything about her demeanor proclaimed that Sebastian was a stubborn fool who'd questioned her integrity for no good reason, since he wasn't about to find anything that would help him to understand what had happened to Amanda.

Michael's page came immediately after Amanda's, as expected, and Sebastian studied the brief entry.

Boy, born August 20, 1844, to Vera Canton, aged twenty.

Sewn to the page was a small, sealed envelope. Despite Matron's obvious disapproval, Sebastian opened the envelope and extracted the contents. Inside was a brass cross on a thin chain. Usually after all these years brass would have tarnished, but, since the cross hadn't seen the light of day, it looked much as it would have the day it had been left with the infant. The pendant wasn't the usual, simple four-point cross that represented the Church of England. It had three crossbars of varying lengths, the lowest one slanted from left to right. Every bit of space was carved with images and symbols, the vertical bar depicting Jesus, a halo around his head, his arms outstretched across the middle crossbar with the letters IC on the left and XC on the right. Four more letters were carved above his head, but they were like no letters Sebastian had ever seen. The top crossbar bore two bowing angels with what had to be the Heavenly Father at the very top, a cross held in his left hand, the right hand raised in benediction, and a halo encircling his head and bearded face. There was a skull beneath Christ's feet, and another etching beneath that looked like roots or a plant of some kind. The slanted bar was level with the feet, and a medieval church was etched into each arm.

Sebastian turned the cross over and examined the back, which was smooth to the touch, except for an inscription that ran along the longest crossbar. The words weren't in English, and the engraving was worn away, presumably from prolonged wear. Sebastian's pulse quickened. This was a connection not to be ignored, and had to be a confirmation that the ring wasn't a randomly scavenged piece of jewelry but part of a greater whole, a compass whose needle unwaveringly pointed toward the east. Sebastian would never have been able to join the two dots were it not for Gemma, who had found the first crucial piece of evidence that helped him to slot this new evidence into place.

Matron looked from the cross to Sebastian, probably expecting an explanation. Her earlier skepticism, which had been written all over her face, had been replaced by an expression of awe, which was quickly followed by a nod of certitude that Sebastian had to be on the right track.

"Has Michael ever seen this?" Sebastian asked.

"No. No one has."

"Not even your predecessor?"

"No," Matron replied. "The letters left for the orphans by their mothers are private. If the envelope were sealed, Matron Rowe, who was in charge when Michael was admitted, would have no reason to open it."

"Who took over when Matron Rowe left?"

"I did," Matron Holcombe replied. "I became matron eight years ago, and I have never opened anything that wasn't addressed to me." Her gaze shifted to the stunning object in Sebastian's hand. "Have you ever seen such a thing before?" she asked.

"No, but I believe this is a Russian Orthodox cross that suggests a connection between it and the insignia on the ring found in Amanda's dress."

Matron looked perplexed. "Even if Michael's mother was Russian by birth, what does that have to do with Amanda's death?" Her eyes widened as understanding suddenly dawned. "Was it Michael? Did he murder Amanda?"

The obvious answer was yes, but, having spoken to Michael, Sebastian could not square the gentle, sensitive boy he'd met with someone capable of such violence. That didn't mean Michael couldn't be guilty. Sebastian wasn't so cocksure that he would dismiss Michael as a suspect based on nothing more than instinct, but he wasn't ready to arrest the boy. Arresting Michael would tip off whoever had given him the ring, and Sebastian wasn't ready to show his hand just yet. Michael wasn't going anywhere tonight, and, as long as no one was the wiser, the killer believed themselves safe.

"He may have," Sebastian said. "But until I'm certain, I have no plans to take him in." He replaced the necklace in the envelope and slipped it into his waistcoat pocket, where it would be safe. "You will get it back," he hurried to reassure Matron Holcombe, who looked like she was about to raise objections.

"And Matthew Campbell? Will we get him back as well?"

"If he's in no way complicit, Mr. Campbell will be released in due course," Sebastian replied. "You are not to tell anyone about what we've discovered, Matron. Especially Michael."

"I understand." Matron stood and blocked his exit, her

fearful gaze searching Sebastian's face. "I will have your word that you will not go to the press, Inspector Bell."

"You have it," Sebastian replied. "I will not do anything that will have an adverse effect on you or the hospital. But I will catch this killer. You have my word on that as well."

"Then go with God," Matron said, and stood aside.

THIRTY-SIX

It was nearly five o'clock by the time Sebastian walked out through the gates of the Foundling Hospital. It was cold and very dark, the night moonless and silent, the streets beyond the hospital nearly empty. This last week of the year always felt strangely slow, everyone biding their time until the new year began and they returned to their lives with a renewed sense of purpose. Sebastian didn't lack purpose, but what he needed was more time. He briefly considered his next step, then found a cab and directed the driver to take him to Mrs. Poole's. He hadn't had anything since the tea he'd shared with Mrs. Ramsey, the pain in his shoulder had intensified, and he needed time to analyze what he'd learned before reporting back to Lovell.

"You're back early," Mrs. Poole said when Sebastian let himself in.

She was wearing her Sunday gown, a navy and cream striped satin, and there was a black velvet ribbon wrapped about her throat with a cameo positioned directly beneath her wobbly chin. Bouncy ringlets framed her flushed face, and there was a sparkle in her eyes that bordered on maniacal. She looked expectantly at Sebastian, as if she hoped he would comment on her appearance, but he wasn't about to fall into that trap, not when an innocent compliment could be mistaken for flirtation or, worse yet, an invitation.

"I need an early night. Would it be possible to have a tray in my room?" he asked with exaggerated politeness.

The last thing he wanted to do was spend an hour making banal small talk with the other lodgers, who were both middle-aged clerks, the most exciting thing to happen to whom all day was the boiled cod Mrs. Poole was making for dinner. A fishy smell permeated the house and was probably driving poor Gustav wild with longing.

"And a piece of fish for Gustav," Sebastian added.

"That will be an extra charge," Mrs. Poole snapped.

"Yes, I'm aware." Sebastian was amazed that she didn't charge him extra for the mice Gustav caught, since she would consider that a contribution to the cat's sustenance rather than a benefit to her that should be rewarded with the occasional treat.

"You'll have to eat early if you want a tray, Inspector, since I will be busy serving supper later and it might take longer than usual." Mrs. Poole smiled in a way Sebastian found distinctly unnerving, since she wasn't a woman to smile without reason and extra work didn't normally merit glee.

"Is everything all right, Mrs. Poole?" he asked despite his earlier resolve not to react to whatever was making her vibrate like a tuning fork.

Mrs. Poole's smile grew wider. "We have a new lodger. Mr. Quince moved in just this afternoon. He's to have Mr. Wright's old room."

"What happened to Mr. Wright?" Sebastian asked, and almost expected Mrs. Poole to tell him that Mr. Wright had passed. The previous occupant of Mr. Wright's room, Herr Schweiger, had died in his sleep, leaving poor Gustav trapped in the room with the dead man, meowing desperately to be let out and fed. Sebastian had broken down the door to let the poor creature out and the undertakers in, and had earned Mrs. Poole's fleeting gratitude and Gustav's less fleeting affection. According to Gemma, Sebastian and Gustav were now bound for life.

"Mr. Wright has left us. He's retired from his position at the bank and has decided to spend his remaining years with his widowed sister in Devon."

Sebastian nodded, relieved to hear the man wasn't dead and would hopefully spend his twilight years in a more pleasant setting and with someone who actually cared for him.

"And a good thing it is too," Mrs. Poole said. "I wouldn't want that old fool underfoot all day long, demanding extra coal and endless cups of tea."

"An outrage, indeed," Sebastian agreed, but the sarcasm was entirely lost on his landlady.

"Come into the parlor and meet Mr. Quince," Mrs. Poole invited him. "He's a real gentleman and has lovely manners." *Unlike you* seemed to hang in the air.

"I'd really rather—" Sebastian began, but Mrs. Poole glared at him.

"Really, Inspector Bell. Would it kill you to say hello to a new neighbor? You hardly speak to the other lodgers. One would think I take in lepers the way you carry on."

"I do apologize for my rudeness, Mrs. Poole, but I'm rather busy these days," Sebastian replied. The truth was that he would rather walk on hot coals than endure an hour of having to appear interested in the trials and tribulations of his neighbors.

"Surely not too busy to spare a moment to welcome Mr. Quince to our humble home."

Chastened by Mrs. Poole's rebuke and wishing only to get the introductions over with, Sebastian marched into the parlor, which for once was actually warmer than a crypt. A merry fire blazed in the grate, the curtains were drawn against the winter night, and a decanter of brandy and a cut-crystal glass stood on a low table before Mr. Quince, who seemed to be getting a very warm welcome. The reason for Mrs. Poole's generosity became immediately obvious. Mr. Quince was no older than forty and had neatly oiled dark hair, a pencil moustache that crawled across his upper lip like a particularly furry caterpillar, and dramatically arched eyebrows over hooded dark eyes. Although not classically handsome, he was just the sort of man to appeal to a lonely widow, an unexpected gift since Sebastian had clearly just been demoted in the hierarchy of Mrs. Poole's affections.

"Mr. Quince, allow me to introduce your neighbor, Inspector Bell," Mrs. Poole purred. "I must say, I sleep better at night knowing he's there to keep me safe."

"A pleasure to meet you, Inspector," Mr. Quince said, rising to shake Sebastian's hand.

"Likewise," Sebastian replied. "And what is it that you do, Mr. Quince?"

"Mr. Quince is a well-known writer," Mrs. Poole exclaimed, and clasped her hands to her bosom in an uncharacteristic display of girlish ecstasy.

Mr. Quince colored under Sebastian's gaze. "I actually work at King's Cross. I'm a porter," he explained. "But I do dabble in the arts," he added with a self-deprecating chuckle.

"Oh," was all Sebastian could manage.

"I write penny dreadfuls under the name B.E. Ware," Mr. Quince went on, lowering his voice conspiratorially. "Lots of inspiration at King's Cross. I meet all sorts."

"Isn't that clever?" Mrs. Poole exclaimed. "Beware," she intoned with a dramatic shudder.

"Ware is my *nom de plume*, but B.E. is for my Christian name," Mr. Quince explained. "Bertram Everett."

"Such a proud name," Mrs. Poole exclaimed and shot Sebastian a sharp look. Clearly he was expected to make some appropriate comment.

"Yes, that is very clever, Mr. Quince," he said.

"I say, Inspector, if you're a fan of the old penny dreadful, perhaps we can work together," Mr. Quince suggested, all the while watching Sebastian much like Gustav did when he thought sardines might be on offer. "A mutually beneficial collaboration, if you will. The writer and the detective. Think of what we could accomplish. We could take my stories to a whole new level. Spine-tingling suspense," he said dramatically, and made the sort of theatrical gesture a magician might resort to after making a dove disappear. "For a share of the profits, of course."

"I'll give it very careful thought," Sebastian promised. "I prefer novels myself. Dickens, Thackeray, Trollope."

"Stirring stuff to be sure, but do not underestimate the power of sensationalism, my dear Inspector. It appeals to the masses, and those pennies do add up." Mr. Quince rubbed his hands together and smiled suggestively. "Are you in the midst of a case right now?"

"He certainly is," Mrs. Poole cried. "Why don't you tell us all about it, Inspector Bell?"

"I am not at liberty to discuss ongoing cases."

"We don't need the names," Mr. Quince replied. "Just the basic facts. Come now. There's a good man."

"Do excuse me," Sebastian said. "I have an early start tomorrow." He had to leave before he said something he might regret and unexpectedly found himself in search of new lodgings.

"Well, if you change your mind, my door is always open, Inspector," Mr. Quince said with an oily smile. "I can't imagine that an inspector earns enough to turn down a tidy little infusion every month."

"I wish you both a pleasant evening," Sebastian said, and headed upstairs.

His tiny sitting room was freezing, the only illumination coming from a streetlamp down the street that cast a pale halo onto the ground beneath. Mrs. Poole didn't care to waste coal to heat an empty house and spent most of her day in the kitchen and downstairs parlor, which were warmed by the kitchen range. Sebastian didn't bother to light a lamp. He hung up his coat and hat, cracked the crust of ice on the water in the pitcher, and washed his hands and face. The icy water revived him somewhat. He then lit a fire in the grate, grateful to Hank, who worked for Mrs. Poole, for leaving him more coal, since his scuttle had been empty.

By the time the fire took hold, Mrs. Poole had arrived with Sebastian's dinner tray. She shoved it into his hands and left without a word. She didn't like to cater to her lodgers' requests and frequently reminded the residents that she wasn't running a fine hotel but a modest, respectable boarding house, but today she appeared to have an additional reason to have her nose out of joint. Perhaps she had hoped to impress Mr. Quince with her ability to foster a profitable partnership between the two men, or maybe she had hoped to make Sebastian jealous with her obvious interest in the new tenant, or vice versa, but she had failed on all counts and would have to devise a new plan to get her man. Sebastian sincerely hoped that Mr. Quince would take a romantic interest in Mrs. Poole; it would make Sebastian's own tenancy at the boarding house a little less fraught with the sort of drama he'd rather avoid.

Sebastian set the dish of cod before an ecstatic Gustav, then took his own plate and settled by the fire, the tufted side of the armchair soft against his aching shoulder. The cod was cold and bland, the boiled potatoes undercooked, and the peas dry, but Sebastian dutifully ate his supper, then set the dish aside. He'd take Gemma out for a nice meal to celebrate the new year. He liked to treat her since she never went out, both because she was a single woman and going out by herself was unseemly, and because she was in mourning and her life was currently limited to work and her room at her own boarding house.

Sebastian would have loved to discuss the case with Gemma, but he had to make do with Gustav, who jumped into his lap and got comfortable, resting his head on his paws, the flame reflecting in his pale eyes. Sebastian stroked the cat's silky black and white fur as he stared into the flames, his mind returning to what he'd learned that afternoon. As far as he knew, Michael was the only person at the Foundling Hospital who had a connection to Russia, which strongly suggested that someone must have given him the ring. It would make sense that Michael would give the ring to his beloved to seal their promise to each other, but why would he then want it back? Could it be that someone had got wind of what he had done and didn't approve? If that were the case, why had they given the ring to the boy in the first place, particularly while he was in a place where it could be discovered and taken off him, either by the other boys or by one of the teachers?

Since the children had virtually no contact with the outside world, someone would have to have found a way to identify Michael and speak to him, even if for just a few moments, in order to explain the details of his parentage and pass him the ring. It could also be possible, and maybe more likely, that Michael had got the ring from one of the teachers. Might it have been a token of another kind of love? It wasn't unheard of for men to fall in love with boys in their care, particularly when they had no access to women and spent all their time in the company of their own sex. Having accepted such a gift from an adult, Michael could have in turn given the ring to Amanda, another gesture of love that would instantly transform Amanda into a grave threat to the original owner of the ring.

It wasn't very likely that Archie Wilson had made contact with Michael, but Matthew Campbell had daily access, and Michael seemed to like and respect the man. Perhaps Campbell had taken Michael under his wing and was grooming the boy to become an intimate companion, despite his admission that he and Miss Parish had feelings for each other. There were individuals who were drawn to both sexes. If Amanda had started asking questions, she could have cost Campbell not only his livelihood but possibly his freedom too. Sodomy was a crime and, even if he wasn't charged, Campbell's reputation would be tarnished for life.

There was also another possibility. Perhaps Michael had been approached by his mother, in which case Sebastian needed to learn all he could about the ring and the cross. The inscription on the back of the cross could help him track down Vera Canton. Both items were valuable and, if Vera could afford to leave such an irreplaceable token with her son, perhaps her situation had not been as dire as she might have led the Foundling Hospital to believe, and she'd had other reasons for leaving her child. Now that Michael was practically a man, she might be ready to forge a relationship with the son she'd given up.

Before he threw Matthew Campbell to the wolves, Sebastian had to be certain that the man had really been involved or prove that the evidence against him was purely circumstantial. He felt safe in eliminating Archie Wilson from his inquiry for the time being, since his involvement would require knowledge and actions that currently seemed quite improbable.

The first thing Sebastian needed to do was learn more about the items in his possession. He thought the cross was Russian, based on the crest on the ring, but it could also be Greek, and he needed to be certain. Sebastian knew of two Orthodox churches in the vicinity. There was the Greek Orthodox church in Little Winchester Street and the Russian Orthodox church on Welbeck Street. Given the obvious origin of the ring, it made more sense to start with the Russian church, so he would pay a visit first thing in the morning. Once he was better informed, he would ask to speak to Michael.

The plan was a start, but Sebastian was well aware that he

was still in danger of hitting a brick wall. The ring and the cross might yield nothing of value, and, if Michael knew who had killed Amanda, he just might decide to feign ignorance and wait for the investigation to come to a natural end. Perhaps Michael was protecting the killer, or maybe he had changed his mind about a future with Amanda and had demanded she give back the ring. An argument between the two could have led to a violent altercation that resulted in Amanda's death. If that was what had happened, Michael would hang for murder, so his best defense was to keep silent. It was the only way to save his life and ensure he had a future. Whichever way tomorrow went, it would be a crucial day for the investigation, and Sebastian would either close in on the killer or be forced to admit defeat.

Set on a plan of action and ready to give his mind a break, Sebastian leaned against the back of the chair and shut his eyes, but his turbulent thoughts weren't quite done with him. His shoulder was still hurting, the earlier throbbing ache now punctuated by moments of sharper pain. He couldn't get Amanda out of his mind or rest easy knowing that Gemma might be shut in with the killer, who was clearly clever and resourceful, and possibly privy to the details of Sebastian's investigation. Sebastian didn't think Matron would reveal what she had learned, but people's judgment was often clouded by trust, and she had to have confidants among the staff. What if one of those familiars was the killer?

And then suddenly the memory of Anne Ramsey standing barefoot and nearly naked before a stone effigy, her expression rapturous with love for a husband who was gone, swam to the surface of Sebastian's mind, and his sorrow for Anne and Colin reminded him how fragile and fleeting life was, even for those who managed to live to old age. Life was so brief and so cruel, and to lose one's mind rather than deal with the grief of losing a loved one was an effective shield against pain, one Sebastian had once tried to build with the help of spirits and opium. He missed the peace he'd enjoyed after smoking the pipe and the vivid dreams that had followed, in which he had been happy and loved. Those hours spent floating outside himself had been a balm to the soul and the only thing that had offered him a respite from grief.

Overcome with frustration and tired of being in pain, Sebastian settled his gaze on the small writing desk by the window. The only item on it was a bottle of cheap brandy, the amber liquid that resembled molten gold in the light of the fire taunting him with the promise of oblivion. He had been surprised when Mrs. Poole had given him the brandy as a Christmas gift and knew then that he should dispose of it before he gave in to temptation, but instead he had left the brandy in plain sight, a test to his newfound sobriety. He tilted his head to the side and studied the bottle. He had been true to his word and had not touched opium or laudanum-based tonics in nearly two months, but surely a man was entitled to an occasional drink without giving in to addiction.

Sebastian shooed Gustav off his lap and pushed to his feet. He reached the table in three strides and picked up the bottle. He used his teeth to pull out the cork, lifted the bottle to his lips and took a long swig, and then another. The brandy smelled sour and tasted flat, but a pleasant warmth spread through his chest, and the sharp pain in his shoulder began to fade, the familiar sense of well-being settling over Sebastian like a warm blanket.

THIRTY-SEVEN

Gemma glanced out of the infirmary window as she passed, and saw nothing but impenetrable darkness beyond. As a girl she had always loved this time of the year, when she could spend the evenings by the fire, reading, chatting with Victor, or just daydreaming about the future. She had felt ensconced in safety and unwavering affection, never imagining that the bedrock of her existence would crumble so soon, leaving behind nothing but bittersweet memories of times gone by and of people who were never far from her thoughts, benevolent specters who watched over her from beyond the grave.

These days, she found the darkness oppressive and only wanted December to end so the days could grow longer, and spring, with its sunny days and renewed life, wouldn't seem so far away. Her friend Lydia used to call this sort of melancholy the midwinter of the spirit, but Lydia was gone, just like the rest of them, her spirit having flown to a place Gemma had no wish to follow. Perhaps the same place where Amanda's soul had gone only a few days ago. Would she meet the mother she'd never known in life, or was the promise of eternal life and heavenly reunion simply a lovely story people told so that death wouldn't seem so final and terrifying? Would Sebastian be reunited with his wife and son? And if he were, what would that mean for Gemma if she allowed herself to love him?

Checking the time, Gemma saw that it was past six and wondered where Sebastian could be. Had he pressed on with the investigation after she'd seen him at the hospital, or had he finally permitted himself to go home? She hoped he had. Sebastian's face had looked drawn, and he had very obviously been in pain. His shoulder was not yet fully healed after the brutal beating that had left his tendons torn and his collarbone fractured. He wasn't eating properly or taking enough rest, but at least he didn't seem to be imbibing spirits or relying on opium. His resolve was surprisingly strong, she thought, given how unrelenting the grip of addiction could be.

Sebastian would prevail, and maybe in time he would take his rightful place as superintendent, his talents finally recognized. Because if they weren't, he just might leave; his long-standing plan to go to America and join the Pinkerton Detective Agency would give him the excuse he needed to start over in a place that held no painful memories or bureaucratic limitations. And if Sebastian went, where would that leave Gemma? Alone, desolate, and without any hope for the sort of future she'd dreamed about during those long, cozy nights by the fire.

Ignoring the sadness that tugged at her heart, Gemma checked on the children before settling them for the night, then, when Ella returned with supper, sat down at the table. There was a bowl of stew and a slice of buttered bread, and a cup of liberally sweetened tea and two pieces of lavender shortbread, probably a thank-you from Matron for staying the night, since Gemma didn't expect to see the extra hours reflected in her wages. Miss Landry had barely made an appearance all day, claiming she must have caught croup from the children and was ill and needed to stay in bed. Gemma didn't bother to explain that croup was an illness of small children and she had never come across an adult afflicted by it. Miss Landry probably wanted some time off, and, since she hadn't been terribly helpful to begin with, Gemma had decided to let her off the hook.

Gemma had just started on the stew, which was no worse than the fare Mrs. Bass served to her lodgers, when Miss Parish staggered into the infirmary. Her skin looked chalky and her pupils were dilated. Her hand trembled as she grabbed the back of a chair to steady herself.

"Miss Parish, are you all right?" Gemma asked as she sprang to her feet and hurried to help the woman.

"I'm afraid I don't feel well, Miss Tate." Miss Parish put all her weight on her hands and bent her head over the back of the chair, taking deep breaths as if to stave off nausea.

"Can you tell me what's troubling you?"

"I have a terrible headache, my vision is blurred, and I feel awfully weak, like I'm going to faint." Miss Parish was slurring her words slightly, which was worrying. "I also feel a bit bilious. Perhaps it's the sugar sickness."

There had been a nurse in Scutari who'd suffered from sugar sickness and had described having similar symptoms when she experienced a particularly severe bout during her time on the ward. She kept the affliction at bay by drinking sweet tea and eating as often as possible, but it hadn't always worked. Miss Nightingale had threatened to send her home if her condition grew worse, but the woman had managed to remain until the end of hostilities.

"Miss Parish, do you normally suffer from sugar sickness?" Gemma asked.

"No, this is the first time I've experienced anything of this nature, but my father was often ill."

Gemma had read that sugar sickness was treated with laxatives, emetics, and sometimes a few days at the seaside, but, although she could supply Miss Parish with castor oil, or a spoonful of ground mustard seed mixed with warm water to help her vomit, she didn't think she should jump to baseless conclusions. If Miss Parish continued to experience symptoms, she could consult a physician, who would be better equipped to offer long-term care.

"I think you had best lie down," Gemma said. "I will get you a headache powder and keep an eye on you over the coming hours."

"I don't want to put you to any trouble, Miss Tate," Miss Parish moaned.

"It's no trouble at all. In fact, I think you should stay the night."

"That's very kind," Miss Parish replied weakly.

"Not at all."

"Perhaps it's just a megrim," Miss Parish suggested.

"Do you often suffer from megrims?"

"From time to time, especially when it's my time of the month."

"And is it your time of the month now?"

Miss Parish nodded miserably.

Perhaps Miss Parish should have started with that, but Gemma supposed the poor woman felt too ill to think clearly. A period of rest should do the trick but if she still felt unwell in the morning, Gemma would ask Matron to summon the doctor.

She went to the cabinet where the medicines were kept, took out a packet of headache powder, and mixed the contents into a glass of water. Once Miss Parish had drained the glass, Gemma helped her remove her gown, crinolines, and boots, and helped her into bed.

"The best thing for a megrim is quiet and dark," she said. "Try to rest."

"Thank you."

Miss Parish's eyelids were already fluttering, so Gemma left her to sleep. She looked to be suffering even in sleep, her fair curls damp against her forehead. As Gemma looked on, Miss Parish's face began to relax, and her breathing grew deeper. Gemma had a sudden silly thought and had to suppress a smile. Miss Parish reminded her of Little Bo Peep in the storybook her mother used to read to Gemma and Victor when they were children. Bo Peep had the same pinched look as Miss Parish, her fair curls sticking out from her straw bonnet and her pale hands clasped to her breast. Gemma had often thought that there was something helpless about Miss Parish, as if she had found herself in a world not entirely her own and wasn't sure how to go on. Gemma supposed such a sentiment was common to women who found themselves suddenly destitute and had to find employment, working long hours instead of living in comfort and being waited on hand and foot. It wasn't easy to adjust and admit that, whatever dreams for the future one had once harbored, life would now follow a very different course.

Leaving Miss Parish to sleep, Gemma returned to the table, eager to finish her meal before it grew cold. The corridor outside the infirmary was quiet, with everyone still in the dining hall, and despite her loneliness Gemma relished the moment of peace. She finished her stew, then drank some lukewarm tea and ate one shortbread. She dunked the second biscuit in the tea, then changed her mind and set it back on the saucer. She didn't much care for lavender as a flavor. It smelled too much like soap and left an odd taste in her mouth.

She had nearly finished the tea when she began to feel woozy and heavy-limbed. Ella's round face swam in and out of focus as the girl walked in and stopped near the door, watching Gemma's distress with maddening detachment. Gemma's vision began to dim, and she'd just managed to stumble over to an empty cot and tumble down onto it when Ella loomed over her. Her face was too close, her mouth opening and closing, the smell of onions and stewed meat still clinging to her clothes. Gemma thought Ella had said something that sounded like "policeman" but wasn't sure, and then darkness overtook her, and Ella's voice dissipated, leaving behind nothing but a silent void.

THIRTY-EIGHT

WEDNESDAY, DECEMBER 29

It was the whimpering that woke her. One of the children, Joe, Gemma thought, was asking for a cup of water. Gemma heard Miss Landry's soothing voice, and then the crying stopped. She heard the swish of Miss Landry's skirts as she walked toward the window and pulled open the curtains so the weak light of a winter morning filled the room with a milky haze.

Lying perfectly still, Gemma took stock of the situation. Her brain was most definitely awake, if a bit sluggish, and she could hear and smell, since she thought she'd got a whiff of porridge as the children started on their breakfast, and there was a full chamber pot somewhere quite close. Gemma's limbs felt like lead, and she couldn't seem to pry her eyes open. The lids felt as heavy as if coins for the dead had been placed on her eyes just before she was dispatched across the River Styx. The thought served to jolt her fully awake as memories of last night began to crystallize in her foggy mind.

Gemma had just started on her supper when Miss Parish had arrived, looking very ill and clearly in need of help. Gemma had assessed the situation and had done the only thing she could think of under the circumstances. Once Miss Parish had fallen asleep, Gemma had returned to her meal, and had managed to finish the stew and drink most of the tea before she'd suddenly felt as if all the strength had been drained from her body and her brain had simply begun to shut down as she passed out on one of the cots. The last thing she could recall was Ella Boone hovering over her. Had she said something about a policeman, or had she said, "Are you all right, ma'am?" Gemma couldn't recall, but Ella had clearly left her on her own and hadn't asked anyone to fetch Sebastian.

A terrible sense of dread stole over Gemma as the events of last night began to form a discernible pattern. As a nurse, she was familiar with the effects of laudanum and the severity of the reaction based on the dosage. Had someone given her a few drops, she would have simply felt tired and slept peacefully through the night. The only side effect would be some vivid dreams and maybe a slight wooziness when she first woke. What she had experienced last night had hit her like an oncoming train, which meant that whoever had tampered with her food had not wished to err on the side of caution. The very idea that she had been taken completely unawares and had been made so vulnerable during the hours of unconsciousness left her trembling with horror. She had been left to sleep off the effects of the drug, but whoever had given it to her could have done anything, anything at all, and she would not have been able to stop them. Like most unmarried women, Gemma had fears about her safety, but to find herself unconscious and at the mercy of some unknown culprit had to be one of the very worst. She had to gather her wits and figure out exactly what had happened. Understanding was the only way to combat her growing dread.

Gemma carefully reviewed what she had eaten and tried to recall the taste and the texture of the food in her mouth. She hadn't noticed anything wrong with the stew, but the dish had contained root vegetables that the cook used to bulk up consis-

tency and create more volume so that it would stretch to more
people. Turnips in particular had a slightly bitter taste, but
Gemma didn't think the stew was the culprit. It had to have
been the tea. It had been fine, although maybe unusually sweet,
when she had first tasted it, and when she'd drunk it with the
lavender shortbread it had tasted a little strange. She had
attributed the peculiar taste to the presence of lavender in the
shortbread, but perhaps it was the laudanum that she had
tasted. Which brought her to the next and much more important question. Who would want to drug her, and why?

Cook had no reason whatsoever to tamper with Gemma's
food, and probably hadn't been the one to prepare the tray.
That would be Ella or one of the other kitchen servants. And
there were many. Ella had brought the tray upstairs, which gave
her both opportunity and access. Ella had known Amanda.
They had been in the same dormitory until Ella came of age.
Might the two girls have had some sort of falling-out? Ella
would also have access to keys, which would enable her to get
into the laundry if she had a mind to.

And then there was Miss Parish. She was the only other
person to come to the infirmary around the same time as Ella.
Miss Parish had not come near the food, but Gemma had gone
to fetch the headache powder, which meant that she had turned
her back on the other woman for about two minutes. Was it
possible that Faith Parish had added laudanum to Gemma's tea?
But why would she do that? And what reason would she have to
harm Amanda and Gemma?

Gemma took a deep breath and moved her arms experimen-
tally. They still felt heavy and unwieldy, but a little less than a
few minutes ago. The drug was wearing off, and it was time she
got up. For one thing, she desperately needed the toilet, and for
another, she had to get to the bottom of this outrage before
Sebastian returned to the Foundling Hospital. She wasn't about
to tell him that someone had drugged her but she didn't know

who or why. She didn't want to worry him unnecessarily, nor did she want to admit that she had been caught unawares and neatly dispatched for what had to be about eight hours. Sebastian would send her home and insist that she remain there until he thought it safe for her to return, but she wasn't ready to leave.

Pride was one of the deadly sins. That had been drummed into Gemma since she was a child; but her reason for investigating wasn't because her pride had been wounded. She would do it not only to protect herself from further attack but to help Sebastian, since whatever had happened last night had confirmed what he had been saying all along. The killer was among them, and as long as he or she remained at liberty no one was safe.

Finally feeling strong enough to rise, Gemma sat up, waited until the initial dizziness had passed, then stood up slowly. The cot Miss Parish had occupied last night was empty, her clothes and shoes gone. Gemma shook out her skirts, patted her hair into place and made sure her lace cap was still affixed to her hair, then walked over to Miss Landry, all the while assessing the acuity of her senses. She felt a little lightheaded but otherwise like her normal self.

"Miss Tate, I am so very sorry," Miss Landry exclaimed when she saw Gemma.

"What about?" Gemma asked carefully.

"I have let you down and left you on your own. I really should have realized how tired you were after taking so many consecutive shifts. Ella said you fair collapsed with fatigue last night. Out like a light, she said. So I let you sleep and looked after the children. Don't you worry, Miss Tate," Miss Landry hurried to reassure her. "Everyone has been washed, fed, and dosed with balsam. I do believe Tommy and Joe are on the mend. Henry and Peter are still poorly, but they're no worse, which is always a plus in my mind."

Miss Landry cocked her head to the side like a curious little bird and studied Gemma. "I hope you will forgive the observation, Miss Tate, but you do look rather unwell. I think a strong, restorative cup of tea should do the trick. With lots of sugar. Shall I fetch you one?"

"Thank you, Miss Landry, but there's really no need," Gemma replied. Her tongue felt like wet flannel in her mouth, and she would have killed for a cup of tea, but she wasn't about to allow anyone access to anything she ate or drank this morning. "If you've no objection, I will get it myself. I need to stretch my legs, and maybe there's some porridge left."

"Of course. Thoughtless of me," Miss Landry replied. "You will want your breakfast. Well, don't you fret, Miss Tate. I'm here, and the children will be looked after. Take as long as you need."

"Thank you," Gemma replied. "Did you happen to see Miss Parish this morning?"

"Miss Parish left just as I arrived. She said she was terribly unwell last night, and you had been an absolute angel and allowed her to stay the night, but she was feeling much better. She asked me to convey her thanks and hoped you hadn't succumbed to something catching."

"Why would she think that?" Gemma asked.

"Miss Parish said she tried to wake you, but you were dead to the world, Miss Tate. That's what she said. Dead to the world," Miss Landry blathered on.

"I think you're right, Miss Landry. I was just very tired."

"Well, I'm glad you were able to get some rest and slept through all the hullabaloo this morning."

"What hullabaloo?" Gemma asked, her stomach clenching with foreboding.

"Mrs. Baker couldn't wake Lucy, so she sent one of the girls to fetch you. When Joan saw you were sleeping, she came to find me."

"What?" Gemma cried, horrified. "Is Lucy all right?"

"Not to worry, Miss Tate," Miss Landry hurried to reassure her. "Lucy was just sleeping very deeply and was tearful and groggy when she finally woke, but nothing seemed to be amiss. Perhaps she had trouble sleeping during the night and fell into a deep sleep toward the early hours. Strange thing, though," Miss Landry mused. "Her right hand smelled of lavender and her mouth looked a bit sticky."

Gemma's gaze flew to the table where she had sat last night, but the tray had been removed and the only dish on the table was an empty saucer. Matron did not condone waste, so food was never thrown out, with leftovers being utilized the following day. Instead of throwing the uneaten shortbread into the rubbish bucket, Ella must have left it on the saucer in case Gemma wanted it later. Was it possible that Lucy had snuck out again and had helped herself to the biscuit before returning upstairs? If she had, she must have taken the shortbread with her and eaten it in bed, otherwise she would have succumbed to sleep long before she'd reached the door to the dormitory.

Dear God, Gemma thought as the full impact of what could have happened dawned on her. Lucy could have been seriously hurt, died even, if she had finished Gemma's tea as well. She could have grown drowsy and fallen down the stairs, or, if she had ingested a large enough amount, could have failed to wake altogether. A child her age, who also happened to be underweight, would not be able to tolerate such a high dose and might have slipped away in her sleep. Gemma balled her hands into fists to keep them from shaking, and tried to look calm, but her distress wasn't lost on Miss Landry.

"You do look a bit queer, Miss Tate," she observed. "You go on now, before all the porridge is gone. You should eat something nourishing. It's sure to make you feel better," she went on, her face a mask of concern.

"Yes, I believe you're right," Gemma stammered. "I'll go down in a minute."

She poured water into a clean cup, swallowed it down, drank another cup of water slowly, then poured some into a basin. She washed her hands and face, which made her feel more alert, then stopped by the cloakroom before heading down to breakfast. The dining hall was full, but the children were unusually quiet, their heads bowed and their gazes fixed on their bowls of porridge. Amanda's funeral would be held shortly after breakfast, and everyone was expected to attend the service, which would be held in the chapel where Amanda had sung only a few days ago. One of their own was dead, and they were more aware of it today, on the morning of the funeral. Knowing someone was gone and watching them being put into the ground were two vastly different experiences, and every child in that hall had lost friends during their tenure at the hospital and knew they could very easily be next.

Gemma scanned the vast room until she caught sight of Lucy's fair head. The child looked listless and pale, but she was spooning porridge into her mouth, which was a good sign. Lucy saw Gemma standing there and gave her a watery smile, all the confirmation Gemma needed that the girl was on the mend. Relieved, Gemma headed toward the tables reserved for the faculty and staff.

The teachers and masters were just as subdued. No one was conversing or exchanging bits of news and gossip with their coworkers. Some sat in silence, while others looked around, their eyes reflecting just how lonely and lost they felt in this huge room filled with humanity. Gemma was sure everyone had noticed Mr. Campbell's absence by now and had probably drawn their own conclusion, that a man they had known and trusted was a killer. And now Mr. Frain seemed to be missing as well.

Gemma looked toward the head table, where Matron normally sat during meals, but she was also absent. Perhaps she had some last-minute details to see to before the burial. Gemma hoped Matron had asked a few of the older boys to dig the grave, since it would be too much for a man of Mr. Fletcher's age to hack through near-frozen earth and haul out six feet of soil. At any rate, the coming days would surely test Matron's mettle, and Gemma suspected that changes would be made to the way the hospital was run and how strenuously new employees were evaluated. The directive would no doubt come from the governors who sat on the committee.

Gemma glanced toward the female teachers' table. Miss Parish sat with Mrs. Dixon and Miss Baker, and gave Gemma a grateful smile before instantly rearranging her face into a mask of sorrow befitting a woman who was about to attend a funeral. Ella normally served that side of the room, but she was nowhere to be seen. Perhaps she was in the kitchen, waiting to be sent out with fresh pots of tea or getting ready to collect dirty plates and bring them back to the kitchen to be washed.

Gemma found an empty seat and helped herself to porridge from a nearly empty pot. She then poured a cup of tea, which she tasted before adding sugar. The tea tasted as it should, so she added two lumps of sugar and a splash of milk, then mixed butter and honey into the quickly cooling porridge. She wasn't particularly hungry, but it was important that she eat if she wanted to rid herself of the after-effects of the laudanum. She needed something in her belly to absorb the remnants of the tainted tea and give herself energy for the coming day.

Gemma finished her meal and poured another cup of tea, all the while scanning the room for Ella and replying to questions from the other women at the table, who were concerned about a wider outbreak of croup as well as the ongoing investigation. No one said anything about Mr. Campbell, but the women's gazes kept straying to the table where he normally sat, and they shook their heads and tut-tutted to each other, as if condemning him before he had even been charged would somehow right the wrong that had been done to Amanda and by extension the Foundling Hospital.

"Will you be going to Amanda's funeral, Miss Tate?" Mrs. Monk asked, her eyes dancing with mischief.

"Of course she will be, Mathilda," Mrs. Dyer replied, her gaze also fixed on Gemma. "If only to see that policeman. I expect he will be there, to see who acts twitchy as the vicar eulogizes Amanda. I tell you, that Inspector Bell can question me anytime. Where on earth did you meet him, Miss Tate? Or do you have a dark past none of us know about?"

"I met Inspector Bell during the investigation into my brother's murder."

That was the first time Gemma had revealed anything of a personal nature about herself. The other women were aware that she had been a nurse in Crimea, but that was the extent of their knowledge, and hearing that Gemma's brother had been murdered seemed to render them speechless. They looked away, embarrassed to have blundered so badly. Gemma finished her tea, bid them a good morning, and crossed the dining hall, approaching a young server named Sal. She knew her to be friendly with Ella and thought Sal might be able to help.

"Good morning, Sal. I was looking for Ella. Is she in the kitchen?" Gemma asked as soon as she got the girl's attention.

Sal shook her head. "Sorry, Miss Tate, but Ella is not here this morning."

"Where is she?"

"It's her morning off. She likes to take off early."

"Do you know where she goes?" Gemma asked.

Sal grinned. "She goes to see her young man. He works at a livery, and they're that sweet on each other. I think Ella might be one of the lucky ones and actually escape from this place, and not into service."

"Where did they meet?"

"Right here. In the courtyard. The lucky cow," Sal said under her breath. "He's lovely, he is. Wish I'd seen him first."

"Do you happen to know which livery Ella's young man works at?" Gemma asked.

Sal fixed her with her dark gaze. "Why so curious about Ella, Miss Tate?"

"No reason. I just wanted a word."

"Well, she'll be back after lunch, so you can talk to her then. I have work to be getting on with."

"Thank you, Sal."

"Not at all, Miss Tate," Sal said. She turned away and returned to stacking dirty crockery on her tray.

Gemma tried to look casual as she strode from the dining hall, but her mind was buzzing. Ella was involved with a young man who worked at a livery and who had come to the Foundling Hospital at some point in the not-so-distant past. Surely that was too much of a coincidence, given what Sebastian had told her about Archie Wilson; but there were several liveries in the area, and Gemma could hardly assume that Ella and Archie were a couple without proof. She couldn't question the girls who worked with Ella without arousing suspicion, and it was time she went back to the infirmary.

As she neared the door, Gemma came upon Miss Parish, who again smiled at her gratefully.

"I do hope you're feeling better, Miss Tate. You looked absolutely worn out last night. It's no easy thing, looking after the sick, especially children."

"I'm quite all right. Thank you, Miss Parish. And you? Are you feeling better?"

"Much. I felt miraculously restored this morning. I wanted to thank you for looking after me before I left, but you were fast asleep, so I spoke to Miss Landry instead. I hope she passed on my thanks."

"She did."

"Well, I had better be off. I need to stop by my room before the funeral to get my cape, bonnet, and gloves. What a sad day," Miss Parish added.

"It is indeed," Gemma replied.

They walked out together, then parted ways after wishing each other a good morning. Gemma was just about to head upstairs when she heard a commotion coming from the direction of Matron's office. Curious, she skirted the banister and hurried toward the office, all the while wondering if Sebastian might be the cause.

THIRTY-NINE

Matron stood just outside her office, hands on her hips, face flushed with anger, and eyes blazing with an unholy fire. Her breath came in great pants that put Gemma in mind of an incoming locomotive. Sebastian was nowhere to be seen, but several people, teachers who'd got wind of whatever was happening and two porters, were milling about. Just as Gemma approached, Mr. Frain came running, a tool chest beneath his arm.

"What happened?" Gemma inquired of Mr. Timmins, who was closest to her.

"Someone broke into Matron's office last night. And quite forcefully too," Mr. Timmins said. "There's some considerable damage."

"Was anything taken?" Gemma asked, doing her best to show nothing but natural curiosity.

"Someone forced the drawer where the most recent register is kept," Matron Holcombe said, having overheard their conversation. She looked mystified as she sucked in a sharp breath. "First the girls' dormitory, and now this."

"What happened in the girls' dormitory?" Gemma asked.

Matron didn't seem inclined to answer, but outrage finally won out, and the reply came out in a gush of words. "Someone stole Amanda's things. Now we don't have anything to bury her in. What would anyone want with her smallclothes and dress?" she exclaimed. "They even took her stockings and shoes." She huffed with frustration. "I suppose we'll have to make do with a winding sheet. I can't justify wasting a new dress and shoes on a corpse."

"You need to inform Inspector Bell right away," Gemma said, doing her best to ignore Matron's callous words.

"What on earth for?" Matron demanded. "This is theft, pure and simple."

"Someone clearly wanted a look at the register," Gemma argued.

"What they wanted, Miss Tate, was valuable tokens left by heartbroken mothers for their children. What they didn't realize was that most of the items have no monetary value."

"The thefts could be related to Amanda's death, ma'am," Gemma insisted. "Perhaps someone was looking for something specific."

She didn't want to mention the ring, since that would implicate her in retrieving it from Amanda's hem, but she needed to impress upon Matron just how important it was that she send for Sebastian. Someone knew about the ring and must have been searching for it when they stole Amanda's things. The ring was the key, and whoever had given it to Amanda had been in the building last night.

"Really, Miss Tate, you do have quite the imagination," Matron exclaimed. "No doubt as a result of your association with that policeman. I would consider your reputation if I were you. Once lost, some things can never be replaced, such as one's good name."

"The same could be said for whatever was taken from your office, Matron," Gemma snapped.

"Mr. Frain will repair the door, and that will be the end of the matter."

There didn't seem anything left to say, so Gemma left Mr. Frain and Matron Holcombe to discuss the repairs. Matron would assume she was on her way back to the infirmary, but Gemma had a different destination in mind. Thankfully, she still had a few hairpins left.

FORTY

Despite his moment of weakness the night before, Sebastian felt reasonably well and ready to focus all his energies on the case. A few months ago, he would have finished the entire bottle and fallen into a dead sleep, an outcome he had desperately desired, but yesterday he'd set the bottle of brandy aside after two swigs. The brandy had helped him to sleep, and a good night's rest had done its work on his aching shoulder. It was still sore, but not nearly as painful as it had been yesterday, a clear indication that the damage had been superficial and the bone was intact.

Sebastian set off for Welbeck Street immediately after breakfast. He hoped there would be someone at the church who could answer his questions. It was a weekday, and he didn't know how often or at what time an Orthodox church normally held services.

His route brought him up behind the church, and he stood back to take in the view.

The Church of the Dormition was an oddly shaped building, painted a gleaming white. It seemed to consist of a cluster of asymmetrical add-ons topped with brown eaves that resembled raised eyebrows. A stubby tower that culminated in a blue and gold onion-shaped cupola rose above the roof, topped by an Orthodox cross that glinted in the morning light. A structure atop the roof that resembled a Greek temple or some rich man's folly housed several bells that were currently still and silent. Sebastian followed the fence and eventually came to the front of the building, which was shaped like a castle keep and boasted one long, rounded window directly above a rounded archway that led to the door.

The church was a classical architect's nightmare, and the lack of symmetry made Sebastian feel momentarily queasy and unbalanced at the wrongness of it all. This wasn't the norm for churches built in the East; he had seen depictions of ancient churches in Jerusalem and Constantinople and found them beautiful, with their gleaming cupolas and pleasing proportions. Perhaps this style was particular to Russia.

The door was unlocked. Relieved, Sebastian walked in. The interior was surprisingly spacious and not nearly as chaotic as the outside, probably because there were no pews or windows to fill the space. An iron chandelier was suspended high above, the candles lit to cast a flickering light onto the brilliantly colored icons on the far wall. Candlelight reflected off the gold leaf, giving the impression of movement and light. The narrow windows that dotted the tower allowed in feeble daylight, and there were two banners and recessed alcoves on either side of the business end of the church. A man of middle years wearing a floor-length black cassock and a black cylindrical headpiece came toward him, the elaborate cross that hung from a thick chain and reached nearly to his waist swaying gently as he walked.

"*Dobroye utro, moi sin,*" the priest said, and held out his right hand, palm down, the hand too high for a handshake. He seemed to expect Sebastian to kiss it.

"Good morning, Father," Sebastian said, but made no move

to take the man's hand or to kiss it, if that was what was expected.

The priest withdrew his hand and folded both hands across his middle. He studied Sebastian, his head cocked to the side. "I don't believe I've seen you here before," he said in English.

"My name is Sebastian Bell. I'm an inspector with Scotland Yard."

"Sebastian like your venerated saint?" the man said with what looked like a derisive smirk.

He clearly didn't think much of St. Sebastian, who had attained sainthood by first being shot full of arrows and then getting bludgeoned to death as soon as he had recovered from his injuries. Perhaps Russian saints had faced more romantic challenges, but Sebastian didn't know anything about the priest's faith and wasn't about to debate the merits of sainthood. He did suddenly recall that Simian used to refer to St. Sebastian as the "human pincushion" when he wanted to poke fun at his younger brother's name. An insult he had been forced to give up when Sebastian got big enough to knock him flat.

"Yes," Sebastian replied. "Like the saint. And you are?"

"Father Vitale. How can I help you, Mr. Bell? It's not often that we see a representative of the law in our holy church."

"I'm investigating the murder of a young girl, and I was hoping you might be able to answer a few questions for me."

"Is a member of our congregation a suspect?" Father Vitale asked, then his tone became more urgent as an alternate possibility presented itself. "Or the victim?"

"The victim is not of your faith, but perhaps the killer is."

"I will help you in any way I can," the priest said, but he wore a closed expression Sebastian had seen many times. Until the man knew precisely what Sebastian was after, he would not reveal anything that might incriminate a soul in his care.

Sebastian withdrew the ring and the cross from his pocket

and held them out for Father Vitale to see. The man bent over Sebastian's hand, peering at the objects in obvious surprise.

"How did you come by these items?" he asked.

"The ring was discovered hidden in the hem of the girl's dress, and the cross was left as a token by the mother of a boy consigned to the Foundling Hospital. What can you tell me about them?"

Father Vitale reached for the ring and studied it carefully, before returning it to Sebastian and picking up the cross. The chain dangled from his hand as he held up the cross to catch the light coming from the chandelier. He remained silent for several minutes, his expression thoughtful as he turned the cross over to check the back, then dropped it into Sebastian's outstretched hand.

"The cross is made of brass, but it's far from a cheap trinket."

"So, you're saying that these items would belong to persons of quality?" Sebastian asked.

"No simple peasant would possess such items unless he stole them," Father Vitale said. "The ring would be worn by a member of the nobility. And the cross is also worth quite a bit."

The priest's words were encouraging, since they supported the conclusions Sebastian and Gemma had already come to.

"What do these letters mean?" Sebastian pointed to the IC and XC on the longest crossbar.

"They stand for *Isus Christos*. Jesus Christ," Father Vitale explained. "The letters are Greek."

"And these? I don't recognize these letters," Sebastian said as he pointed to the four symbols above Christ's head.

"The letters are from the Cyrillic alphabet, and they mean Jesus of Nazareth, King of the Jews."

"So, would this cross belong to someone who's Russian Orthodox, or could the owner be Greek?" Sebastian asked, unsure what the two different languages meant in terms of the investigation.

"Definitely Russian," Father Vitale replied. He turned the cross over and showed Sebastian the inscription on the back. "This says, 'To our beloved son, Alexei.' This might have been given to a child on the day of his baptism, or perhaps later in life, a token of love to keep him safe." Father Vitale's dark eyes probed Sebastian's face. "You think the mother who left this cross is a member of this congregation?"

"She could be. Are there many Russian immigrants in London?" Sebastian asked.

"Not very many, and few are of noble birth. Of course, both items could have been stolen and smuggled into England. Do you believe they belong to the same person?"

"I think that's possible, given that they were both found at the Foundling Hospital. How likely is it that a member of the Russian nobility would leave a child at the Foundling Hospital in London?"

"Not very," Father Vitale said. "If a man of noble birth fathered a child out of wedlock, he would most likely see that the child was raised on his estate."

"Would he acknowledge the child?" Sebastian asked.

"No, but nor would he have reason to send the child to England to be brought up in an English orphanage."

"Unless the mother was English," Sebastian replied. "Do many British subjects visit Russia?"

"There are envoys to the Tzar's court, craftsmen, and sometimes tutors and nannies. The children of the nobility are well educated and encouraged to learn several languages. English is not uppermost on the list—French is the preferred language of the Russian nobility—but English and German have their place."

"The Russian nobility speak French?" Sebastian asked, confused.

Father Vitale smiled sadly. "Russian is perceived as coarse. The language of the peasants. To converse in French is to show one's refinement," he said with obvious disdain. "But this rejection of the mother tongue is also a grave insult to our history and our Church, so French is not spoken within these walls."

"I see," Sebastian said. "And what is the language of the Church?" He wasn't quite sure if the services were conducted in Russian, Greek, or possibly even Latin.

"The services are conducted in Church Slavonic. It's the language of our religion. Our *vera*," Father Vitale said reverently. "And our faith in the Redeemer is unshakable. There's even an icon that commemorates our undying devotion."

Father Vitale pointed a long, thin finger toward an icon mounted on the back wall. It was the head of Christ, but this Christ did not resemble the Jesus Sebastian was accustomed to seeing in religious paintings. His hair was darker, his gaze direct, and his face not nearly as gaunt. The background was solid gold leaf. "That, Inspector, is the Vera Icon. Not the original, of course. That one was painted in the twelfth century and will never leave Russia, but it is not to be confused with the one painted by that Dutch fellow," the priest said with a dismissive wave.

Sebastian stared into Christ's eyes and felt an unexpected sense of calm as the pieces of the puzzle slowly rearranged themselves in his mind, hazy outlines and muted colors beginning to form another religious image. Madonna and Child.

"Thank you, Father Vitale."

"You're welcome, Mr. Bell. I hope I was of help to you."

"You were," Sebastian assured him, but he was already on the move, sprinting toward the exit.

FORTY-ONE

Gemma walked sedately down the corridor, looking for all the world like she was precisely where she was supposed to be. This end of the corridor held several staff bedrooms, the last of which on the left belonged to Miss Parish. Until last month, Miss Parish had shared a room with Miss Brook, but Miss Brook had left to take up a position as a governess at a country house in Kent. Matron Holcombe had not yet hired a replacement, so Miss Parish was in the room alone.

Although Gemma had every intention of finding out the name of Ella's beau, she would have to wait until she saw Sebastian to discuss her suspicions. The opportunity to drug Gemma had been there, but she didn't know enough about Ella to decide if she'd had a motive. In the meantime, she meant to look more closely into Miss Parish, whose odd behavior had set off alarm bells in Gemma's mind.

Last night was the first time Faith Parish had come to the infirmary, and, although she had looked ill, Gemma supposed it wasn't impossible that she could have faked her symptoms. Since Gemma had no reason to suspect her of lying, she hadn't questioned her motives, but now that she had more information she couldn't ignore the facts. Miss Parish had complained of having a severe headache, and Gemma had turned her back on the woman to get her a headache powder, giving Miss Parish an opportunity to add laudanum to Gemma's tea. Gemma strongly suspected that Miss Parish had given her more than was necessary because she wasn't sure how much it would take to render her insensible and she'd needed her to sleep through the night.

Miss Parish had then stayed the night in the infirmary, and left in the morning in full view of Miss Landry and after making a comment about how tired Gemma had seemed. If she were seen wandering about in the middle of the night, she could simply say that she had needed to go to the cloakroom, since she had let it slip to Gemma that it was her time of the month. This gave her a solid alibi for a night during which Matron's office was broken into and the drawer containing the register forced. Coupled with Amanda's clothes being stolen, that could mean only one thing: Faith Parish had been searching for the ring and possibly another item, one that would be safely hidden within the pages of the register. What reason would she have to drug Gemma on a night when Miss Landry wasn't there if not to cover her tracks?

Although physically recovered, emotionally Gemma was still reeling. She was furious with Miss Parish, all the more so because Lucy could have been badly hurt by her actions; but Gemma was also angry with herself. She had lowered her guard, and her desire to help a woman in distress had blinded her to danger and left her open to serious harm. This was precisely the sort of thing Sebastian was always warning her about, and he would have a thing or two to say if he found out how easily she had been duped.

Taking a calming breath, Gemma pushed her feelings aside. She needed to focus on the task at hand or she would find herself at a disadvantage once again. She wasn't sure what she would find in Miss Parish's room, but a theory had begun to form in her mind, and what she needed more than anything was proof that she could present to Sebastian. She didn't think Faith Parish was foolish enough to leave anything in plain view, but perhaps she kept letters or a journal, or maybe Amanda's things were even now in her room, waiting to be disposed of.

Faith Parish would not have found the ring, because Sebastian had it, but perhaps she had taken whatever else she had been looking for. Would that be enough, or would she continue to search for the one object that she obviously thought could incriminate her? Since she wasn't aware that Gemma had found the ring in Amanda's dress and had turned it over to the police, Miss Parish might continue her efforts, desperate to reclaim what had to be hers.

Gemma slowed her step and waited to make certain she was alone. All the teachers would be on their way to Amanda's funeral, but Gemma had no desire to be caught breaking and entering in broad daylight with no ready excuse should someone be running late and happen to pass by. The corridor was quiet, no one about, so Gemma pulled out two hairpins and bent one. Having had a lot of practice, she was able to pick the lock much quicker this time, and then slipped inside before anyone could come along and ask what she was doing.

The room was spartan, the two beds neatly made, the writing desk by the window bare except for an inkwell and a pen. There were few personal belongings, and Gemma found nothing incriminating when she opened the desk drawers, then checked the trunk at the foot of the bed. There was a change of linen, two gowns, one wool and another muslin, spare stockings, and a pair of shoes. There was also a valise, but it was empty. Gemma turned in a circle, upset with herself for feeling so disappointed. She had been so sure that she would find something in Miss Parish's room, but perhaps the woman was innocent after all and Gemma was simply desperate to fit someone for the crime.

It was time she returned to the infirmary, so she walked to the door and put her ear to the seam between the door and the jamb, listening for any sound of movement outside. It was only when she turned her head to press it to the wood that she noticed a reflection in the window. The object stood on the windowsill and was hidden from view by the thick curtain, which was pulled back but not all the way. The windowpane behind it mirrored a sliver of bright red.

She walked over to the window and pulled aside the curtain, and nearly cried out in delight when she saw the object. It was a wooden doll, much like the one that had been clutched in Amanda's hand, only much bigger. The face was easier to make out, and the doll was taller and wider but had no limbs, only a painted body. Gemma lifted the doll and examined it more closely. She noticed a seam in the wood that ran right round the center of the doll, dividing it into a top and a bottom half. Gemma twisted the top and it came off, revealing an identical doll inside, only a little smaller. She repeated the process and before long had six dolls, the belly of the last one empty. The one that had been in Amanda's hand must be the seventh, smallest doll, which had to be the baby, since the dolls all bore the same face and seemed to represent a family. A terrible thought struck her; could Amanda have been with child? Or did the size of the doll not mean anything at all?

Whatever it meant, the dolls in Faith Parish's possession were a direct link to the little dolly found with Amanda. Gemma replaced the dolls inside one another, then set the thing where she'd found it, hiding it behind the curtain. Only then did she leave Faith Parish's room, shut the door without bothering to lock it, and hurried down the corridor. If her hunch proved correct, she knew precisely where, in about half an hour, she'd find Faith Parish.

FORTY-TWO

"You should go to the funeral," Miss Landry said. "I will remain with the children."

"Thank you, Miss Landry. That's very kind," Gemma replied, pleased that Miss Landry had offered. She had gone out of her way to be accommodating and Gemma didn't want to take advantage of her desire to help.

"If nothing else, at least you will get some fresh air. You still look peaky, Miss Tate," Miss Landry observed. "Perhaps you're sickening for something."

"It's been a distressing few days," Gemma replied as she reached for her cape and bonnet.

"That it has. Between you and me, I don't think that policeman is going to solve the case. You mark my words, Miss Tate. We won't be seeing him again after today."

"I think you might be right, Miss Landry."

"These policemen are all witless and useless, if you ask me. Can't manage to do a decent day's work, so they strut around, pretending to know something we don't. And what does he know, I ask you?" Miss Landry went on. "Nothing any of us didn't know already."

"If you will excuse me, Miss Landry. I don't want to be late for the funeral."

"Of course. I do wonder if there will be mourning biscuits," Miss Landry mused. "I wouldn't say no to a biscuit and a nice cup of tea."

"I will be sure to bring you one if there are," Gemma promised, and made her escape.

She bowed her head as she walked down the stairs, her mourning bonnet obscuring her face as she blended with other black-clad women and pale-faced orphans on their way to the chapel. No one paid Gemma any mind as she stopped to lace up her boot, taking her time until everyone had passed. Alone at last, she hurried toward the door that led to the cellar and made her way down the stairs as quietly as she could.

The passage was silent and almost completely dark, and Gemma wished she had a lantern, but it would have looked suspicious if she had brought a lantern to a funeral, and she didn't want to waste time going back. She could make out the distant glow of the sconce by Mr. Fletcher's room, the meager light of one candle just enough to navigate by. Gemma passed several storerooms, then slowed her step as she approached the laundry. The door was closed, but there was enough of a gap between the wood and the flagstone floor to see a narrow strip of light from within.

Gemma stood perfectly still, listening. She heard footsteps, then saw a shadow pass in front of the door. Someone was inside the room, and she didn't think it was one of the children. Gemma looked around, searching for a weapon, but, other than sacks of potatoes and onions and the iron sconce that was affixed to the wall, there was nothing to hand.

She could almost hear Sebastian's voice in her head, telling her to walk away and wait for him to arrive, but she just couldn't. In her infuriating ignorance, Miss Landry had struck a nerve, unwittingly voicing Gemma's own concerns.

The trail had gone cold, and once Amanda was buried Lovell would be under pressure to close the case. If Gemma didn't present him with irrefutable proof of guilt, Sebastian would have no choice but to admit defeat and walk away without solving the case. He was doing his best with the evidence he had, but Gemma was here, on the inside, and privy to information Sebastian couldn't hope to attain when there were those who'd see his inquiry obstructed in order to protect their own interests. Gemma was certain that the person within the room was the killer, and this was her only chance to confirm what she suspected and present Sebastian with a name.

After today, things would change. With Amanda buried, Matron would do everything in her power to thwart the investigation, and, even if the truth came to light, the governors would no doubt prefer to deal with the culprit internally and administer their own brand of justice. There were ways to destroy someone without paving their way to the gallows, especially if that someone happened to be a woman. To end one's life in a workhouse was a worse fate than the few moments it took the condemned to die. It was years and years of physical and emotional hardship with no escape in sight, the only way out in a pine box. The only bit of luck such a person could pray for was a premature death rather than prolonged suffering that would result in precisely the same bitter end.

Given what she was currently engaged in, Gemma realized she should worry more about her own prospects than the immediate future of the person within, but she couldn't let a child's death go unpunished. That went against everything she was and everything she believed in.

Realizing she might be at a disadvantage, she removed her bonnet and cape and set them on a nearby barrel. The cape would limit her mobility, and her mourning bonnet allowed her all the peripheral vision of a horse with blinkers on. Her heart thumped loudly and her hand trembled as she finally reached out to open the door.

The outer corners of the room were lost in shadow, but a figure clad in black crouched by the far wall, a lantern held just above the floor to illuminate the flagstones and the space beneath the drying rack. Fair hair glowed golden in the light of the flame, and a pale hand frantically patted the stones and swept beneath the rack.

Miss Parish whipped around at the sound of the opening door and for just a second looked deeply annoyed, but then she quickly rearranged her face into an expression of bland incomprehension.

"Miss Tate, what are you doing here?" she asked pleasantly.

"I could ask you the same question, Miss Parish."

"I came down here a few days ago and dropped a jeweled hairpin." Miss Parish pushed to her feet and set the lantern on a nearby stool. "It's only bits of colored glass really, but it's a pretty thing, and I was sorry to lose it."

"What were you doing in the laundry?" Gemma asked.

An expression of panic flitted across Miss Parish's face, but she recovered her composure almost immediately. "I came down to get a washboard."

"What use is a washboard outside the laundry? Do you launder your things in your room?"

"Oh, it's not for that," Miss Parish replied with an amused chuckle. "I wanted to use it in class. Everyday household items have been used to make music for centuries. People play the washboard, wooden spoons, and even bits of reed. They make them into whistles. I thought it would broaden the children's horizons."

"How clever," Gemma exclaimed. "Have you ever seen these instruments played?"

"I have."

"Was this while you were abroad?"

Faith Parish's expression instantly changed, and Gemma knew she'd made a terrible mistake. She'd revealed too much, and now the woman knew she was in danger. Seeing as she had already betrayed herself, Gemma pressed on.

"Why did you kill Amanda, Faith? Was it because she wouldn't give back the ring?"

If Faith Parish was surprised that Gemma knew about the ring, she didn't show it. All Gemma saw was single-minded determination to turn the situation to her own advantage.

"Give me the ring, and we'll say no more about this," Miss Parish said, her tone wheedling.

"But it seems there is so much more to say," Gemma countered.

"Do you have it?" Miss Parish demanded, all pretense at friendliness gone.

"I did, but I gave it to Inspector Bell."

Miss Parish's face twisted with fury. "You stupid woman! Why'd you have to go and do that?"

"Because a child is dead, and the killer can't be allowed to go free."

"It didn't belong to her," Miss Parish shrieked. "I asked her to give it back, and to release Alexei from his promise."

"Is that Michael's real name?" Gemma asked. "Alexei?"

Faith's eyes widened when she realized she'd revealed too much. "How did you know it was Michael?"

"Because he admitted to planning a future with Amanda, and because, now that I know the truth, I can see the resemblance. You are Michael's mother."

"Alexei." She said it softly, and the name sounded like a prayer that came straight from the heart. "That's the name I called him in my heart. But I wasn't permitted to use it. Not ever. Everything I did was to protect my son," Miss Parish cried. "Surely you can understand that."

"I can understand everything short of murder," Gemma replied.

Miss Parish's face twisted with anger, the delicate features of a beautiful woman transforming into the predatory snarl of a lioness. Her gaze was fixed on Gemma as though she was evaluating her options and deciding where best to strike. As long as Sebastian didn't know who the ring belonged to he wasn't an immediate threat, but if Gemma got the chance to tell him what she'd learned, Faith Parish was bound for the gallows. Her eyes resembled chips of blue glass, her glare pulsating with purpose, and it was to kill or be killed.

Gemma's thoughts slowed, her breathing becoming even and deep as some primal instinct took over, reducing her entire existence to one all-important moment. Gemma had never intentionally hurt anyone in her life. She had chosen nursing because she longed to help those in pain and ease their suffering, but she knew she would have to resort to violence in order to survive this day. Whatever act of savagery she was forced to resort to would have to count, because she wouldn't get a second chance.

Faith charged, flying at Gemma like a deranged wildcat. Her lips were pulled back, her eyes blazing with murderous intent. Time seemed to stand still when in fact only a few seconds had ticked by as the space between the two women narrowed. Faith's best bet would have been to strike Gemma with the heavy lantern, but the thought had clearly not occurred to her, which gave Gemma an advantage. She dipped down and grabbed the handle of a coopered oak bucket that had been left by the wall.

Swinging her arm out, Gemma whipped the heavy bucket around with all her might. The wood created a blurred arc as it passed through the glow of the light from the lantern. Miss Parish roared with pain as the bottom of the bucket collided with the side of her head, knocking her against the stone wall and bringing her to her knees.

The blow was enough to stun and to hurt, but not to immobilize the woman for long. Gemma knew she had mere moments before Faith was back on her feet and angrier than before, her desperation now fueled by physical pain. Gemma dropped the bucket, since she had no intention of bludgeoning the woman to death, and threw herself at Faith, forcing her onto her stomach and wrenching her arms behind her back until Faith gasped with shock. Gemma straddled Faith to keep her down, but she had nothing to bind her wrists with and couldn't afford to release her for even a second since that would give her an advantage she would no doubt exploit. She was thrashing wildly and growling with the effort to free herself. Her temple was the color of raw liver, and a trickle of blood crept down her cheek from where the bucket had punctured the skin.

Suddenly seeing an opportunity, Gemma bent low and used her teeth to pull on the ties of Faith's pinafore, releasing the bow. Once the ties were free and lying between Gemma's knees, she used her thighs to keep her prisoner's arms in place and quickly wrapped the ties around Faith's wrists, securing them as tightly as she could without cutting off the woman's circulation.

It was at that moment that the door burst open to reveal Sebastian, with Constable Bryant just behind him.

"Blimey!" Constable Bryant exclaimed when he saw the two women wrestling on the floor.

Gemma almost burst into hysterical laughter when she registered Sebastian's expression at seeing Miss Parish's wrists bound with the strings of her own pinafore and Gemma straddling her like a pony. His face was a blend of shock, disbelief, admiration, and, dare she say it, pride.

"Constable, cuff her," Sebastian instructed, then strode

toward the two women and lifted Gemma off her prey, the reckless move causing him to groan with pain.

Gemma's legs wobbled, and the hair that had come out of its remaining pins fell into her face. Her cap was on the floor, her pinafore was creased and not quite centered, and there was a long tear in her stocking from where it had snagged on the corner of a flagstone.

Momentarily free, Faith Parish flipped onto her back and tried to kick Sebastian, but Constable Bryant grabbed her beneath the arms and hauled her to her feet, pushing her up against the wall in case she should try again to fight her way out.

"Are you all right?" Sebastian asked as he took in Gemma's disheveled appearance.

Her breath was coming in short gasps, and she no doubt looked completely feral. She nodded, and saw relief in Sebastian's eyes. He had been frightened for her. Reassured that Gemma wasn't hurt, he now looked incensed.

"What did you think you were doing?" he demanded. "You could have been seriously hurt."

"She murdered Amanda," Gemma sputtered.

"I know," Sebastian said, unwittingly taking the wind out of Gemma's sails.

"You know? How?" She gaped at him, her chest still heaving, as she waited for an explanation.

"She's Michael's mother. But you solved the case," Sebastian was quick to point out. "You caught the killer, Gemma."

That pacified her somewhat, but she wasn't quite finished. "I found proof in her room. She has the same wooden dolly, only larger. I think it might be Russian since the doll is painted wearing what looks like a Slavic costume."

"There's other proof as well," Sebastian said. "I paid a visit to the Church of the Dormition and learned some interesting things."

"I'm coming with you to Scotland Yard. I want to be there when you charge her."

Sebastian looked like he was about to argue, but then the urge seemed to pass and his eyes glowed with pride as he smiled at her.

"You've earned this, Inspector Tate," he said.

Gemma grinned like a loon at the unexpected form of address.

Now that she was safe and all the fight had gone out of her, she began to tremble, her eyes filled with tears, and her lips quivered as she tried desperately not to cry. She didn't want to give in to hysterics, but her emotions overwhelmed her, and she didn't know how to come to terms with what she had just done.

Recognizing her distress, Sebastian pulled her into his arms and held her close, brushing his lips against her temple as he promised her that all would be well. Gemma was glad Faith Parish wasn't there to see her fall apart—Constable Bryant had already maneuvered her out of the laundry and toward the stairs.

"Come now," Sebastian said. "We need to get her to Scotland Yard."

Gemma retrieved her cape and bonnet, rewound her hair, and pinned it up before putting on her bonnet and following Sebastian up the stairs and out into the courtyard. The morning was cold and overcast, tiny flurries swirling in the air and landing on her nose and cheeks when she lifted her face to the colorless sky. Gemma inhaled deeply, grateful for the bracing freshness and the wide wings of the bonnet that hid her face from the mourners who, now that the funeral was over, were filing into the courtyard. Everyone stared, amazed to see Miss Parish escorted outside by a policeman and handed into the police wagon that waited near the door.

Gemma caught sight of Faith Parish just before Constable

Bryant shut the doors. She was sitting on the bench, her face deathly white, her hair in disarray, and an old, moth-eaten blanket carelessly draped over her shoulders for warmth. She had the look of a prisoner heading to their execution, and Gemma realized that such a scenario probably wasn't too far-fetched.

Constable Bryant climbed onto the bench and reached for the reins.

"We'll find our own way back, Constable," Sebastian informed him. "See that Miss Parish remains cuffed."

"Yes, sir," Constable Bryant said, and snapped the reins. The wagon lurched forward.

"We could have fitted," Gemma said as she watched the wagon make its stately way toward the gates and turn into the street beyond.

"We could have, but I think you are in need of a strong drink, Inspector," he teased.

"I won't say no to a small sherry," Gemma replied shakily.

"Then a sherry you shall have."

"Where on earth do you think you're going, Miss Tate?" Matron Holcombe called out as she approached them, her cheeks pink with outrage against the black satin of her bonnet and her skirts swishing violently in the gathering wind.

"I'm afraid Miss Landry will have to cover for Miss Tate for the remainder of the day, Matron," Sebastian said. "She solved the case and has apprehended the perpetrator. She is coming to Scotland Yard to give a statement."

Matron's mouth fell open, and she glared at Gemma, but she refrained from saying anything since the mourners returning from the graveyard were beginning to gather around them.

"I trust we will see you tomorrow, Miss Tate?" she inquired instead.

"Of course, Matron."

"Good day to you both, then," Matron said, and marched inside.

Sebastian offered Gemma his arm, and they walked along at a relaxed pace, as if they were promenading in the park rather than heading to a tavern to imbibe spirits before noon and then to Scotland Yard to question a killer.

FORTY-THREE

Sergeant Woodward and Constable Forrest followed Gemma's progress across the duty room with mute incomprehension, but didn't dare comment. Gemma thought that Constable Bryant had filled them in on the details of Faith Parish's arrest and they were probably shocked, or more likely appalled, by the role she had played in subduing the suspect, and clearly couldn't fathom what she was doing at Scotland Yard or why she was heading toward the interview rooms.

Gemma averted her gaze, because despite the outcome she was quite embarrassed. Never before had she engaged in a physical altercation with anyone, at least not since she and Victor were about four years old and had come to blows over the rocking horse they had received as a birthday present from their grandparents. Victor wouldn't let Gemma have a turn, and she had pulled him off the horse and shoved him to the floor. She had climbed on before their mother could intervene, and had enjoyed a merry ride until she was lifted off by their father and sent to the nursery for the rest of the day as punishment for her bad behavior.

"Is Superintendent Lovell in his office?" Sebastian asked.

"Just came back from lunch, as it happens," Sergeant Wood-ward replied. "And pleased as punch that you've made an arrest."

"You always get your man, or woman," Constable Forrest gushed.

"It was Miss Tate who solved the case and apprehended the suspect, and I have invited her to sit in on the interview," Sebastian said.

"So we heard," Sergeant Woodward replied, his eyes dancing with amusement. "Will it be bare-knuckle fighting next, Miss Tate? I reckon that would draw a lively crowd."

"Mind your manners, Sergeant," Sebastian growled. "You're speaking to a lady."

"I can think of a few names for women that carry on like men, but a lady ain't one of them. What's next, women on the police service?" Sergeant Woodward muttered under his breath. Gemma felt Sebastian stiffen beside her, and laid a restraining hand on his wrist.

"The world will surely go to hell in a handbasket then," Constable Meadows, who'd just walked in, joked, and grinned at Gemma approvingly. "Shall I release Matthew Campbell, then?"

"Not yet," Sebastian replied. "I'd like to hear what Miss Parish has to say before we let him go. Perhaps she had an accomplice."

"That's good thinking, that is," Constable Forrest said. The young man was clearly a bit starstruck.

"Constable, please bring Miss Parish to interview room one," Sebastian told Constable Meadows.

"Yes, sir."

"And you and I will have a quiet word later," he told Sergeant Woodward. "In the alley."

"I was just joking, Bell," the sergeant said, and smiled nervously, but Sebastian clearly wasn't amused and looked like he had every intention of teaching the sergeant some basic manners.

"You will apologize to Miss Tate this minute, Sergeant," Sebastian said, his voice low but deadly.

Sergeant Woodward looked like he might have soiled himself a little. He rearranged his face into an expression of toadying civility. "Please, accept my apologies, Miss Tate."

Gemma inclined her head but refrained from answering. The last thing she wanted was for Sebastian to engage in an altercation with the sergeant on her behalf. She felt conspicuous enough as it was, but the man had been terribly rude and she wasn't about to let him off the hook.

"Please, let's not speak of it again," she said to Sebastian, who was clearly still angry but realized that she wanted only to forget the insult and leave the duty room.

Sebastian glared at Sergeant Woodward one last time, then escorted Gemma down the corridor and into a utilitarian room furnished with a scarred wooden table fitted with an iron ring and surrounded by four chairs. There was also a coat rack in the corner, so Gemma took off her cape and hung it up, then removed her bonnet and patted her hair into place. She would need to purchase a few more hairpins, since the ones she had used to pick the locks were too bent to be of further use.

Sebastian hung up his coat and hat as well, then pulled out a chair for Gemma and took a seat next to her. There was nothing particularly oppressive about the room in itself, but, like so many places that had been witness to strong emotion, the very walls seemed to radiate despair. Gemma could just imagine how many suspects had sat in those chairs, their hands cuffed to the table, their fate sealed. Some had been executed, their remains tossed into paupers' graves, while others had gone to prison or been transported to Botany Bay, where they'd still perished, only much slower as they starved to death or fell victim to illness.

Gemma watched as Constable Meadows escorted Faith Parish into the room and held out a chair for her. Faith looked confused, her gaze darting from Sebastian to Gemma, as if she couldn't quite work out why she was there. The heavy cuffs dragged her wrists down so her shoulders drooped, and when she sat down she seemed to fold in on herself, drawing in her head like a tortoise.

"You can uncuff her, Constable," Sebastian said, his gaze on the frightened woman before him. "Try anything and I will change my mind," he told Faith.

She nodded and held out her hands, and shook them out when the iron cuffs were removed. Constable Meadows handed the cuffs to Sebastian along with the key, and Sebastian set them on the table, the iron clattering against the wood.

Faith Parish stared at the cuffs with obvious fear, then folded her hands before her like a timid schoolgirl. Her delicate wrists were red and raw from the cuffs, even though she'd worn them for no more than an hour, and her gown reeked of sweat despite the cold ride she must have endured in the police wagon. Gemma knew that odor. It was the smell of fear and defeat. Faith bowed her head and stared at her hands, but looked up again when Sebastian addressed her.

"What is your name?"

"Faith Parish."

"Your real name," Sebastian countered.

Faith looked surprised, and then nodded as if acknowledging that she had been found out. "Vera Canton," she replied calmly.

"Clever," Sebastian said, seemingly impressed with whatever it was Miss Parish had done.

Gemma shot him a questioning look.

"Vera means belief, or should I say faith, in Russian. I just learned that from Father Vitale at the Church of the Dormition. And canton is another word for parish, so Vera Canton became Faith Parish when it suited her to disguise her identity."

The explanation seemed to surprise Miss Parish, or Miss Canton, and Gemma saw a spark of admiration in her gaze— and something else. A flash of desire, followed by a slow, seductive smile. Gemma felt an unexpected jolt of anger, but quickly tamped down her jealousy. Sebastian did not belong to her, but neither would he belong to the likes of Vera Canton. She was simply trying to unbalance him, a tactic that would never work; Sebastian was too clever by half and not susceptible to calculated female flattery.

He completely ignored Vera's feigned admiration and continued. "I assume you changed your name in order to obtain employment at the Foundling Hospital?"

"You tell us," Miss Canton replied tartly. "You seem to be the one with all the answers."

"All right. If you insist."

Sebastian took out the ring Gemma had found, and a chain, and held up the latter so that the two women had a clear view of the cross that swayed gently beneath Sebastian's hand. Gemma had never seen anything like it and tried to make out the details. She was astounded by how many symbols and images fit together in such a limited space. The workmanship was truly impressive, and the necklace had to be very valuable. Vera blanched when she saw the items, and her eyes shimmered with tears. Her reaction appeared to be sincere, but she remained silent, unwilling to offer an explanation.

"Still don't want to tell me?" Sebastian asked softly.

Vera shook her head and used the back of her hand to wipe away the tears that silently slid down her cheeks.

"All right. Then I will tell you the story I have pieced together, and you can tell me if I got it right."

Vera stared at Sebastian, as if willing him to be wrong, but Gemma could see in her eyes that she was genuinely frightened. She hadn't expected to be presented with damning evidence and had probably only just realized that Sebastian knew more than she had initially thought and could build a convincing case against her.

"Approximately fifteen years ago, you found yourself in Russia," Sebastian began, his voice melodious as if he were telling a bedtime story rather than driving nails into the coffin of a condemned woman. "I expect you went there to work as a governess, or perhaps you had accompanied someone on a trip since you must have been very young. Around sixteen?" he asked, and Vera nodded. "You met a Russian nobleman whose Christian name was Alexei."

"How do you know that?" Vera cried.

Sebastian turned the cross over and pointed to the inscription on the back. "It says so right here. *To our beloved son, Alexei.* At first, I thought you might have commissioned the inscription before leaving the cross at the Foundling Hospital and it referred to your own beloved son, but the inscription is smooth to the touch, which tells me that this cross was worn for many years before it came to you. A fresh inscription would feel serrated."

Vera bowed her head and nodded. "Yes," she whispered at last.

"I assume you had an affair, since your lover gave you a cross that was clearly precious to him, as well as his ring," Sebastian mused. "Or maybe you stole the items and brought them back to England, either as keepsakes or as insurance should the situation become dire. I don't know about the cross, but the ring is solid gold and would fetch a respectable sum."

"I didn't steal anything," Vera cried, her cheeks growing a mottled pink with outrage.

"All right," Sebastian conceded. "So he gave you the items willingly. Presumably this man loved you?"

Vera nodded again and sniffled miserably.

"You left the cross as a token for your boy and kept the ring, since it was too valuable to part with. Now, my theory is that once Michael, or Alexei, as you have always thought of him, got older and came closer to leaving the Foundling Hospital, you devised a plan. You obtained a position as a music teacher so you could have access to the child you had given up. I expect you wanted to forge a relationship with your son before you told him the truth, so that he wouldn't reject you and blame you for giving him away. Then, when you judged the time to be right, you told Michael the truth of his parentage and gave him the ring to support your claims."

Vera's head bobbed up and down in confirmation.

"But Michael, whose affections had been engaged elsewhere since he was a small boy, gave the ring to Amanda, as a token of his love," Sebastian said, finally eliciting a verbal reaction.

"Amanda had no right to that ring, or to my Alexei. He has a bright future ahead of him. More so now."

"Why now?" Gemma asked.

Vera gave her a sneering look. "Because he's Prince Alexei Sorokin's only surviving son."

"Prince Sorokin?" Sebastian repeated, his brows knitting as he clearly tried to recall something. "I've seen that name quite recently."

Vera brightened. "Alexei's father and his son, Oleg, were killed in a railway crash in November. Alexei is now free to acknowledge his firstborn."

"Does he know he has another son?" Gemma asked.

"He does now," Vera replied, and smiled slyly. "I wrote to him as soon as I read about the accident."

"Did he reply?" Sebastian asked.

Vera shook her head, but she didn't seem disappointed or upset by the lack of communication. "It takes a long time for a letter to reach St. Petersburg, especially during the winter months. But he will," she replied confidently. "Alexei will write to me."

"How did you meet Alexei?" Gemma asked.

She was genuinely curious. To her, Russia seemed as far away as the moon, a land of thick forests, wide rivers, and windy steppes, its people foreign and rugged, and tragically oppressed. Her only point of reference was the stories she had heard from some of her patients at Scutari, but even from them it wasn't difficult to deduce that Russia was a land of great extremes. It was much like England, where the wealthy spent a fortune on hothouse flowers and imported delicacies while the poor could barely afford food or coal, and feared the winter months, since they were a true test of endurance for anyone who led a hand-to-mouth existence.

Vera's cheek and temple were red and bruised from where Gemma had hit her with the bucket, and her left eye was beginning to swell, but her good eye clouded with what had to be a beautiful memory because, when she began to speak, her words seemed more for herself than for the two people in the room with her.

"My father was an architect. Philip Canton. He was quite well known in his day," Vera said, her voice tinged with pride. "Alexei's father had visited England when he was a young man and had fallen in love with the Georgian manor house where he'd been a guest. It couldn't compare to the baroque splendor of the palaces in St. Petersburg, but he wanted to recreate the house on his estate near Levashovo. It was to be his summer residence, what he called his *dacha*, and he chose Father based on glowing testimonials from his friends in England." Vera sighed, the pride now replaced by sorrow.

"My mother had died the year before Father was offered the commission, so he brought me along. Father thought it would help us in our grief and would be a good way to slowly come out of mourning." Vera gave Sebastian a defiant look. "It's no small thing to design and build a house, especially in a country that has a rhythm all its own and where the workers answer only to their masters. Father had to rely on Prince Sorokin's serfs for labor, but they had other jobs to do on the estate. These men were mostly farmers, not skilled builders, but they were free labor as far as Prince Sorokin was concerned, so Father had to make do. Only a few had experience in construction, and they knew how to build mostly wooden cabins, not brick manor houses. And of course there was the problem of obtaining the bricks, since they weren't as popular in construction there as they are in England and had to be specially ordered and shipped. It was quite an undertaking."

Vera sighed.

"I hardly saw Father. He was always on-site, while I was left behind at Prince Sorokin's St. Petersburg residence. It was finer than any manor house I had ever seen before or since. Of course, I was treated with every courtesy, but I wasn't part of the family, or one of the servants, which left me only the children's governess to converse with, and she spoke mostly French. And then I met Alexei."

Vera smiled wistfully, and Gemma got the impression that she was no longer looking at the two people across from her but had turned inward and was reliving cherished memories that she probably hadn't shared with anyone in fifteen years for fear of betraying her shame. Perhaps the only person who knew the truth was Michael, but the version she had presented to him might have been altered to make Vera appear tragic and respectable.

"Please, go on," Sebastian invited her when Vera paused and glanced toward the small window that bathed the room in a nearly white light. Snow had begun to fall, and the world beyond looked pure and white, and as unspoiled as a bride on her wedding day. Probably much as Vera herself had looked when she'd first met the man who'd changed her life.

"Alexei had just graduated from the Military Academy and would be joining his regiment in September. His parents wanted him home for the summer so he could attend the various entertainments organized by their friends and spend some time with his younger sisters," Vera explained. "Nina and Sveta worshipped him, and dreamed of marrying one of his friends so they could always move in the same circles."

Her expression grew sad. "Alexei realized right away that I was terribly lonely and felt out of place. Days can be very long when you have no one to talk to—or even a book to read, since all the books in the library were in Russian or French. Alexei had learned some English at the Academy and made it a point to speak to me whenever he was at home, which was mostly in the mornings since he had various social engagements later in the day. He was kind, and so beautiful."

Vera was now absentmindedly pleating the fabric of her sleeve, clearly agitated despite the precious moments she was recounting. "Alexei couldn't invite me to social gatherings, since I wasn't of his class and questions would be asked by the parents of the titled girls who would be his prospective brides once he was ready to marry, but he showed me the city he loved and took me to all the places only a native would be familiar with. He rented a boat and rowed us out on the Neva, and even took me fishing when we visited Levashovo. We were completely alone, just sitting side by side on a riverbank dappled in sunshine, the only sounds the rushing of the river and the singing of the birds. Those days were absolute bliss."

"But they didn't last, did they?" Sebastian said.

Vera shook her head, her gaze fixed on the falling snow. "In the autumn, Alexei reported to the 1st Guards Corps to begin his military service. The corps was part of the Imperial Guard and was stationed in St. Petersburg, so we still saw each other. Alexei frequently dined with his parents, since the barracks were just a few streets over from Prince Sorokin's palace, and he had a few days' leave every month. Alexei said he loved me. And I loved him. I wanted to stay in Russia forever," Vera said, her expression dreamy. "Oh, I loved it, with its vast skies, silver birch forests, and fields ripe with wheat. I can still hear the peasants singing as they worked in the fields. Their songs were always mournful. A cry of the soul, someone once called them, and then I understood, even though I couldn't follow the words. They were songs about freedom."

"The songs of slaves usually are," Sebastian said sharply.

"These people didn't know any other life," Vera said with a delicate shrug. "They loved their masters and saw them as benevolent benefactors, like parents assigned to them by God. I suppose you think that's barbaric, but they were certainly better off than the multitudes who don't know where their next meal is coming from or if they will survive the winter," she went on defensively. "They were looked after."

"So, what happened then?" Sebastian asked, clearly not interested in debating the pros and cons of indentured servitude. "Did this man seduce you and leave you?"

"No," Vera said simply. "He asked me to marry him."

She smiled, and her battered face lit up with the remembered joy of that moment. "It was in December, and the world was white, but not like this," she remarked, gesturing toward the window. "Alexei came to collect me from the house in St. Petersburg. He had a sleigh pulled by a white troika waiting outside. The horses were perfectly matched, and the harness was painted with bright colors and fitted with bells. And the sleigh looked like some magical ship. We sped across the wintry landscape, the deep snowdrifts no match for the sleigh's runners. There was only the snorting of the horses and the jingling of the bells to disturb the silence. And the wind. Always the wind."

Gemma could sense Sebastian's mounting impatience. He wanted facts, not detailed descriptions of pretty horses and

Russian sleighs. But if he wanted the truth, or Vera's version of it, he would have to allow her to tell the story in her own time.

"Please, go on," he prompted again when Vera seemed to have retreated into a daydream.

"Alexei took me to a lovely old church. It was just there, in the middle of nowhere, an ancient wooden building with six copper domes all clustered together like mushrooms. There were crows perched on the crosses, and they watched us as we pulled up, and then they took off, squawking as if they could foretell my doom, their wings black against the pale blue sky."

Vera's gaze cleared and she looked directly at Gemma, as if she somehow thought Gemma would understand what she had felt that day. "I thought Alexei took me out because it was Christmas and he wanted to acknowledge that, since Christmas is not celebrated in Russia until January seventh, but he had a different plan," Vera gushed. "It was to be our wedding day. The elderly priest and the peasant who drove the sleigh were our witnesses, and we signed our names in the register as Alexei Sorokin and Vera Sorokina. We were man and wife, and no one could put us asunder. Or so I thought," she added sadly. "After the ceremony, we met Alexei's friends in a nearby village. They had taken over the tavern, and there was vodka and food and hot, sweet tea with *pryaniki*, and a band of gypsies playing fiddles and balalaikas and singing. Their songs weren't mournful," Vera reflected. "They were fast, and joyful, and pulsating with passion, and the women stomped their feet as they danced and twirled their colorful skirts until I was dizzy with happiness. It was the most magical night of my life."

"So, what went wrong?" Sebastian asked, a tad sarcastically.

But Gemma didn't need to ask. She could imagine all too well what had happened once Prince Sorokin discovered that his naïve young son had married the daughter of the English architect in a secret ceremony. It wasn't uncommon for wealthy and powerful men to bed the servants, but one didn't marry them, not when a glittering future lay ahead. Alexei would take his place among the Russian *ton* and eventually inherit his father's title and estate, unless his regiment wound up in Crimea and his blood was spilled onto its rocky soil.

Vera began to cry softly, tears rolling down her pale cheeks. This was no longer a beautiful memory but the worst day of her life, the day that had changed everything and led to this moment, this stark room, and Vera's terrifying reality.

"Ivan Ilyich—that's Alexei's father—said that the marriage wasn't valid because I was never baptized into the Russian Orthodox Church. He told Alexei that the entry in the register had been erased, the priest sent to Siberia for performing a marriage he knew would not be sanctioned by the groom's parents, and the coachman whipped for acting as witness. The summer house was nearly finished by then, only the interior still required some finishing touches, so Father and I were told to leave, our trunks packed within the hour, and a plain brown sleigh waiting by the back door to take us away. Alexei pressed his cross and his ring into my hand and swore he would convince his father to change his mind, but I never saw him again," Vera said, her voice flat now, as if she were recounting simple facts.

She sighed heavily, her shoulders drooping. "There were no trains in Russia then, the Neva was frozen solid, and no captain in his right mind would set sail until late spring. Father found us lodgings on the outskirts of the city, and we remained in St. Petersburg until April, when the river finally began to thaw, and we were able to find passage to England. By the time we arrived in London, it was May and I was five months along, so there was no hiding the truth. I had tried writing to Alexei, but I'm certain my letters were destroyed. He would have replied had he known."

"So, it was your father's decision to give Michael to the Foundling Hospital?" Gemma asked, feeling sympathy for the woman despite everything she had done. Her life had been destroyed, her child ripped from her, while Alexei had eventually gone on to marry and father a son, and possibly a few daughters.

"Yes," Vera said simply. "I begged and pleaded and promised Father that he'd never have to see the child if he allowed him to remain, but he refused. He said I had shamed him, and he wouldn't allow me to raise a bastard in full view of the neighbors and his friends. He thought Alexei had tricked me and the marriage was just a cruel prank. If I refused to take the child to the Foundling Hospital, Father said, he would leave him at some other, far worse place. The only concession Father made was to allow me to say goodbye and to leave Alexei's cross for my son. He made me promise never to seek him out."

"But you broke that promise," Sebastian pointed out.

Vera smiled sadly. "I thought of my boy every minute of every hour, and prayed that he was alive and that someday I would have the chance to know him and love him. Father died two years ago, and I was finally free. I assumed Alexei was married, but I finally had a chance to find my son, and I wasn't going to let anything get in the way of that."

"And then Alexei's father and son died unexpectedly," Sebastian said. "Did you think you would return to Russia and Michael would take his rightful place?"

Vera nodded. "Alexei would acknowledge him. I was sure of it. And with his second son dead, our boy would inherit the title and the estate."

"That was a lovely dream," Sebastian said. "And maybe it would have come to pass if you hadn't murdered the girl your son loved."

"I never meant to kill her!" Vera cried. "I only wanted to talk to her. To explain. But she wouldn't listen to reason. And she refused to return the ring."

"So you attacked her, slammed her against the wall, and then drowned her in a tub of icy water," Sebastian spat out.

"I did it to free my son," Vera exclaimed. "I did it for my Alexei. He was always destined for greater things."

"So you murdered one child to free another," Gemma said.

"Only one child mattered to me," Vera replied unapologetically.

"This was in Amanda's hand when she died," Sebastian said. He took out the tiny dolly and set it on the table.

Vera nodded. "I gave that to Michael. It was the baby from a nesting doll. A *matryoshka*. Predictably, he gave that to Amanda as well."

"Why was it in her hand?" Gemma asked.

"Because she tried to give it to me," Vera replied. "But I didn't want a peg of wood. I wanted Alexei's ring. I turned out her pockets, but the ring wasn't there. I expect Amanda hid it in a safe place, but the dolly was of no value, so she carried it in her pocket like a talisman. Much good it did her," Vera scoffed. "Where did you find the ring?"

"It was sewn into the hem of Amanda's dress," Gemma replied. "I found it, and I found the nesting doll in your room. That's what gave you away."

Vera sighed again, only this time with disappointment. "I genuinely liked you, Miss Tate. You seemed like a nice woman, the sort who would understand another woman's plight and feel sympathy for what she had suffered through, but you turned out to be quite the Judas, didn't you?"

"You liked me so much that you drugged me in order to create an alibi for the night you broke into Matron's office?" Gemma retorted. "How did you manage to look so ill?"

For a brief moment, Vera looked quite pleased with herself. "Oh, it wasn't hard. I applied rice powder to my face and used atropine drops to dilate my pupils. You can find the drops at any chemist, did you know that? Some women use them to enhance their appearance. Such vanity," she said with disgust.

"Yes, I'm familiar with atropine," Gemma admitted. She was annoyed with herself for not having considered the possibility that Faith had used drops derived from belladonna to dilate her pupils.

"I had to get the cross back," Vera went on. "And you looked like you could use a good night's sleep." A spiteful smirk crossed her face.

"Why did you ask Amanda to meet you down in the laundry?" Sebastian asked.

"Because it was a quiet, private place. Michael's handwriting is very similar to mine, so she thought the note was from him. That was the only reason she came."

"And the water in the tub?" Gemma asked. "Did you prepare that in advance?"

Vera shook her head. "The water was there. Someone forgot to empty out the tub. The drowning wasn't premeditated, if that's what you're thinking, but once I went for Amanda I couldn't allow her to live. She would have told Matron, and the truth would have come out."

"So what if it did?" Gemma exclaimed. "Michael is fourteen. You could have worked on your relationship with him once he left the Foundling Hospital."

Vera shot Gemma a derisive look, as if she were an even bigger fool than Vera had taken her for. "First, I would never find another respectable post, not once Matron was done with me, and I do need an income, Miss Tate. And second, I had to separate my son from that girl. As long as she held on to him, he would never agree to travel to Russia to meet his father."

"Did you have any accomplices, Miss Canton?" Sebastian asked.

Vera shook her head. "I allowed Matthew Campbell to court me because I was lonely, but I have remained faithful to Alexei. We might not be together, but he's still my husband in the eyes of God, and in my heart." Vera exhaled heavily. "I never told Matthew the truth, even though I don't think he would have judged me too harshly. I would have broken things off with him once Alexei and I were ready to leave."

"What about Ella Boone?" Gemma asked. She never had found out what Ella's beau's name was and if he was in any way involved.

"Ella Boone? What's she to do with this?" Vera asked, very obviously surprised by the question.

Her reaction was enough to put Gemma's mind at ease on that score. Even if Ella knew Archie, their association did not seem to have any bearing on the case.

"How much did Michael know of what transpired in the laundry?" Sebastian asked, deftly redirecting the conversation. Gemma noticed that he refused to call Michael by his Russian name, and thought he did it to annoy Vera. An angry woman was more likely to talk.

"He knew nothing. I swear," she cried. "Alexei would never forgive me if he found out I killed Amanda."

"Yet he was ill on the morning Amanda was found dead. Quite a coincidence," Sebastian replied.

"Alexei is a very sensitive boy," Vera said. "He must have sensed that something was wrong. It's not a crime to feel ill, Inspector."

"And you told him nothing once he realized that Amanda was dead?" Gemma interjected.

"No, of course not. I offered him love and support. Alexei would never understand that I did it all for him, so that he could have a family at last."

"And now he will be left all alone in the world," Gemma said softly. "With no mother to love him or Amanda to build a future with."

"He knows about his father. Alexei will take his rightful place!" Vera cried.

"I hope for his sake that his father will be willing to help him, or Michael will become just another foot soldier in an army that uses young men as cannon fodder and dumps them in unmarked graves," Sebastian replied cruelly.

"Please, don't question him, Inspector Bell," Vera begged. "I swear to you on Alexei's life that he knew nothing. He's hurting enough as it is without being accused of withholding information in order to protect his mother."

Vera began to weep in earnest, and Gemma had to admit that she could understand her pain. Love and hope for the future had been the driving forces in Vera's life since her baby had been born, and to know that she had failed and would never get to see her son grow into a man and reconnect with his heritage had to be heartbreaking.

"Will I hang?" Vera asked suddenly, the gravity of her situation finally sinking in.

"I don't pass the sentence," Sebastian said. "That's up to the court."

"But you have enough evidence to prove my guilt?" Vera asked, her eyes wide with horror.

"I do." Sebastian stood and faced her, his expression grave. "Vera Canton, I hereby charge you with the murder of Amanda Carter, aged fourteen. You will be transferred to Coldbath Fields Prison to await trial."

Vera continued to sob as Sebastian opened the door and summoned Constable Meadows, who would take her down to the cells to await transportation.

"Release Mr. Campbell," Sebastian told the constable. "He's free to go."

"Yes, sir," Constable Meadows said, and disappeared down the corridor, Vera's heels clicking on the wooden floor as she walked dejectedly next to him.

. . .

"May I take you to a celebratory lunch?" Sebastian asked Gemma once Vera had gone.

"I don't feel much like celebrating," Gemma said. "I certainly don't condone what Vera Canton has done, but I can understand the feelings that drove her to such desperation."

"That's why they call them crimes of passion," Sebastian said. "Love can make one kill just as easily as hate."

"They're two sides of the same coin."

"Yes, they are. Can I see you home, then?" Sebastian asked.

"I'll find my own way. I think someone is waiting to speak to you."

Superintendent Lovell had just approached the door, his face wreathed in smiles. "Well done, Bell. Well done, indeed."

"It was Miss Tate that figured it out," Sebastian said.

"You really are too kind, Sebastian," Lovell said, giving Gemma a patronizing smile that was meant to dismiss her. "A word in my office?"

"Go on," Gemma said, and reached for her things. She couldn't wait to get outside. The air inside the room was sour and oppressive, and she longed to be outdoors.

Despite the falling snow, Gemma didn't bother to look for a cab. She needed to walk a while, to think on what had happened and try to understand the sequence of events that had led Vera to commit murder. Was there really such a thing as a crime of passion, or were certain people naturally predisposed to violence, seeing it as the only alternative in a situation where reason might have prevailed? Would Vera have killed Gemma in that cellar in order to get away? Gemma thought she knew the answer to that. She would have, and, by the time Gemma's body was discovered, Vera would have established an alibi. And her conscience would have been untroubled by the loss of yet another life.

Gemma couldn't help but wonder if Vera's lover had been heartbroken, or relieved to have been saved from his youthful mistake, and how he would feel to learn he had a son by a woman he hadn't seen in fifteen years. And was Michael really the kind, sensitive boy Gemma had thought him to be, or had he inherited his mother's ruthlessness? And would he mourn the mother he'd so recently come to know?

Gemma was sure Vera would hang, an outcome that could have been avoided had she simply waited. Vera had had the love of a good man, a beautiful son who had survived into adolescence and had probably been happy to be reunited with his mother, and a future in which the three could have become a family. All she'd had to do was bide her time until Michael left the Foundling Hospital, at which point she would have no longer had to guard her secret. Instead, she had murdered a child over a ring, and had destroyed not only her son's hopes for the future but any chance of a life in which they could have made up for the time they had lost.

Was it folly? Ambition? Or something darker that couldn't be controlled? This was the sort of evil Sebastian came across every day, and yet he still managed to remain honorable and kind, and capable of great compassion. Gemma didn't think she would want to battle such corruption of the spirit every day, but she had to admit that it had felt incredibly rewarding to right a wrong and obtain justice for a child who could no longer speak for herself. Was that how Sebastian felt every time he collared a murderer?

Gemma drew in a deep breath of snow-scented air and allowed herself a small smile. She wouldn't want to join the police service even if women were allowed, and she certainly didn't care to deal with patronizing men who could never recognize the worth of a woman without feeling the need to crush her spirit. But she had to admit that *Inspector Tate* had a very nice ring to it, and seeing the admiration in Sebastian's eyes after she had subdued a killer had been even sweeter. That was how life was, a delicate balance between life and death, good and evil, darkness and light. And today she had experienced all three.

Feeling somewhat more at peace, Gemma hastened toward a cabstand. Her feet were growing numb with cold, and she was suddenly very hungry. Instead of directing the cabbie to take her back to the boarding house, she asked him to take her to a lovely tearoom she had often passed by on her way to work. She would treat herself to a pot of tea and a scone with strawberry preserve. She had earned it, by God!

FORTY-FOUR

FRIDAY, DECEMBER 31

Gemma snapped her valise shut, took one last look around the bare room, then took the beloved watercolor she'd taken from the house she shared with Victor off the wall. The room looked shabby and forlorn now that all her personal possessions had been removed, and Gemma wasn't in the least sorry to leave it. It was a good thing she hadn't paid the rent for January. Even though she would be gone before the first of the month, she had a feeling Mrs. Bass would not have returned the money and would have instead claimed that she would keep it in lieu of notice. Gemma was in no doubt that a new lodger would move in before the week was out. Someone had come asking for a room only last night.

Although ready to surrender the key, Gemma couldn't seem to walk out just yet, and sat down on the bed, suddenly feeling tired and terribly sad. The past two days had been unexpectedly difficult, even though Sebastian had been there to support her and Colin had offered a lifeline that would keep her from sliding further down the steep slope that began with genteel poverty and ended with outright penury. In reality, Gemma was nearly there already, but she wasn't ready to contemplate a future in which she might have to consider more drastic options.

Matron Holcombe had had quite a lot to say when Gemma returned to work on Thursday morning. The conversation kept replaying in her mind, and she wished she could get Matron's cold glare out of her thoughts, but the interview would stay with her for a long time. She had never been sacked before and had never been made to feel like such a failure, a woman who couldn't be relied on and wasn't worthy of a second chance.

"Well, well, well, if it isn't Miss Tate," Matron had said as soon as the door closed behind Gemma. She did not invite her to sit but left her standing before her desk to be berated like a wayward child.

"First, allow me to begin by congratulating you on solving the crime. Bravo! Now, thanks to you, the Foundling Hospital will be forever associated with the name of a murderess, our reputation tainted, and our benefactors wary of supporting an institution that could allow such an individual to grace its halls for two whole years. The story is in every paper, as I'm sure you're well aware, and I hear there's rather a graphic depiction in the *Illustrated News* this morning. We will also be known as the institution that hired a seemingly respectable woman who engaged in behavior so unbecoming of a member of staff as to leave one speechless. Not only did your actions border on the criminal, but you neglected the children in your care and engaged in a physical altercation in which you nearly killed Miss Parish with a bucket. The only thing worse than having that woman hang would be to know that you'd be carted off to prison."

Matron sucked in a shuddering breath at the thought of such an outcome. "You will collect your things and leave immediately. Because I don't want to see anyone brought low, no matter their character, I will pay the wages you're owed, Miss Tate, but you will not receive a character reference from me or anyone else associated with the Foundling Hospital. You are not deserving of one."

She skewered Gemma with a vicious stare. "You are not to converse with any members of staff or say goodbye to the children. If you attempt to seek out Lucy, whom I know you have grown fond of, I will have Lucy whipped."

Gemma gasped and opened her mouth to protest, but Matron held up her hand. "Yes, I realize that seems unnecessarily cruel, but I believe that is the only measure on my part that will discourage you from disobeying my orders. If you are not out of the building in ten minutes, I will have Mr. Fletcher forcibly evict you. Is that understood?"

"Yes, Matron."

"Very good. And happy new year, Miss Tate," she added acidly. "May it be a better one for us all."

Gemma didn't have anything to collect, since she had left no personal items in the infirmary. She went to the door and walked out. Dozens of eyes followed her from the windows as she crossed the courtyard toward the gates. She was glad they couldn't see her face, or the tears that streamed down her cheeks and immediately turned icy cold in the gusty wind. She had taken out her handkerchief and rubbed at her eyes, ashamed to display such weakness in public. It wasn't until she got back to the boarding house that she locked herself in her room and gave vent to her grief in private.

She had many reasons to cry. For one, she was deeply ashamed. She had behaved in a manner unbecoming a woman in her position; she couldn't argue with that. She had done precisely what Sebastian had warned her not to do and had paid the price. She could have waited for him to arrive, shared her suspicions with him, and told him what she had found, but instead she had decided to confront Miss Parish herself, an act of such monumental stupidity that Gemma was lucky to be alive. She could hardly blame Matron. She'd had no choice and was probably terrified of losing her own position, since someone always had to take the blame. Dismissing Gemma seemed to satisfy the powers that be, but Matron Holcombe could have also been sacked.

Burying her face in a pillow, Gemma allowed herself to acknowledge the real reason she felt so wretched. Lucy. Sweet little Lucy, who'd think that Gemma had abandoned her without saying goodbye. Yet another adult in her life who had cared for her and then left her to fend for herself in a world where no one much cared about a sickly little girl whose disreputable start in life was going to haunt her for the rest of her days. Gemma wished she could have at least explained and told Lucy that she had cared for her, but what would be the point? She would not be allowed to visit Lucy or see her ever again. And to make promises she couldn't keep would be even crueler than walking away without a backward glance.

Gemma cried for hours, and afterwards her face was so blotchy she couldn't bear to go down to dinner and face the other lodgers, so she took to her bed. It was as the night closed in and the boarding house grew quiet that she finally began to drift, pathetically grateful that the awful day had finally come to an end. She wasn't sure if the thought was conscious or if she had started to dream already, but an old nursery rhyme echoed in her mind, the shrill voices of children as they recited the words making her shiver, for this ancient version of the rhyme seemed to encompass Amanda's murder, almost as if the poem had been written expressly for that purpose.

Or perhaps terrible things happened again and again because as long as there were people there would be passions that couldn't be controlled, and secrets deemed worth killing for. Gemma mouthed the words into the darkness, and the darkness echoed them back to her, almost as if it agreed with her assessment.

One for sorrow,
Two for joy,
Three for a girl,
Four for a boy,
Five for silver,
Six for gold,
Seven for a secret never to be told.
Eight for a wish,
Nine for a kiss,
Ten a surprise you should be careful not to miss,
Eleven for health,
Twelve for wealth,
Thirteen beware it's the Devil himself.
Fourteen for love.
Fifteen for a dove.
Sixteen for the chime of a bell.
Seventeen for the angels' protection.
Eighteen to be safe from hell.
Nineteen to be safe from a crime.
Twenty to end this rhyme.

Gemma fell asleep with the rhyme swirling in her head and woke feeling just as shattered as she had the night before. But she didn't have the luxury of staying in bed or giving in to her melancholy. That was reserved for women of means. She splashed cold water on her face, got dressed and had her breakfast, then called on Colin Ramsey, ready to plead her case if he had reservations about offering her the position. But Colin was overjoyed and asked her to move in immediately, grateful to have someone he trusted look after his mother. Gemma swore then and there that she would do nothing to betray Colin's faith in her or risk losing another position because of her penchant for sticking her nose where it didn't belong.

Ready to leave at last, she put on her bonnet and cape,

picked up the valise with one hand, and tucked the painting beneath the other arm. Sebastian would meet her downstairs in a few minutes and would take her to Colin's house. Gemma liked Colin immensely, and Mabel was a lovely girl, but the thought of looking after a patient who was only bound to get worse and suffer endless emotional torment left Gemma's heart feeling heavy. She had enjoyed the company of children and had felt like she was making a difference to their lives, especially the younger children, who longed for a bit of motherly affection. Anne Ramsey needed her too, though, and Gemma promised herself she would do her best to make Anne's final years bearable and safe.

Sebastian was already waiting for her outside. He smiled and reached for the valise.

"How's your shoulder?" Gemma asked as he helped her into the waiting hansom and settled in beside her.

"Much better. No permanent damage done."

"I'm glad to hear it." Gemma knew she shouldn't ask, but she had to know, and she was curious to know if Sebastian had been to the Foundling Hospital since she had left. "Have you heard anything about Vera and Michael?" *And Lucy*, she wanted to add.

"Vera Canton will be tried in the new year, and, when I spoke to Michael yesterday, he expressed a desire to go into the army."

"I had hoped he wouldn't do that," Gemma said.

"So did I, but I think he wants to be as far away from London and his mother as it is possible to get. The only way he can move forward is by distancing himself from what happened. He's still in shock."

"That poor boy," Gemma said.

Sebastian laid his hand over hers, and she felt the warmth of his skin through her kid glove. "Where there is life, there's hope, Gemma. Michael is very young, so don't write him off just yet.

Or Lucy," he added. "She is sad, but she will be all right. And perhaps there will be other children you might care for."

Gemma didn't ask him what he meant, and Sebastian didn't elaborate.

"It's New Year's Eve, and tonight we should celebrate," he said instead. "Colin has prepared several bottles of champagne, and Mabel is making roast beef and Yorkshire pudding."

Gemma nodded. "I'm more than ready to see this awful year out."

"Surely it wasn't all bad," Sebastian said, a smile hovering at the corners of his mouth.

"No, it wasn't all bad," Gemma said, and smiled back.

Gemma set aside the book she had been reading to Anne Ramsey and crept from the room. Anne would sleep for at least an hour, and Gemma longed to go for a walk. It was the only time during her day that she was truly alone, and she cherished these stolen moments, desperate for a bit of solitude to think her own thoughts and breathe her own air. She was glad she no longer had to follow rigid hospital rules or be mindful of what she shared with the other members of staff, but Anne was like a small child who required constant vigilance, so the position came with its own set of trials, both emotional and physical.

The sunny day outside beckoned, and Gemma thought she might walk by the river. One of the reasons she enjoyed strolling by the Thames was that there weren't any newsboys yelling themselves hoarse along her route. As much as she took an interest in the news, sometimes the horror was just too much to bear.

And there were always the details that didn't make the papers. Only yesterday, Sebastian had told Gemma that Vera Canton had been found guilty of the murder of Amanda Carter. The verdict came as no surprise, but the sentence did.

Vera was to be transported to the penal colony at Botany Bay by the end of the month. The journey took months, and many died during the voyage, but Gemma had a feeling Vera would reach her destination. And as Sebastian had said, where there was life, there was hope. Perhaps Vera would find a way to thrive.

The other bit of news was that Sebastian had visited Michael at the Foundling Hospital to bring him news of his mother's trial, since Matron did not allow the children to read the newspapers and Michael had been kept in the dark. The only other person who might have passed on the news was no longer employed at the hospital. Matthew Campbell had moved on and was now teaching at some remote school for boys near Dartmoor. Gemma had an image of him strolling along the moor like Heathcliff from *Wuthering Heights,* his dark hair whipping in the wind and his coat flapping dramatically about his legs. She didn't know for certain, but she suspected that Matron had denied him a reference as well, to punish him for his involvement with Vera Canton and pacify the governors of the hospital.

Michael would also be leaving London soon. He had been in contact with his father and, now that the elder Sorokin was no longer there to object, Alexei, who was widowed, had acknowledged his first marriage to Vera Canton and had drawn up papers that would legitimize his son. Michael had decided to keep his Christian name, possibly to get back at his mother, who called him Alexei, but now pronounced it the Russian way, according to Sebastian, who found it endearing. Mihail Alexei-ivich Sorokin was now the heir to a great fortune and was about to embark on a life he had never dreamed of. Sebastian had mentioned that Michael's first order of business was to start learning Russian and French so he could communicate with his extended family and the serfs on the estate. He would also be going to university once he was proficient enough to keep up with the lectures.

Gemma had just put on her cape and was tying the ribbons of her bonnet when Colin came upstairs from the cellar, probably to get a cup of tea. He smiled shyly at her and stopped to chat, something he did several times a day. Today he looked somewhat uncomfortable, and Gemma hoped it wasn't bad news.

"I wonder if I might ask a favor of you, Miss Tate," he said.

"Of course. How can I help?"

Colin stepped from foot to foot, making Gemma wonder about the nature of this favor.

"It's Mother's birthday next week," Colin said at last. "She has always loved the theater, and I thought it would be a wonderful surprise if I could take her to see a performance." He looked down for a moment, then lifted his head, his gaze searching Gemma's face. "I realize you're still in mourning for your dear brother, and I really hate to ask, but would it be completely out of the question for you to accompany us? You're so good with Mother, and she feels safe with you. Of course, if you feel it's too soon, I will completely understand," Colin added.

Gemma considered the request. It was too soon really for her to start going out—Victor had died only four months ago, and it seemed disrespectful to his memory to start gallivanting around London. But she had come to care for both Mrs. Ramsey and Colin and really wanted to do this for them. Colin asked for so little, and Anne didn't have much time left to enjoy the wonderful things life had to offer. She spent more and more time lost in her own head and rarely delighted in anything anymore.

"Yes," Gemma said. "I will be happy to accompany you to the theater."

"If you're sure," Colin replied.

"If I'm going in my capacity as a nurse, then I'm not dispensing with mourning."

"Excellent," Colin said, and smiled happily. "I will purchase the tickets. Do you have any objections to me inviting Sebastian?"

"Sebastian?" Gemma repeated.

"Believe it or not, Sebastian has never seen a Shakespeare play."

"Is that what we will be seeing?"

"*Romeo and Juliet*," Colin replied, beaming. "Mother's favorite. My father took her to see it when she was a young bride, and she never forgot that day. She's been bringing it up, so I thought she would really enjoy it."

"I think she will too," Gemma said. "And I don't have any objections to you inviting Sebastian. In fact, I'm rather curious to see what he will make of it."

"So am I," Colin said. "So am I. But please, don't let me keep you from your walk. It's very pleasant outside today."

"It is," Gemma agreed, and stepped outside.

Now that she had agreed, she realized she was looking forward to the outing. She hadn't been to the theater in years, and it would be nice to step away from their daily routine and enjoy a performance. A peaceful evening with the three people she liked best, where the only drama would be pretend.

A LETTER FROM THE AUTHOR

Huge thanks for reading *Murder at the Foundling Hospital*. I hope you were hooked on Sebastian and Gemma's latest case. Their adventures will continue. If you want to join other readers in hearing all about my new releases and bonus content, you can sign up for my newsletter.

www.stormpublishing.co/irina-shapiro

If you enjoyed this book and could spare a few moments to leave a review, that would be hugely appreciated. Even a short review can make all the difference in encouraging a reader to discover my books for the first time. Thank you so much.

Thanks again for being part of this amazing journey with me and I hope you'll stay in touch—I have so many more stories and ideas to entertain you with.

Irina

irinashapiroauthor.com

 facebook.com/IrinaShapiro2

x.com/IrinaShapiro2

 instagram.com/irina_shapiro_author